COLONY OF THE LOST

By Derik Cavignano

Praise for *Colony of the Lost*

"A solid horror story with appetizing characters."
– *Kirkus Reviews*

Colony of the Lost

Copyright 2015 by Derik Cavignano

All rights reserved.

For more information about the author, visit:

www.amazon.com/author/cavignano

www.dcavignano.wix.com/cavignano-stories

E-mail the author at:

dcavignano@hotmail.com

Other books by Derik Cavignano:

The Righteous and the Wicked

COLONY OF THE LOST

In memory of my father, Fred Cavignano

For Bella and Ben (when you're a few years older)

Acknowledgements

I'd like to thank my wife Mary Ann—my most dedicated reader—for all of her love and support and for not strangling me whenever I asked her to read a dozen variations of the same paragraph (which was often). I'd also like to thank my test readers going back to 2002 when a version of this book was first released under the title *Where the Dark One Sleeps*. There are far too many of those readers to name, but I'd like to mention Gail Cavignano, Jen Campbell, Chris Coxen, Nicole Wing, and the Okomski clan. I'm also grateful to Kirkus Reviews for their constructive feedback on the manuscript, much of which has been incorporated into the final product. Thanks are also due to Ed Campbell of the Danvers Police Department for his guidance on law enforcement matters in the state of Massachusetts. Any mistakes in that regard are mine, not his. And finally, I'd like to thank Jen Campbell for the great cover photo portraying Washaka Woods.

PROLOGUE

The tall man stared into the dark and wondered about the voices. It seemed that lately he could think of little else. They haunted him at home. They haunted him at work. All hours of the day. Whispered promises of death's dark purpose.

Shadows draped his living room. Darkness stretched its tentacles into every corner, every crevice. The blinds were drawn tight, shutting out the pale light of dusk and the fluorescent glow of the street lamps.

He hadn't cleaned in weeks. Dishes loomed over the sink in teetering stacks, rising from a cesspool of stagnant water. A bag of trash overflowed beside the refrigerator; its rotting contents buzzed with flies.

He barely noticed the stench. He was far too used to it by now, far too absorbed in his problems to even care.

He was losing his mind.

Bit by bit.

It happened in a span of weeks. The seed of madness had taken root and blossomed, sprouting spidery vines that wormed into his brain. It seemed hard to believe that his sanity could slip away so suddenly. More likely, he'd always been crazy and just never knew it.

But who could he ask? Ever since Mary died, he had all but broken off from the rest of the world. He had no children, no immediate family to speak of ... at least not since his brother died in that car wreck on I-95. He had no friends at work. Just acquaintances. And he'd stopped joining them months ago for the occasional beer after his shift.

He lowered his face into his hands. *Please God, let me be insane. Let this all be part of some crazed delusion.*

But it wasn't a delusion. A small part of him knew that. He had imprisoned the truth in the darkest corner of his mind, had bound it in chains and locked it away from the rest of his consciousness.

But sometimes it escaped.

Images appeared when he least expected them, grisly scenes too horrifying to watch. Flashes of light, bursts of sound…phantom memories of events he wasn't conscious of at the time.

Fact or fantasy? Reality or madness?

Only the prisoner in his mind knew for sure.

Eventually, he'd have to confront the prisoner and discover the truth, but would he be ready to hear what the prisoner might say? Or would it be the last words he heard before the thread of his sanity snapped, and he plunged headlong into the abyss?

His eyes slipped shut, and suddenly the images appeared. He tried in vain to force them away, to resist the horrors he knew would be revealed, but his efforts proved futile.

***

Leaves and twigs crunched beneath his feet as he picked his way through the midnight forest. Starlight filtered through a canopy of skeletal limbs, the trail ahead steeped in shadows. Ragged clouds of breath plumed before him, lingering for a moment before vanishing into the dark.

His respiration was heavy, his lips salty and slick. His arms struggled to restrain their writhing burden. The child jerked and squirmed and tried to scream, but the duct tape pressed over its lips muffled the sound.

Laughter echoed through the forest. Voices circled his mind in a maddening frenzy.

He staggered toward a moonlit glen, drawn toward the mouth of the gaping earth, strung along by the whisper of death's dark purpose, the promise of life begun anew. His shoes rasped against a rocky floor as he wound through a drafty passageway and spiraled down, ever down, toward the restless voices and the beating of an ancient heart.

He emerged into a cavern adorned by seeping stalactites. A phosphorescent glow emanated from the walls and floor, illuminating a subterranean pool in the center of the chamber. The water was onyx black, its surface as smooth as glass.

The whispering voices became a chant, and all at once he could hear them everywhere, an urgent susurration that compelled him nearer to the pool. He shuffled toward the water's edge, stooped down, and drew a knife from the sheath at his ankle.

The chanting built into a guttural swell, into a dark symphony of madness. The blade reflected the ghostly light. Steel plunged into flesh, again and again, spattering hot ribbons of blood across his face.

The child's screams became a choked garble. The chanting ceased. The cave fell quiet. All that could be heard was blood dripping into the pool, swirling and rippling its black waters.

When the child's lifeblood was fully drained, he released the body and watched the once-still water begin to bubble and roil.

CHAPTER ONE

"Go ahead," Jay Gallagher said. "Pack your things and get out. See if I care."

The room was hot, hotter than it had any right to be this early in April. From where he lay sprawled on the bed, Jay could see Crystal reflected in the mirror above the dresser, her eyes swollen and damp. Tears mingled with her mascara and traced sooty lines down her cheeks.

All of her crying was giving him a headache. He wished she would just shut up and get the hell out so he could have a drink.

She yanked the drawers open and shoved her clothes into a suitcase, not even bothering to fold them first. He clenched his hands into fists and stared at the ceiling. How could she be leaving him?

I can't take this anymore. I've had it! Her words. *You promised, Jay. And like a fool I believed you. It's over. This time for good.*

Buckles buckled into place. Zippers zipped shut.

Crystal slung a bag over her shoulder and stooped to pick up another. She didn't even have the decency to look him in the eye.

"I'll be back for the rest of my things."

"Good for you," Jay said. He rolled off the bed and stalked into the bathroom. Slammed the door behind him.

Crystal yelled something unintelligible, then stormed through the living room and out the front door. The force of her exit rattled every window in the house.

Jay massaged his forehead. Who needed her anyway? If she couldn't love him for the man he was, then the hell with her. He gazed into the bathroom mirror and studied his face in the flickering light of a dying bulb. For one unpleasant moment, he mistook it for the face of his father.

The illusion passed when he blinked his eyes, and then it was only him again—a hazel-eyed twenty-eight-year-old with high cheekbones and rugged good looks. Only right now, he didn't look so good.

Sweaty cords of hair hung in his eyes. The rough beginnings of a beard bristled on his cheeks, the longer hairs tinged with red. Dark circles underscored his eyes, half moons prominent on a face that looked too pale.

He shuddered at the image, for a moment considering the possibility that there might be something wrong with the way he lived his life. But he shrugged it off. Who wouldn't look this bad after all he'd put up with?

He drew a deep breath and opened the cabinet beneath the sink. After sliding aside the back panel, he reached behind the pipes until his hand closed around a square glass bottle. "Gotcha," he said, grinning at the familiar black label.

"Looks like it's just you and me tonight, Jack."

A third of the way empty when he pulled it out, the bottle drained below the halfway mark before he collapsed onto the bed. Liquid fire blazed a trail into his stomach. A tingling sensation followed, spreading to his extremities until he felt so numb it seemed as if he was floating. The nasty business with Crystal washed away like the tide rising to cover a rocky coastline.

No need to hide his stash anymore. And no more listening to Crystal's constant complaining. Hell, this was a good thing. A great thing.

It wasn't his drinking that bothered her—she'd been looking for a way out of the relationship already. Drinking was just her excuse.

What a cowardly thing to do—accusing him of being drunk just so she could provide a reason for walking out. She must have seen the boy. He was right outside the window, for Christ's sake. Standing there at the edge of the woods, staring into the bedroom. What the kid was doing out there at midnight, Jay didn't know, but for her to say she didn't see anyone ...

He swallowed the last mouthful of whiskey. Tossed the bottle onto the floor.

He wasn't even drunk when he pointed out the boy. He'd only had three beers at Malley's. That's what annoyed him the most—that she'd accuse him of being drunk when he clearly wasn't. He hadn't been drunk in front of her for months, ever since he'd agreed to quit. He always waited until after she fell asleep before he got started on the real drinking.

The boy was out there, though. It wasn't a drunken hallucination like she claimed, although what the kid would be doing at the edge of the woods so far after dark was anybody's guess, especially with that Brakowski kid missing.

It didn't matter. She'd come to her senses eventually, and if she didn't, so what. He'd find someone who loved him for the man he was, someone capable of loving him despite his faults. After all, wasn't that what true love was supposed to be?

True love. What a joke.

The boy was there, Crystal. How could you not have seen him?

Sometime later, after day faded into night, he climbed out of bed. A void had opened in his stomach, and it ached to be filled. He shuffled into the kitchen, already feeling slightly detached, a passenger in his own body. When he reached the jar of flour, he yanked off the lid, chucked it to the floor.

How do you like that, Crystal?

He thrust his hand into the powder and retrieved a fifth of scotch. Thanks to Crystal, tonight's ritual had started a little early. But that was all right. A little more was always better than a little less...just like his dear old dad used to say.

12

He shook his head. How could she just walk out on him? He brought the bottle to his lips and chugged it down in three quick gulps. The wall hit him as he lurched into the bedroom. He spun away from it, too tired to be angry, and collapsed onto the bed.

The boy was there.

The thought pursued him into the sucking spiral of sleep.

***

5:45 A.M.

Screams.

Over and over again.

Jay sat bolt upright, his heart hammering. A nightmare?

The sound repeated itself, but it wasn't exactly screams—more like an electronic wailing.

The alarm clock!

He flopped back onto his stomach and smacked the snooze button, silencing the alarm's annoying cry. God, he felt like crap. He rolled onto his back and cradled his pounding head. A film of saliva caked his lips. His mouth tasted sour and yeasty.

He glanced at the empty side of the bed, and the events of last night returned to him in a flood. Tears stung his eyes, and through their hazy blur he could see something sparkling on the dresser: Crystal's engagement ring.

That stupid kid. Why did he have to be outside our *window?*

He came awake with a start, unaware he'd fallen back to sleep. According to the alarm clock, it was 7:30. He jumped out of bed and did the math quickly in his head. He should've been at work ten minutes ago.

The sudden movement upset his stomach. Bile rose into his throat, and he dashed into the bathroom. A fit of dry heaves doubled him over as he crossed the threshold. He sank to his knees and cradled the toilet, waiting for the spasms in his stomach to subside. When he finally managed to climb to his feet, his whole body trembled.

13

COLONY OF THE LOST

He cranked the faucet all the way, doused his head, and brushed his teeth.   Fifteen minutes later, he was dressed and out the door, sunlight blinding him as he raced to his car.   It started right away— something the LeBaron rarely did—and he peeled away from the curb with tires squealing.

At two minutes shy of eight, he pulled up to Glenwood High. Someone had taken his assigned spot, so he was forced to park adjacent to the upper fields.   The students in first period gym class huddled on the grass nearby, choosing sides for softball.

He slammed the door shut and hurried across the parking lot. This was all Crystal's fault.   If she hadn't run out on him, she would've been there to get him up on time.   Now he had to sneak into class before Principal Hoffman found out he'd missed homeroom.

He entered the school through the gym doors, bypassing the main entrance and the administrative offices.   The halls were empty, not a student in sight.   He could hear snippets of his colleagues' lectures as he rushed past their classrooms, their voices rising and falling as he progressed down the hall.

He reached his own classroom a few moments later, relieved that his honors geometry students had enough sense to close the door. When he stepped inside, he found that half the class had gone AWOL. The remaining students sat on top of their desks, engrossed in conversation.

Brian Mossler leaned back in Jay's chair, his feet propped up on the desk.   Graffiti adorned the blackboard behind him—a few smiley faces, a *Melissa loves Mark 4-eva*, and a huge proclamation in red chalk: *Geometry is 4 Queers!*

"Hey, Mr. G!   Glad you could make it."

Jay dropped his bag next to the desk and squinted at the clock. Forty minutes late.   Christ.   But had anyone besides his students noticed?

"You look like hell, Mr. G."

14

"Thanks, Brian. Your honesty is always so refreshing. I just wish I could say the same for your cologne."

"Maybe you should take a rest," said Maria Renaldi. "Teaching will only make you feel worse."

"Yeah, Mr. G," said Julia Chapin. "We don't want you to get sick. We went over the problems while you were gone, anyway."

"Sure you did." He was about to boot Brian out of his chair when he felt his stomach lurch. "Uh, I've got to step out for a minute. You guys behave yourselves and I won't give you any homework."

"We love you, Mr. G."

He forced a smile and whirled around, anxious to get to the teachers' room so he could puke up whatever remained in his stomach. He rushed past a group of teachers in the lounge, barreled into the bathroom, and dropped to his knees inside the stall.

After he finished, he trudged to the sink and rinsed his face.

The door to the other stall swung open. "Feeling a bit under the weather today, are we Jay?"

Jay sucked in his breath and cursed his bad luck. "Sorry, Ron. I didn't know anyone else was in here."

The principal shrugged. He walked to the adjacent sink and rinsed his hands. "We need to talk."

Jay swallowed. "What about?"

Hoffman dried his hands. "After class, Jay."

"I can't help it if I'm sick."

Hoffman balled up the paper towel and tossed it into the trash. "Go back to class, Jay. I'll see you in my office in half an hour." He adjusted his tie and walked out without a glance.

*　*　*

Hoffman's office had to be the brightest room in the school. Jay sat in a cracked plastic chair opposite the windows and struggled to keep from squinting.

"Do you know why I called you into my office?"

Jay shrugged. *Because you're an asshole?*

Hoffman leaned back in his chair and sighed. "I called you here because ... well, why don't I just come right out and say it. I'm afraid I have no choice but to terminate your employment."

Jay recoiled as if he'd been slapped. "What? I was late for class because I didn't feel well. How is that grounds for termination?"

"Let's cut the crap, Jay. You're an alcoholic. Signs of it have crept up in your work in the past. Today was just another example."

"That's ridiculous, I'm not an alcoholic! How could an alcoholic have the second highest test scores in the state? And let's not forget I was voted teacher of the year for three years running. Admit it, Ron. I'm a good teacher, probably the best you've got."

"*Were* a good teacher," Hoffman said. Splotches of red had bloomed on his cheeks. "I gave you the benefit of the doubt. When I found out you were in AA I was willing to give you a chance."

"Who the hell told you I was in AA?"

"It doesn't matter who told me. What matters is two months ago I found you stumbling around in the copy room with liquor on your breath. What matters is you came in late today with a hangover. I can't let this go on any longer."

"I can't believe this. I've never had a drink at work. That day in the copy room I fell because I tripped over a box of paper. If there was any liquor on my breath, it was from the night before. And today I threw up because I caught a twenty-four hour bug from my girlfriend. You're making excuses, Ron. What's the real reason you're firing me?"

"That is the real reason. If the school committee catches wind that you're an alcoholic, they're going to force me to fire you anyway. Nobody wants their kid alone in a room with a drunk. I'm sorry if that sounds blunt, but it's the truth. I'm looking out for you, Jay. I like you—I always have—but at the same time I have to do my job."

16

Hoffman leaned forward. "No one outside of this room knows about this. What I suggest is you resign quietly. If you do that, I'll put nothing of your problem in your employment file. I'm doing you a favor, Jay. A big one. You quit, get your act together, and you'll find another job just like that. Because you are a great teacher."

"It's always about politics, isn't it?" Jay stood up. "Thanks for nothing, Ron."

CHAPTER TWO

Sunlight streamed through Sarah Connelly's bedroom window, painting her butterfly bedspread in a patchwork of gold. Mr. Whiskers lay sprawled between her feet, purring so hard his body vibrated. Sarah stroked her cat's fluffy head and stared into the woods where the wind blew the budding branches back and forth.

"When those grow into leaves, it will be summertime."

"I know," Jenny said. "I can't wait."

"Me neither," Sarah said. "Then we can play by the stream all day."

Mr. Whiskers rubbed his face against her knees, and Sarah giggled. "I wish I could stay home with you today."

Mr. Whiskers rolled onto his back and licked a paw. "Why don't you?" she imagined him saying. "You're old enough to do what you want."

Sarah folded her arms and stared at him. "You try telling that to my mother."

Mr. Whiskers spread his toes and licked the spaces in between. "Your mother doesn't understand cat language. She hasn't the intelligence."

A voice floated up from downstairs. "Sarah?"

Sarah glanced from Mr. Whiskers to Jenny and wrinkled her nose.

"Hurry down to breakfast, Honey. Your toast is getting cold."

"I'll be right there." She grabbed her backpack off her desk and trudged downstairs to where Dad sat reading the paper.

"Hi, Honey. Ready for school?" He set down his coffee and adjusted his glasses.

Sarah plopped into a chair next to Dad and chewed a corner of toast, trying her best to look sad. "Can't I stay home? Please? Just for today?"

"Oh no," Mom said. "You'd better not start this up again."

Dad smiled. "Sarah, you know Mommy and I have to go to work. We can't leave you here alone."

"But I won't be alone. Jenny will be with me."

Mom huffed and shook her head. "When are you going to outgrow Jenny? You're nine years old, for God's sake. She's not real. Can't you see that?"

"Margaret, leave her alone. You're upsetting her."

"Her? I'm upsetting *her*? I'm going to make an appointment with the doctor. This has gone on long enough."

Dad took off his glasses and rubbed his eyes.

He always looks so old when he does that. Just like Grandpa when he was still alive.

"Why don't we talk about this later," he said. "I've got to get to the office." He tapped Sarah on the shoulder. "Want a ride?"

***

Sarah sat with her hands in her lap and stared out the car window. She thought about asking Dad again if she could stay home from school, but then decided against it. Whenever she asked him for something, he always had to check with Mom first. And Mom never let her do anything.

A few minutes later, they arrived at Glenwood Elementary. Sarah stared at the school and frowned.

At least I didn't have to take the bus.

She hated the bus even more than she hated school. Susie Jenkins was always calling her Snake Girl and saying that she had no friends. Some of the boys teased her too, boys like Bobby Peterman and Joey Cobb. They called her Snake Girl because she used to have a

19

bad lisp. Two years of speech therapy had cured her of the lisp…but boys like Bobby Peterman and Joey Cobb never forget.

They'd hiss at her the whole bus ride. Sometimes, they'd shoot spitballs into her hair or throw paper airplanes at the back of her head. She tried to ignore them, tried not to cry, but it wasn't easy. And if she did cry, the teasing got worse.

"Come on, Hon. Give me a kiss good-bye."

Sarah frowned and glanced over her shoulder. When the coast was clear, she leaned in and pecked Dad on the cheek.

"Have a good day," he said.

"You too." She climbed out of the car and watched it pull away, then walked to the school with her head down. She hadn't even reached the first step when she heard Bobby Peterman's cackly voice crying out for the whole world to hear.

"Aw, isn't that cute? Giving Daddy a kiss bye-bye." He clutched his stomach and laughed, his freckly face scrunching up.

A group of third graders stopped to look at her. They started laughing too, and Sarah felt her face burn. Third graders! She fought against the stinging in her eyes and turned to use the door at the west wing.

"Where you running to, Snake Girl? Going home to kiss Mommy?"

Sarah realized then that she was running, but she didn't care. She had to get away from them. She just had to. The stairway leading up to the west wing was deserted, and Sarah allowed herself a sigh of relief. "I hate them."

"So do I," Jenny said. "They're just plain mean."

Sarah was about to say something more, but then three kids she didn't know passed by, and she kept quiet. She continued walking with her head down, following the trail of gray and green diamonds on the floor tiles. Kids laughed and shouted as they pushed through the corridor, the roar of their voices mingling with the sound of locker doors slamming shut.

A group of fifth grade boys suddenly ran past her, tossing a baseball hat back and forth, keeping it away from the red-faced boy trailing after. "Hat head! Hat head! Billy's got a hat head!"

Sarah watched them melt into the crowd and disappear. She didn't know the boy whose hat had been stolen, but she hoped he would get it back.

Why weren't there ever any teachers around when you needed them?

Her locker was next to the boy's bathroom. She never bothered to memorize the number—all she had to do was look for the words 'Snake Girl' scribbled across the top in black marker. Bob the Janitor had quit cleaning it a long time ago, since the words had a funny way of reappearing the next day.

Sarah glanced at her Disney Princesses watch and shrugged off her backpack. She had to hurry to make it to class on time. She tossed her lunch into her locker, slammed the door, and headed into the classroom.

Most of the kids were already seated, and she had to pass them to get to her desk, all the while looking down and pretending not to hear them hissing and whispering, "Snake Girl".

She sank into her seat and felt heat blooming on her cheeks. *I wish they'd let me stay home. They don't know what it's like here.*

She turned toward the window and stared at the giant oak looming over the playground. A robin flew around the budding branches, chirping and singing.

That's what it's like to be free. No one telling you where to go or what to do.

A book slammed against a desk.

Sarah whirled around to see Mrs. Melvich frowning at her students.

"Good morning, class," Mrs. Melvich said, the tone of her voice suggesting that it was anything but.

The class mumbled something in return, and Sarah glanced around to make sure no one had caught her flinching.

"All right, settle down and be quiet for the morning announcements."

Bobby Peterman muttered something under his breath, but shut up when Mrs. Melvich glared at him. Sarah allowed herself a secret smile. Mrs. Melvich never took crap from anyone—not even from Bobby Peterman.

Mrs. Melvich was in the middle of telling Mikey O'Donnell to stop making faces at the other kids when the intercom cut in with a crackle of static. Everyone turned toward the dented metal speaker as Mr. Vincent began the morning announcements in the bored and toneless voice that every kid in Glenwood Elementary had imitated at one time or another.

After rambling on about Spirit Day and the importance of turning in field trip consent forms, Mr. Vincent led the school in the pledge of allegiance. Bobby Peterman and Joey Cobb cracked up behind her like they always did during the pledge, switching the word *flag* with *fag*. They were such mean jerks, but for some reason the other kids liked them. It didn't make any sense.

Mr. Vincent cleared his throat. "As you know, Ryan Brakowski has been missing for over a week now. I'd like you all to pray that he returns home safely."

Sarah stole a glance at the empty desk in the back row and wondered where Ryan could be. He was probably dead. That's what most of the kids thought, and for once she agreed with them. The grownups thought he was lost in Washaka Woods, but kids like Sarah knew better. The woods were pretty big, but if you walked ten miles in any direction you would come to a town. All of the grownups thought that kids were too stupid to realize this, that Ryan wandered in and got lost, walking around in circles so that he never got out.

She lowered her head. Ryan was dead. She just hoped he hadn't died in any of the ways the other kids had suggested.

When the announcements ended, Mrs. Melvich ordered them to take out their grammar books and turn to page 175. Sarah frowned and reached into the back of her desk. Grammar was the worst. There were too many rules, and that made it boring.

The lesson dragged on forever. She knew it better than most of the other kids, so she didn't need to listen much. She sat quietly at her desk and doodled in her notebook, glancing up every so often to show Mrs. Melvich that she was paying attention.

She scribbled a picture of two girls wading in a stream and thought about what Mom had said earlier. *When are you going to outgrow Jenny? She's not real.*

Sarah sighed and drew frowns on the girls' faces. In a way, she could understand why Mom was so mad—she was worried that her daughter might be crazy.

But Sarah wasn't ready to give in to her just yet. Jenny had been her best friend for as long as she could remember. Jenny was her first friend, her only friend. Why should she have to lose her just because she wasn't real? What was so bad about pretending, anyway? Wasn't a pretend friend better than no friend at all?

That's what Mom didn't understand. She didn't have any imagination. Not like Sarah who could imagine things so vividly that it was like watching them come to life on a movie screen.

She hunched over her notebook and sketched a kitten sniffing a daisy. She chewed her pencil and studied what she'd drawn. She supposed she could admit to Mom that Jenny wasn't real, but, of course, then she'd have to explain that the reason she clung to Jenny was because she couldn't make any real friends. Mom could probably handle that, but Sarah didn't think she could handle it, herself.

Thinking something was one thing. Saying it out loud was another. When you said something out loud, it made it real. Made it forever.

If she admitted to Mom that Jenny wasn't real, it would never be the same again. Once she admitted it out loud, Jenny would just fade away, and for the first time in her life she really would be all alone.

When the lesson ended, Mrs. Melvich switched to science. And then that was over too, the lunch bell ringing so suddenly that Sarah jerked in her seat and smacked her knees against the underside of her desk. The kids around her giggled, and she saw Joey Cobb stick out his tongue and hiss.

Sarah found a place on the wall to stare at until the other kids had packed up and left the room. When the last kid disappeared from view, she tucked her books into the back of her desk and headed out of the classroom.

A sea of bodies crammed the halls, moving as one toward the cafeteria. Sarah grabbed her lunch bag from her locker and followed the crowd. After buying chocolate milk, she found an empty table near the back and took a seat. She unwrapped a peanut butter and jelly sandwich and ate in silence.

Overhead, a fluorescent light flickered. Sarah stared at the interplay of darkness and light on the table, her eyes studying the shadows as they swelled and contorted like monsters taking form out of the dark.

And an instant later, they were monsters.

Three of them rose up from the table, their bulging bodies oozing a tar-like goo as their eyes darted left and right in search of prey. They leaped to the floor, claws clicking against tile as they crept toward where Joey and Bobby sat eating their lunches.

Bobby laughed with his mouth full—globs of tuna glistened against the pink of his gums. Joey laughed too, slapping the table with an open palm, making a carton of milk jump.

The monsters attacked.

They ripped Joey and Bobby from their seats and hoisted them into the air, holding them up for everyone to see.

Everyone in the cafeteria watched. They knew Joey and Bobby deserved to be punished.

The boys squealed like babies when the monsters popped them into their jaws like popcorn and swallowed them whole.

It got real quiet for a moment, and some kid muttered from behind her, "Good riddance to bad rubbish." After that, all the kids went back to talking about what they wanted to play at recess.

Sarah sipped the last of her chocolate milk. Next time, she would make the boys beg for their lives first.

The bell signaled the end of lunch.

Sarah rose to her feet.

Recess. The worst time of day.

A handful of teachers' aides couldn't really police three hundred kids running around like lunatics. Nowhere was safe. Not the blacktop, not the ball field. Her only chance was to stay near one of the aides, but even that didn't guarantee safety. As soon as the aide turned to yell at someone, she would be left open to anyone who felt like picking on her.

And that's exactly what happened today. One of the aides ran across the field to break up a fight and left Sarah standing alone on the blacktop. When Sarah turned to find another aide, she found Susie Jenkins and Bobby Peterman standing right next to her.

Susie wrinkled her nose and glanced at Bobby. "I can't believe how ugly she is."

Bobby nodded, a grin spreading across his face. "She's an only child, you know. Her parents stopped having babies when they saw how ugly she was."

Sarah felt her lower lip quiver. "Leave me alone."

Susie nudged Bobby in the arm. "Look! The Snake Girl's going to cry."

Sarah inched backward. Where was the teacher's aide?

"Fraidy cat!" Bobby shouted, leaping toward her.

Sarah jumped back. She tripped over a loose kickball and went down hard, her head striking the blacktop with a thud. Tears streamed from her eyes, and through a liquid blur she could see Susie and Bobby backing away. One of them muttered something about blood.

A teacher's aide reached her a few moments later and carried her into the school. As they passed through the halls, Sarah could see drops of blood spattering the floor, more of it hitting the tiles every second. She thought about asking the aide how bad it was, but she choked back the words, afraid that it might need stitches.

The nurse saw them coming before they were through the door. She pulled on a pair of latex gloves and instructed the aide to set Sarah down on the table. The aide lowered Sarah onto a sheet of tissue paper that bunched and crinkled beneath her.

Sarah glanced up at the nurse, worried by the look she saw on the woman's face. As the nurse spread apart her hair, Sarah drew a shaky breath. "Does it... need stitches?"

The nurse patted her head with a strip of gauze, pressed down hard, and pulled it away. "I don't think so. It's just a small cut. Head wounds bleed a lot."

"But no stitches?"

"No stitches." She took Sarah's hand and placed it over the gauze. "Keep pressure on that. It'll stop the bleeding." She walked around to the other side of the desk and picked up the phone. "Now, who would you like me to call?"

CHAPTER THREE

Footfalls pounded the pavement. Pebbles ground beneath racing feet.

Tim Hanson ran as fast as he could, gulping the air in great, heaving gasps. Rivulets of blood trickled into his eyes and obscured his vision. He did his best to blink it away, focusing his gaze on the street ahead. Looking for a way out of this mess.

The sun sank behind the trees in the center of town, the last slivers of daylight fanning across the steeple of an old church. Shadows appeared on the street behind him, inching forward and gaining. He could hear them now, muttering threats between winded breaths.

"Make you pay ..."

"Teach you ..."

"... who's boss ..."

Tim willed his legs to move faster, to pump harder, but he might as well have told himself to sprout wings and fly. Randy and his goons were going to catch him, and when they did they'd be certain to finish the beating they so generously began.

Tim could normally summon up enough speed to escape a situation such as this, but a healthy kick to the balls tended to slow him down.

Stand up to them, show them you're not afraid. A good pop to the nose and they'll never bother you again.

His father's advice. It had seemed reasonable enough when he first heard it, but he'd since discovered that punching a bully in the face could make him mad.

Fingers raked the back of his shirt. Tim swore and dodged left, but a hand latched onto his shoulder and dragged him to a halt.

Tim spun around. "Randy, so nice to see you again."

Randy floored him with a punch to the jaw.

Tim hit the ground and rolled onto his side, wincing. "How's your hand feel, Randy? I've got more where that came from!"

Randy's roided out goons yanked him to his feet and pinned his arms behind his back.

"Go ahead," Randy said. "Say something funny. I dare you."

Randy stood a full head taller than Tim and outweighed him by at least forty pounds.

Tim glanced over his shoulder. A quick scan of the street confirmed a lack of witnesses.

Perfect. Outnumbered, outmuscled, *and* alone.

Tim's mom always said he didn't know when to keep his mouth shut. He supposed she had a point, because what he said next was, "Looks like that eye's turning into a nasty shiner. Guess you're not as tough as you think."

Randy thrust a finger into Tim's sternum. "You don't have a clue who you're dealing with, do you? So I guess you'll just have to learn the hard way. First lesson: nobody hits me and lives to tell about it. Second lesson: there's nothing I hate more than a wise guy."

"Why's that?" Tim asked. "Too hard to spell?"

The confused look on Randy's face was almost worth the jab to the stomach that drove Tim to his knees.

"Pick him up," Randy said. "This kid's even dumber than he looks."

The goons lifted him up, and Tim leaned on them heavily.

Randy brandished a switchblade and triggered the release. Four inches of polished steel sprang from the hilt.

Tim went rigid.

Didn't see that one coming.

Randy touched the blade to Tim's forehead. The steel felt cold. And razor sharp.

"Do I have your attention now?"

Tim opened his mouth, but couldn't manage a sound.

"That's the smartest thing you've said all day."

One of the goons cackled. The other one worked Tim into a full nelson.

"Listen real close, Tim. If I catch you talking to Maria again, I'll cut your tongue out. I've got a rusty pair of garden shears set aside special for the job. But since you're new here, I'm gonna let you in on a little secret—I always follow through on my threats. And because you seem like a slow learner, I'm gonna give you a taste of how serious I am."

Randy pressed the blade against Tim's lips. "Open your mouth."

Tim tried to wriggle away, but the muscular goon had an iron grip.

The other goon dug his fingers into Tim's jaw and forced his mouth open.

"I'm gonna cut you, Tim. So I'd advise you to stay real still."

The blade swept across his tongue, cutting into flesh and making him scream. He stared at Randy in disbelief, his heart pumping so fast the beats blurred together. The coppery taste of blood filled his mouth.

"You don't talk to anyone without my permission. You don't even breathe unless I say so." Randy retracted the blade and slipped it into his back pocket. "I'm glad we had this talk, Tim. Because now we can focus on beating the hell out of you. What do you say, Lenny? Feel like giving him a head start?"

"Nah," Lenny said. "I had enough running for one day."

Randy brayed laughter. "What do you say we show the new kid what a Glenwood beating is really like?"

Punches hammered into him from all sides. Knuckles pounded his face, his stomach, his back. He dropped to the ground and curled into a fetal position as three sets of feet kicked up and down his body.

When Randy and his goons finally left, laughing and high-fiving each other, Tim lay on the sidewalk, bruised and bloodied, thankful to be alive.

***

The nurses at Glenwood Memorial Hospital were courteous and efficient, which was fortunate since Tim figured he'd probably be dropping in again soon. With any luck, after his next visit the hot nurse who'd just cleaned his wounds might offer to cure him of his virginity.

Or maybe not… but a guy could dream.

And anyway, it was better than the reality. Today's encounter with Randy had left him with nine stitches, two black eyes, a split lip, and a wealth of bruises up and down his chest and back. Not bad, really, considering the beating he'd taken.

When his parents arrived at the emergency room, his mother was frantic. "Timmy, what happened? Who did this to you?" She always called him Timmy, no matter how many times he said he hated it.

Tim shrugged. "Some guys. I'm not sure who they were."

His father folded his arms and scratched his chin. "Why is it that every time we move, the bullies always seem to pick on you? You've got to stand up for yourself, Tim. Show them you're not afraid. You do that and they'll leave you alone."

"Sure they will—right after they break every bone in my body."

"Timmy! Don't talk to your father that way."

"Can we go home now please? I'm beat."

Tim eased himself off the exam table and hobbled to the door. His whole body hurt, tongue included. The cut didn't require stitches, but it stung like a bastard. He wouldn't be kissing anyone for awhile, that was for sure.

All this over a girl he hardly knew. She was pretty cute, though. It might have been worth another stitch or two to kiss her—at least then he'd have something to show for his pain.

This was his third school in as many years, and everywhere he went it was always the same—the nicest girls always fell for the jerks. Newton should have included it as one of his universal laws.

His mother steered him through the automatic doors and into the parking lot. "I don't want you going out alone anymore."

Tim rolled his eyes. "What are you going to do—walk me to the bus stop in the morning?"

"You'd better watch it," she said, "I just might." She smiled at that, but Tim was pretty sure she wasn't joking.

They piled into his dad's Audi and drove across town, passing through a labyrinth of unfamiliar streets. It still amazed him that his dad could find his way around, having only lived here a week. Unfortunately, Tim didn't possess his father's navigational skills. His last girlfriend liked to joke that he couldn't find his way out of a grocery store, which was totally unfair because it only happened that one time.

Tim still didn't know what to think about Glenwood. Aside from Randy and his goons, it seemed like a nice enough town—huge homes, quiet streets, trees all around. It was a stark contrast to their old neighborhood in Boston's Back Bay, despite the fact that it was only a two hour drive.

Tim massaged his jaw and stared out the window. The sun's passage had trailed a lavender ribbon across the sky. He watched it fade into darkness, dissolving into the shadows stealing over the rounded peaks of the Berkshires.

They were almost home now. Another mile or two and they'd pull down their street—a dead-end fringed by forest. The Audi's GPS showed green space all over the map, a number of sections measuring a few miles square. Their house lay in the shadow of the largest section—Washaka Woods.

When they got home, Tim stalked to his bedroom and flopped onto his bed. A chest-high stack of boxes surrounded the TV. He'd promised to unpack this afternoon, but that was before Randy turned him into a community punching bag.

The guy was a lunatic. What kind of person went around slicing people's tongues just for talking to his girlfriend? He'd have to avoid Maria from now on, and everyone else for that matter. At least until this whole thing blew over.

So much for cashing in on the sympathy factor.

He stuck his tongue out and tapped it gingerly with his finger.

His dad was right about one thing—no matter where Tim went, he was a magnet for bullies. While most people steered clear of bullies, Tim couldn't help but provoke them. People like Randy deserved to be knocked down a notch. Too bad he didn't have the muscle to back up his words.

He'd have to be more careful in the future. He was in high school now. A freshman, which essentially meant he was the lowest form of life inhabiting the halls of Glenwood High. Something akin to plankton. No question that high school was more dangerous than middle school. There were always a few guys like Randy; it didn't matter where you went. And guys like Randy might give you more than a bloody nose or a black eye. If you pushed them far enough, guys like Randy might kill you.

Tim stared at the unpacked boxes and sighed. Just when he started getting used to a place, they would pack up and leave all over again. It was his father's fault—he kept getting promoted. He just took a new position as senior vice president at Greenleaf Insurance. Top management. That meant moving to corporate headquarters.

Glenwood, Massachusetts.

Who the hell had their headquarters in Glenwood, Massachusetts?

He caught a glimpse of himself in the dresser mirror. He was a sorry looking sight—two black eyes, a gash on his cheek, and a bruise on his forehead in the shape of a sneaker print. That last one made him laugh.

"Still better looking than you, Randy," he said, running a hand through his dirty blond hair.

He clicked on the TV and caught a glimpse of the news. He was about to change it, surf around a little, see if maybe they got the Playboy channel here, but then the words *Missing Child Update* flashed across the screen. He'd been following the story since they moved here.

A scrawny newscaster wearing either a bad toupee or a misplaced bird's nest said, "A major turning point occurred today in the search for missing ten-year-old Ryan Brakowski. Earlier, two joggers stumbled upon what police are now labeling a crime scene. We go now live to Brian Jacobsen, who is at the scene with the jogger who made the discovery. Brian?"

"Thank you, Peter. As you can see from the bustle of activity behind me, local officials are crowded behind this cordoned-off section of Washaka Woods in Glenwood. Even at this late hour they are still gathering evidence. I'm here with Ralph Masterson, one of the joggers who made today's shocking discovery. Ralph, what can you tell us about today?"

Ralph, a nerdy looking man in his late thirties, stepped eagerly to the microphone. "Well, I was jogging through these woods with my girlfriend like I do every day. When I ran by this spot, I saw a flash of gold out of the corner of my eye, so I stopped to see if maybe someone had dropped a ring or something. I went to the side of the path where the underbrush looked all trampled down, and I saw a broken necklace with a cross on it. I was going to pick it up, but then I noticed what

33

looked like dried blood on the leaves surrounding it. When I looked closer, I saw more blood and a piece of a shirt snagged on some thorns."

The camera cut back to the anchorman at the station. "What a gruesome discovery, Brian. What else can you tell us?"

"Well, Peter, details are still sketchy, but police tell us that they have located a few torn strips of black and white checkered clothing. Our sources have confirmed that this matches the type of shirt Ryan Brakowski was wearing on the day he disappeared. The boy's family, however, could not be reached for comment. That's all we have for now. Reporting live from Washaka Woods, I'm Brian Jacobsen for Channel 6 News. Back to you Peter."

Tim clicked off the TV and shook his head. He drew back the curtain and stared into the forest looming beyond his backyard. Randy cutting him with a switchblade...Ryan Brakowski murdered in the woods behind his house...maybe Glenwood wasn't such a nice place after all.

CHAPTER FOUR

Malley's.

Malley's and scotch.

That's all Jay remembered about the night he got fired. Except that wasn't exactly right. He'd seen the boy again too.

Last night's events filtered back to him in bits and pieces, like a slideshow of grainy images. He barely remembered leaving the bar and had only a hazy memory of racing down a blackened stretch of the Mass Pike, one eye squeezed shut to prevent double vision.

He rubbed his aching head and rolled over to find a woman lying naked beside him. She had a tangled mane of bleach-blond hair and the gaunt look of a heroin addict. God only knew what he'd done with her, what he might have caught.

He slid out of bed and pulled on a pair of boxers. A shriveled condom lay on the floor by his feet.

It wasn't his. Crystal was on the pill.

He risked a glance back at Jane Doe, who shifted in her sleep, scratched herself, and rolled over.

At least she had sense enough to know what she was doing. Certainly not a drunk like you.

He hung his head and let the words sink in.

You're a loser, Jay. A no-good, worthless drunk. Just like your old man. Maybe you'll even die the same way he did. Wouldn't that be something?

He grabbed his clothes and stomped into the bathroom, hoping the exaggerated noise might rouse the woman from his bed. After washing his face and lingering for a few minutes at the sink, he heard her collecting her things. He waited until the front door swung shut before venturing out of the bedroom, shaking his head as he descended the stairs.

Not my finest moment.

Sunlight pierced his eyes as he stepped onto the porch, the brightness amplifying the pounding in his head. He plodded over to the LeBaron and fumbled for the sunglasses baking on the dash. He slid them onto his face, blinking experimentally.

Sometimes he felt like a vampire. Prowling the streets late at night in search of drink, passing out just before dawn, and in the morning taking refuge from the sun.

He closed the car door and began walking, not sure where he was going, not sure whether he cared. As he passed through the quiet neighborhood, he took an inventory of his life. He'd lost his job and his fiancée, and in both cases it was alcohol that people had blamed.

It seemed ridiculous. Aside from the two times Hoffman had mentioned, alcohol had never affected his work. He might've rolled in with a bad hangover once or twice, but he still did his job better than most of the other teachers at Glenwood High. He hadn't lied to Hoffman when he said he'd never had a drink in work; it was true. Between dinner and 3 A.M. were his drinking hours. He never once strayed from that schedule.

Like Hoffman, Crystal blew his drinking out of proportion. Probably because her mom was an alcoholic. She used to smack Crystal and her sisters around, steal money from their college fund. The whole works. Crystal feared he would become like that one day. But he wasn't even close. He had never hit her, had never stolen from her.

... Not yet, a voice said.

He'd been hearing it for a few years, a sarcastic holier-than-thou voice that he'd give anything to quiet. He wished he could find the section of his brain where the voice resided and cut it out with a scalpel. If he could do that, then he might finally have some peace.

He wasn't an alcoholic like everyone seemed to think. Sure, sometimes he had a little too much to drink, but those times were the exception rather than the rule. He was an expert at walking the line between being drunk enough and too drunk, not like his dad who was always fall-down drunk. Real alcoholics were like his dad. They were bums, people who couldn't hold a job for more than a week, people who didn't care for anyone but themselves and their booze. He might have a slight drinking problem, but he certainly wasn't an alcoholic.

He'd show them all how wrong they were to place that label on him. After a few weeks of well-deserved vacation, he'd get another job. And not some crappy public school job, either. Last year, he had gotten an offer to teach at Philip's Academy up in New Hampshire, an offer he'd turned down because it meant moving away from Crystal. If the position wasn't available any longer, there was sure to be another one like it somewhere else.

On that kind of salary, he'd be able to afford a new car. He'd finally be able to trash the LeBaron. Most times that piece of junk did nothing more than keep a section of his driveway dry when it rained.

He'd show Crystal too. He'd been thinking a lot about the night she left. About how she pretended not to see the boy just so she could accuse him of being drunk.

It sounded funny to put it like that, but what other explanation could there be?

Something about the kid really creeped him out, though. Both last night and the time before the kid just stood there at the fringe of trees, eyes as black as the night around him. Staring at him. Staring through him.

And the glow. What about the glow?

But he forced the thought from his mind. He wouldn't allow himself to think about that.

When he got to the intersection of Maple and Main, he realized he did know where he was going after all. He waited for a lone car to pass—a black Lexus with the license plate *VENTUR CAP*—and then shuffled across the street. With less than ten thousand residents, Glenwood never saw much traffic. It was a nice enough place to live. It had a small town look and small town feel. A good place to raise a family.

He approached Glenwood center. A World War II memorial rose from the traffic circle ahead of him, a massive granite column that loomed over a strip of hedges sheared to spell out the town's name. To his right stood St. Mary's church with its whitewashed walls and wooden steeple, and across from that sat the library—a colonial saltbox with weathered brown shingles.

He strolled past the library and made a left onto Summer Street where a group of boys played whiffle ball. He smiled at their innocence. Those kids didn't have a clue about how life could beat you down. When he was their age, his biggest problem was devising a way to avoid Amanda Fletcher on the walk home from school.

A few minutes later, he reached his destination. He climbed the steps to the old Victorian and rang the bell. It was a monster of a house, consisting of three stories, a widow's walk, and five gables fused together at oblique angles.

A petite brunette answered the door.

"Morning, Gloria."

"Morning, Jay. You're up early."

He shrugged. "You know me—early to bed, early to rise."

"Yeah, right. Steve's out back. Come on in."

Jay followed her inside.

"How's Crystal doing?"

"Uh, good." He averted her gaze and studied a ceramic wall hanging of two pigs touching noses. Its caption read, *Home is where the heart is.*

A scattering of tools surrounded Steve on the deck. He lifted his head at the sound of their approach. Unlike Jay, Steve looked the part of an academic. He wore round, rimless glasses, was dressed in khakis and a golf shirt, and had sandy blond hair that was beginning to recede. He held a wrench in one hand and a steel pipe in the other. He seemed unsure of what to do with either.

"Hey, Jay." He glanced at his wrist. "What time is it?"

Jay shrugged. "Gloria putting you to work?"

"Just bought a new grill. I'm trying to put it together."

Gloria poked her head out of the sliding glass door. *"Trying* being the operative word."

Steve waved her away. After she retreated into the kitchen, he said, "I tried calling you last night. What happened? You didn't really resign, did you?"

"Hoffman found out I was in AA and cut me loose."

"You're kidding—just like that?"

"I never should have let Crystal talk me into those stupid meetings."

Steve looked as though he was about to protest, but then thought better of it. "How'd he find out?"

"I've got a feeling it was Renkin… the little prick."

Steve adjusted his glasses. "I'm sorry, Jay. That really sucks. But maybe it's for the best. Maybe a little time off is exactly what you need. You know, to get things under control."

"Get what things under control?"

"You know what I'm talking about."

Jay shrugged. His head hurt too much to argue. "Maybe you're right." He stared into the backyard. "Crystal left me."

"What? Because you got fired?"

"No. It was the night before that."

"Have you talked to her?"

"She won't take my calls."

"She'll come around. Just give her some time."

"I don't know. It was different this time. You should've seen the look in her eyes."

"Well, it could be worse."

"Yeah, how's that?"

"You could be Ryan Brakowski's dad. They're saying that Ryan may have been murdered."

"They find a body?"

"No. Just shreds of his clothes and some blood in the woods."

Jay grimaced. How could anyone do something like that to a kid? "There hasn't been a murder in Glenwood since we were in elementary school."

"Yeah," Steve said. "I remember. Larry Renquist caught his wife in bed with that tennis instructor and shot them both point blank."

"It's a lot worse when kids are involved."

"Did you hear there's another kid missing? A thirteen-year-old girl. Never came home from school yesterday."

"What's going on with this town?"

Steve shrugged. "I swear the world gets crazier every day."

"You want to know the funny thing? This whole argument with Crystal started over a kid I saw standing in the woods near my house. He was just standing there, staring into our bedroom window. Just a few minutes before midnight. And even though our lights were off, I swear he could see me. You know that feeling you get when you lock eyes with someone from a distance?"

Steve nodded.

"I don't even know if I should tell you the rest."

"Why not?"

"Well, the kid must have been standing in front of a light or something. Blocking it with his body so that all I could see was this blue glow surrounding him like… like some kind of aura."

Steve remained silent for what seemed a long time. Jay could tell he was trying to choose his words carefully. It seemed everyone was doing that around him lately.

"How old did the kid seem?"

Jay shrugged. "I don't know. Ten, maybe twelve?"

"What do you think a ten or twelve-year-old boy would be doing all alone in the woods at midnight?"

"I'm just telling you what I saw. You don't believe me either, do you?"

"I never said I didn't believe you."

"No, but you were going to ask if I was drunk."

"Were you?"

"I had two beers at Malley's. That was it. I swear." He waited for Steve to challenge his drink count, but Steve kept quiet. Jay said, "The kid was back again last night. Standing in that same spot. In front of that same light. It's really starting to creep me out. I guess that's why I'm here."

"What do you mean?"

"I need to borrow your camera. The nice one with the zoom lens."

"You're going to take a picture of him?"

"Yeah, and prove to Crystal that I'm not some crazy drunk."

"What if it's the Brakowski kid? Maybe you should be calling the police."

"I don't think so. I get the feeling he's not from around here."

There was something strange in the way the kid carried himself, the way he just stood there. Motionless. Focused. Jay was beginning to think the kid was a lot older than he looked, that maybe his name was already inscribed in stone, etched into one of weathered tombstones in the old quarter of Woodside Cemetery.

41

CHAPTER FIVE

Tim awoke Monday morning to find the day bleak and overcast. It was his first day back to school since Randy and his goons had run him over with the Glenwood welcome wagon. He had a feeling it was going to be a bad day even before he dragged himself out of bed.

Somehow, the day proved even worse than he expected.

He picked his way through the woods beyond his house and sighed at the memory of the day's events. He knew that everyone would stare at him from the moment he walked through the door. That much hadn't bothered him. After all, what did he have to be ashamed of? It had taken three guys to inflict all those bruises on his face, and once he told everyone that, they'd probably be impressed. All the girls would ask him how he was. They'd hang all over him, apologizing for what happened.

Oh, Tim, we're so sorry. Is there anything we can do to show you how nice a place this really is? Anything at all?

He had every intention of telling people who'd attacked him, but when he finally got the chance Randy stood at a locker right across from him. His black eye was gone—not a trace of bruising anywhere.

So instead of telling the truth, Tim made up a story about going to Boston for the weekend and getting jumped. When the bell rang and the kid Tim was talking to left for class, Randy was still there, his arms folded across his chest. He grinned at Tim, the corners of his mouth twisting into an infuriating smirk. Then he drew a finger over his lips—*Shh!*—and walked away.

Tim felt his face flush at the memory. He'd spent all day avoiding Randy, running away from him like the world's biggest wuss.

42

He hated himself for it, but what else could he do? The guy nearly cut his tongue out with a switchblade.

Later in the day, he'd spotted Maria talking to a pair of cheerleaders, the three of them laughing at some private joke. He pretended not to see her, tried to walk by with his head down, but she called after him.

"Oh my God, Tim! What happened? Did Randy do that?"

"I can't talk to you, Maria. I got to go. Sorry." He plowed ahead without looking and collided with some jock in a football jersey. Fell flat on his ass. He jumped to his feet, feeling like an idiot, certain that his face was glowing neon red. Maria said something, told him not to go, but he turned around without answering and took off down the hall.

Why hadn't he just played it cool and kept walking? Pretended not to hear her?

Whatever. Too late to change it now.

At least the day was over and the sun was shining, the sky a perfect sea of blue. The quiet of the woods had a soothing effect, and as he hopped from stone to stone across a gurgling stream the weight of his problems seemed to dissipate.

When he reached the other side, he turned back in the direction of his house and saw that it had vanished into the trees. It still felt weird to think of it as his house. It seemed more like the latest stop on the road to nowhere.

He sat on a fallen log and pitched a rock into the stream. Why did they have to move? Why couldn't Dad just keep his old job?

It wasn't fair. Just when he started to get close to his new friends, his father would take another job and they would have to relocate all over again. As a general rule, he didn't keep in touch with any of the friends he'd left behind. It was easier that way. He'd learned long ago that you don't miss people as much if you never look back.

His father had promised that this would be their last move until Tim finished high school. The idea had cheered him up at first, but now it depressed the hell out of him.

Four years in Glenwood. It might as well be a death sentence.

He glanced deeper into the woods where the intertwining branches blotted out much of the light. He thought he heard voices coming from that direction, distant cries carried on the wind. It wasn't until he heard barking that he realized it was a search party.

They were looking for those three missing kids. He'd seen it on the news last night. Two more kids had disappeared—a seven-year-old boy and a thirteen-year-old girl. The girl was pretty cute—blond hair, blue eyes. Tanya something. He couldn't remember the boy.

They were probably dead by now, same as the Brakowski kid. A psycho was on the loose in Glenwood. No one disputed that now. Everyone in town was talking about it. You couldn't go anywhere without hearing people whispering their suspicions.

The police instituted a curfew. Nobody under eighteen could go out after 9:00 P.M. unless accompanied by an adult, and nobody other than police or police-sponsored search parties were allowed in the woods.

Randy was probably the first to violate the curfew. Around 11:30 last night, Tim spotted someone lurking around the trees that separated his backyard from Washaka Woods. Although Tim hadn't actually seen Randy, he had seen the little kid Randy was using to pull off his prank.

There was no question Randy was behind it. Who else would do something like that? Randy and his goons were trying to scare him—and maybe they had a little—but he wouldn't let it happen again. He knew exactly what they were up to, dressing up that little kid to look like Ryan Brakowski's ghost.

It was kind of scary at first—the kid actually did look like a ghost—but once he figured out how Randy had done it, he felt like a dork for being so afraid. Randy had used white face paint to make the kid's skin look so pale. The glowing effect must have taken some thought though, so it was clear Randy had help on that one.

But it was really pretty simple when you thought about it. All he had to do was find some of those plastic glow-in-the-dark necklaces, the kind that gave off a phosphorescent glow when you bent them.

He had to give credit to whoever coached Randy on that one. Whoever it was, he was smart enough to wait until the light had faded to the point where you couldn't see the shape of the plastic tubes any more. Just a pale blue blur without definition.

What didn't make sense was why Randy dressed the kid so strange instead of putting him in a black and white checkered shirt. Everyone knew the shirt Ryan was wearing on the day he disappeared.

No sense dwelling on it. Randy just wanted to freak him out. Last night, the kid had motioned for Tim to come outside, and of course, that was the last thing Randy expected Tim to do.

Maybe his father was right. Maybe he needed to stand up to Randy again, even if it meant another black eye or two. What the hell, anything was better than walking through the halls at school all day, too afraid to speak to anyone.

If Randy wanted to play his stupid little game again tonight, he'd play along with him. But this time, he'd play by his own rules. This time he'd teach them a lesson they'd be sure to remember for a long time to come.

CHAPTER SIX

Jay sat with his back slumped against the headboard and waited for darkness to come. He stared at the TV without seeing, his mind a whirlwind of thoughts—none of them pleasant. As the shadows deepened, it became obvious that he was losing his grip on the things that mattered. And he wondered, was this the beginning of a downward spiral... or was it just a bit of a rough patch—the kind of thing everyone goes through at one time or another?

He sipped from a lukewarm mug of coffee and tried not to think about the case of Sam Adams chilling in the fridge. He could picture the dark bottles crowding the top two racks, their sleek necks glistening with condensation.

He needed a drink. And the coffee just wasn't doing the trick.

Face it Jay, you're an alcoholic. Whenever you think about having a drink, you drool like Pavlov's dog. Remember that Christmas dinner with Crystal's relatives?

He didn't want to remember that night, but his traitorous mind took him there anyway, dangling the memory before him like the Ghost of Christmas Past.

He sat at a long table, the meal just started. A dozen of Crystal's relatives flanked him on either side, strangers he met just an hour before. Two bottles of wine went around the table—just two for all those people. He remembered the twinge of panic he felt, sitting there in the stiff wooden chair, gripping the seat while the bottles worked their way toward him with painstaking slowness. Three quarters of a glass was all he got. Three quarters!

It was the only booze in the house, a fact he attributed to Crystal's mom being an alcoholic. He could have understood the rationing had Crystal's mom actually been there, but she'd flown through the windshield of her car and died in a ditch three years earlier.

How could they be so stingy? How could they expect him to sit there for the rest of the night, crammed in with all those strangers, without even a full glass?

By the end of dinner, the need for another drink was so strong that he feigned a stomachache and went home early. That was the first time he'd ever *needed* a drink. But where had that need come from? Why hadn't he noticed it before that day? He never even touched a drink until he was in college, and only then it was because he was tired of being the only person at a party who wasn't clutching a bottle. A few sips here and there so he didn't look like a dork. Not a big deal. He was smart enough not to get hooked on the poison that had killed his dad and ruined his family.

It tasted like piss anyway.

But by the end of his freshman year, beer didn't taste so bad anymore. He'd have five or six on a Friday or Saturday night, get a good buzz going and then stop. He drank more as freshman year slipped into sophomore, and sophomore into junior. But it was normal. Everyone did it. Alcohol was great. It took the edge off his insecurities, gave him the ability to mingle. Hell, it even allowed him to dance without feeling self-conscious. All that and he still got straight A's.

In college he drank because he wanted to. Need was never a part of it. But now need was always with him, an unwelcome companion that shadowed him wherever he went.

Need—the savage beast that roared within the depths of his stomach. He had woken up one day and there it was. Need had replaced want. Just like that.

He had a drinking problem. Lying in bed, staring at the TV, he knew it. But in the back of his mind he also knew that tomorrow, next week, or even ten minutes from now, he would convince himself that he didn't have a problem. There was a constant flip-flop. Only the holier-than-thou voice, that ever-present sober observer, chose one side and stuck to it.

You're a jellyfish, Jay. Spineless and weak.

He chewed a fingernail.

I need a drink. Just one to put me at ease.

What was the big deal, anyway? So he had a problem, so he couldn't live without having a drink. So what? It was just one. It wasn't like he was going to get drunk off it.

He swallowed the last of his coffee and set the mug down on the nightstand next to Steve's camera. He reached for a coaster, but then thought better of it.

Screw it! He didn't need to use a coaster. With Crystal gone, he could do whatever the hell he wanted.

Except have sex with her.

Okay, that was a legitimate downside. But if he decided he *did* want her back, he'd have to focus on the task at hand. He turned toward the bedside window and peered into the backyard. Shadows draped the trees at the fringe of Washaka Woods, their skeletal limbs silhouetted against the darkening sky. A steady wind swept their branches back, and thick clouds blotted out all but a hazy sliver of the rising moon.

If the boy planned to make an appearance tonight, Jay had a feeling it would be soon. He clicked off the light and opened the window, allowing the chill night air to seep into the bedroom. The only sounds from the yard were the wind through the trees and a chorus of crickets strumming their signature tune.

He set Steve's camera to night shot and adjusted the zoom so he'd be ready when the time came. Then he leaned against the headboard and closed his eyes, suddenly realizing how tired he was.

He came awake with a start, not sure what had woken him or how long he'd slept. According to the clock on the nightstand, it was 12:03 A.M.

Just past the witching hour.

The night outside was as black as pitch, the moon obscured by clouds. Maybe it was his imagination, or the lingering effect of a dream, but something felt *wrong*. Maybe the air was too still, or the night too quiet. Or maybe it was the way the crickets had all of a sudden ceased chirping. Whatever it was, it made his skin bristle with gooseflesh and his heart knock hard against his ribcage.

A breeze blew through the window, and the curtains flowed toward him, billowing out like sails. He shut off the TV, and the room plunged into darkness. He sat on the bed, completely motionless, eyes locked forward. A light appeared on the wall over his shoulder. A pale blue glow that pulsed in and out like a creature breathing. He knew without turning that the source of the light was to his right, that a little boy stood within the fringe of trees, his eyes fixed upon the window before which Jay now sat.

Jay's mouth felt so dry he could barely swallow. He could hear the sound of his pulse thudding in his ears. He groped for Steve's camera, drew it into his sweaty palms.

He pictured the kid's sallow face pressed against the bedroom window, his mouth drawn into a sinister snarl.

Should have gotten that drink.

He whirled toward the window.

The boy was there. Closer this time. Standing less than a dozen feet away. A phosphorescent blue glow radiated from his body, his face alabaster white.

The boy focused his gaze on the bedroom window, but he seemed to be staring beyond the shadows. Jay was drawn to the boy's eyes, held fast by a gaze that was as innocent as it was monstrous.

Maybe he's not seeing me, maybe—

49

The boy lifted a finger and pointed.

Right at him.

Jay went rigid. Almost choked on the air.

The boy's finger curled and straightened in an unmistakable gesture.

Come outside.

A screech escaped Jay's lips. He snapped the picture and fell backward onto the bed, momentarily blinded by the camera's flash. When he finally mustered up enough courage to peer over the windowsill, the boy was gone.

He closed his eyes and drew a shaky breath, but the image of the boy was burned into his retinas as a negative, the light and dark reversed. It lingered for a few moments—an image of a boy dead to this world for centuries. An image of a boy who wore Puritan clothing.

***

Jay rubbed sand from his eyes and squinted at the light filtering in through the blinds. No dead little Puritan boy lurked in his backyard. The pasty little ghoul clearly liked to rest during the day so that he could scare the bejesus out of people at night.

Sunlight heliographed off Jay's watch, and he turned his wrist to catch the time. Four in the afternoon. Talk about sleeping in on a Sunday! The only problem was the dial for the date said it was Monday.

But how could that be?

He had a foggy memory of dragging himself out of bed on Sunday afternoon and staggering into the kitchen—straight to his old pal Jack—on a mission to drink that kid's face out of his mind.

Beyond that, everything was a blur.

He sat up and felt a sudden urge to vomit.

It happened before he could react, and suddenly the inside of his stomach glistened on the outside of his sheets. A noise escaped his lips—something between a moan and a sob. He wiped his mouth with the heel of his hand and came away with a sticky line of drool.

"Why do I keep doing this?" he asked the empty room.

Because you're an alcoholic.

"Oh yeah," he said. "I almost forgot."

And you're crazy—you know that?

"Si, señor, soy loco en la cabeza."

Something made a noise nearby, a muffled sort of chirping like the screech of an alarm clock...only this was much faster. It took him a few moments to realize the phone was off the hook, the handset tangled in a knot of blankets. He hung it up and shook his head. Who had he called? Steve? Crystal? The police?

That last thought made him laugh.

Hi, officer, this is Jay Gallagher calling ... yeah, the town drunk. Listen, I'd like to report a dead little Puritan boy in my backyard.

He hoped he hadn't called Crystal and said something stupid, something he would later regret. He'd done something like that with his mom and, unfortunately, they were words he could never take back.

Her cancer had spread fast after the initial diagnosis, ripping through her body like a school of tiny piranhas. He called her after a long night at Malley's, and she started lecturing him about his drinking, told him to quit before he ended up like his dad. That sent him into a rage. He launched into a flurry of curses, told her she had no right to compare him to his dad. Told her to shut up, to hurry up and die.

And that's exactly what she did. His stepfather called the next morning. Jay dragged himself out of bed, fighting off one of the worst hangovers of his life, and made the drive to their house. He didn't even remember the previous night's conversation. But his stepfather pulled him aside before the crowd of relatives grew too large. As it turned out, their outdated answering machine had picked up a moment before

COLONY OF THE LOST

his mom had, and when his stepfather pressed play, Jay was horrified by the words that slurred through the speaker.

The next day he signed up for AA, and at first he went to the meetings religiously. He would sit there in the smoky basement and listen to strangers speak about their trials of addiction. Their patterns of abuse seemed familiar—hiding bottles, lying about how much you had to drink, looking up in a bar and realizing that you were the only one still there. But even so, most of those people had it worse than he did. They'd been drinking longer and harder, couldn't hold a job, had hit rock bottom.

But for Jay, the bottom wasn't even in sight. Sure he'd blurted out something he regretted to his mom, but who hadn't done that at one time or another? Besides, he had a steady job, a great girlfriend. What was he doing at AA anyway? Maybe someday he'd need to go, but certainly not now.

And so he quit going to the meetings and vowed instead to limit himself to three drinks a day. From that point forward, he made sure his drinking was carefully concealed—never at work, never when Crystal was around (unless she was sleeping). Living with her was tricky business. After each drink he'd have to brush his teeth and gargle with Listerine. With her around, he went through bottles of mouthwash almost as fast as he went through bottles of beer.

That, of course, brought up another problem. The trash collectors in Glenwood were Nazis about recycling. They wouldn't take your regular trash if they heard bottles clinking around inside. That forced him to keep a box of empties stored in the attic. Every Saturday when Crystal went to the gym, he'd load the box into his car and throw it into a dumpster across town. Then he'd kill some time before returning home, and if Crystal asked he'd say the AA meeting went well.

And lying here now in vomit-soaked sheets at four in the afternoon, fighting a pounding headache and a raging hangover, he hated himself. All his rationalizations for leaving AA had vanished—no more steady job, no more great girlfriend. And to top it all off, now he was seeing ghosts.

You're screwed in the head, my friend.

"Maybe si, maybe no."

Steve's camera lay on the nightstand, and he switched it on to reveal a picture with a dark and shadowy background. The pines at the edge of his yard rose high into the sky, their slender trunks barely discernible against the night. In the foreground stood the Puritan boy, his body surrounded by an aura of pale blue light. His dark eyes blazed with fierce determination, reflecting twin pinpricks of the camera's flash.

Jay set the camera down and folded his arms. Part of him had hoped to see nothing but trees in that photo.

He pulled his clothes on slowly, testing the strength of his stomach. It seemed okay now. He was pretty sure he was done throwing up. At least until his next bender.

When he got downstairs, he threw the sheets into the washer and set it to sanitary. Hopefully, that would do the trick. They should have been cleaned even before he did Jane Doe, but now he couldn't put it off any longer.

As water sloshed and churned in the washer's belly, Jay dropped a couple slices of bread into the toaster. The smell of it browning awakened him to how hungry he was. He hadn't eaten anything solid in well over twenty-four hours.

A burst of sunlight hit him when he opened the front door, the day so bright it hurt his eyes. He stooped down to grab the newspaper and peered at the street through splayed fingers.

The toaster popped as he closed the door, sending two breaded projectiles sailing over the counter.

The demon toaster strikes again, he heard Crystal say.

God, he missed the sound of her voice. Strong, sweet...always with a touch of sarcasm. She was the best thing that had ever happened to him, and yet he went ahead and screwed it all up. It's not like she hadn't warned him. She threatened to leave a year ago, and even then he knew it wasn't just an idle threat. But did that stop him from taking up the bottle once again?

Why couldn't he stop? Why couldn't he go through an entire day without picturing the beer in the refrigerator? Other people could have one drink, two drinks, and then stop cold.

Why couldn't he do that? Why was he so weak?

He washed the last of his toast down with a gulp of coffee, and then spread out the newspaper before him. His attention turned to a black and white image of a grinning boy wearing a Red Sox cap. The boldface headline to the left of the photo practically leapt off the page:

GLENWOOD YOUTH REPORTED MISSING

Third disappearance in two weeks leaves many parents wondering: *Could my child be next?*

Jay finished the article and shook his head. The whole world was going down the toilet...and it seemed he was going down with it. After leafing through the rest of the paper, he grabbed his keys and drove to Crystal's sister's house. When he got there, he rang the doorbell and switched the bouquet of roses he'd bought from one hand to the other. For a moment, he thought no one would answer...or, even worse, that Crystal would answer with some guy's arms locked around her waist. But after he tried the bell again, the door swung open and Crystal's sister stood looking at him with her mouth hanging open.

"Jay. Hi ... um ... Crystal's not here."

"I know she's here, Denise. Just let me talk to her, okay?"

"She's not here—I swear."

54

"It's okay, Denise." Crystal's voice drifted to them from the kitchen.

Denise turned around, and Jay could see Crystal standing at the entrance to the hallway. "Let him in."

Denise opened the door without a word. She glared at Crystal and then stalked upstairs.

Jay held out the roses.

Crystal seemed reluctant to accept them. "What do you want?" She laid the bouquet on the coffee table.

"Can I sit down?" God, why did she have to look so good?

"I don't think that's a good idea."

The words struck him like a sucker punch to the gut. She wasn't his anymore. It was as if he were meeting her for the first time, as if they had never kissed, never made love. It was as if she had reached inside herself, flicked off some hidden switch and erased seven years of memories.

And suddenly he felt like he might cry. Right here in the living room while Denise listened from the stairs, snickering to herself.

"Are you all right?" Crystal asked.

"No. I just—" He exhaled sharply. "I'm going crazy without you. Please give me another chance."

When she didn't answer, he reached into his pocket and brought out her engagement ring. "You forgot this at the house."

Crystal swallowed. "I didn't forget it."

Jay closed his hand over the ring. "I was afraid you might say that." A tear broke through his defenses and slid down his cheek like an alien kiss. "I don't blame you for leaving me, and I know I don't deserve another chance, but you loved me once. Will you come back if I check into rehab? You can sign me in yourself."

"I can't do this anymore, Jay. Don't you get it? I don't want to get hurt again. Do you have any idea how much pain you've put me through? I need to move on. For my own good." And then she burst into tears.

He wrapped his arms around her, but she pushed him away. Smacked him on the chest. "Why do you have to be a drunk? I loved you, Jay. I wanted to spend my life with you. But you ruined it."

"I'll make it up to you. Please—just give me a chance."

"I told you before, it's either me or alcohol. And you made your choice. So I'm sorry, but I'm done being second to your one true love."

"I'll change, I swear! Look, I'm not drunk now. I'll stay this way. Just give me another chance. Please."

Crystal stared at him, her eyes brimming with tears.

"I want to show you something." He pulled Steve's camera out of his jacket pocket. "I wasn't drunk the other night. I know you don't believe me, but just look at this." He scrolled to the picture of the boy.

She wiped her eyes and stared at it. When she looked up, her face had changed. "Get out."

"What, why?"

"There's nothing in the picture except an overexposed smudge of light. So that means you're either crazy, drunk, or mean. And you know what? I don't really care which one...because we're done."

He stared at the picture. "It's the wrong one," he lied. "Give me a second, I'll find it."

"It doesn't matter. Even if there was a boy that night, it doesn't change the fact that you're an alcoholic. You've broken too many promises. I know you mean them with all your heart—and that's what makes this so hard—but I also know you can't keep them." She shook her head. "It's over, Jay. Good-bye."

She pushed past him and ran upstairs.

"Crystal wait!"

At the third step from the top, she drew to a halt, but didn't turn around. "I think it's best if we never see each other again. And no more phone calls, Jay. Drunk or sober."

CHAPTER SEVEN

Sarah sipped a juice box and squinted down at her math homework. Fractions—ugh! You had to convert them to a common denominator before you could add or subtract them, which was kind of tricky. Almost sneaky. And you couldn't even check your work with a calculator. At least not with the cheap one Mom bought her today.

They got it at the Forest Mall in Gilford. Mom surprised her with the trip after she got home from school. The Forest Mall had much better stores than the mini-mall down the street—Macy's, Dillard's, Saks Fifth Avenue (where Mom said they could look, but not touch), and Brookstone (the store with the cool massaging chairs). The mission had been to find some shorts and some summer shirts for her and some makeup and dress slacks for Mom.

She liked shopping with Mom because it was the only time they really got along. When they went shopping, they were like a family from one of the mushy TV shows that Mom always watched—talking and laughing like best friends, just plain having fun. Not once did Mom bring up Jenny or how Sarah always asked to stay home from school.

It was a great day—one of the best she'd had in a long time. Probably the best since last summer by the stream. She liked to relive that day whenever she felt sad, imagining herself sitting in her favorite spot as the sun warmed her face and the water gurgled around the stones, making mini whirlpools. The air had smelled sweet and clean, like pine trees and flowers. And as she dipped her toes in the water, a Monarch butterfly touched down on her knee, its fuzzy feet tickling her skin. It flexed its wings and then lifted into the air, fluttering higher and higher until it vanished into the canopy.

Sometimes that memory was all she had to keep herself from going crazy, a reminder that no matter how bad things got there was always a place she could go where she felt welcome. A place that was beautiful and peaceful and real. It was her special place, and she'd never shared it with anyone besides Jenny. Someday it would be nice to share her place with, well, a real person, a real friend.

She snapped her math book shut and stood up. Mr. Whiskers blinked sleepily at her from his favorite spot on the bed before settling his head back down between his paws. She glanced at her reflection in the mirror above the desk. Butterfly stickers lined the mirror's edges— bright orange ones, small red ones, fuzzy green ones. They appeared to fly when she tilted her head to the right or to the left.

The girl between the butterflies had shoulder-length brown hair and big, brown eyes. Tiny freckles spattered her face, most of them clustered around her nose. The other day Susie Jenkins had called her ugly ... and maybe she was. Her skin seemed too pale, her head too big. And with two teeth missing, she looked like a beaver.

Most of her classmates already had a full set of adult teeth, but Mom said she was a late bloomer. She lost one of her teeth just the other night. Instead of popping right out, it hung by a sliver of pink flesh that she had to twist and yank until it pulled free. It had hurt a lot, but it was worth it the next morning when she woke up to find that the "tooth fairy" had left her two dollars beneath her pillow.

She'd known the tooth fairy was really her parents since the age of seven. It happened by accident. When she woke up one morning to find a dollar in place of her tooth, she ran into her parents' room to show them. But lying right there on the nightstand beside her sleeping parents was her tooth. She was only seven, but she wasn't stupid. She also knew to keep her mouth shut or else the tooth fairy might stop bringing her money.

From what she could tell, most kids didn't believe in the tooth fairy. Or the Easter Bunny. It was kind of dumb—a giant rabbit hopping around from house to house, leaving painted eggs. Rabbits didn't even lay eggs. And even if they did, why would they want to give their babies away? The tooth fairy, too—what would someone want with a bunch of teeth? Maybe for the silver in the fillings, but not all teeth had fillings. The tooth fairy had taken her teeth, and she'd never had a filling in her life.

Santa Claus was different, though. Her grandmother had told her once that Santa was really an angel that God created to bring happiness to all the kids in the world. Santa Claus had been alive a long time. He had reindeer that flew and magic dust that allowed him to shrink down small enough to slide down any chimney. It sounded crazy, but it all made sense if you thought of Santa as an angel. That's probably why some people called him St. Nick. Besides, everyone believed in God and angels—even grownups. They wouldn't go to church for an hour every Sunday just so that they could fool their kids into thinking Santa was real.

Sarah glanced at the mirror and caught a glimpse of her ugly face. She could almost hear Joey Cobb making fun of her.

Hey beaver face, why don't you go chop down a tree.

She squeezed her eyes shut until the voice faded into the wind that blew through her open window. They were all so mean. Why wouldn't they just leave her alone? No one liked her, no one wanted her as a friend. She glanced out the window at the little trail worn into the grass by the edge of the woods.

The boy wants to be my friend.

The thought came out of nowhere. She had seen him every night for a week, the little boy beneath her window. The boy who wore funny clothes. Something about him seemed weird. Maybe it was just the strange clothes or a trick of the moonlight or maybe just her imagination, but something about the boy made her think of ... well, of a ghost.

She knew she shouldn't believe in ghosts. Dad had told her hundreds of times that there were no such things. Just in movies, he'd say. Dreamed up from someone's imagination. At one time Dad's words would have made her feel better, but that was when she believed he knew everything.

She supposed that up to a certain age all kids believed their parents knew everything. For her, discovering the truth had been a big shock that forced her to doubt everything she had ever learned. How could Dad be alive for so long and still not know everything? Was he stupid, or was there really too much out there for any one person to know? The thought had scared her because if Dad didn't know how electricity was made, how could he know for sure that there were no such things as ghosts?

She shook her head. Ghost or not, she wasn't afraid of the boy. He looked too sad and lonely to be scary. Last night when the boy had motioned for her to come outside to play beneath the stars in the woods, she had almost gone. She wanted to ask the boy who he was and where he came from. But she wasn't allowed out after dark, especially not when her parents were asleep. And with Ryan and the other kids missing, her parents would be worried if they woke up in the middle of the night to find her gone.

But she really wanted to talk to the boy. He wasn't from around here. He didn't know the kids who teased her at school. What if she could make friends with him before any of the other kids made him hate her?

"What if he really is a ghost? What then?"

Sarah turned toward the bed where Jenny sat with her head down, scratching Mr. Whiskers behind the ears. "Are you jealous, Jenny?"

But Jenny didn't answer.

"We can all be friends," Sarah said. "You, me, Mr. Whiskers, and the boy. We can play by the stream all night. Think of all the fun we'll have!"

After a long moment Jenny met Sarah's gaze. "I guess it does sound like fun."

"What about you, Mr. Whiskers?"

The cat blinked at her. "Well, I must admit, I am rather curious about this boy."

Sarah clapped her hands. She looked from Jenny to Mr. Whiskers and back again. "I'm going to meet the boy tonight. Who's with me?"

CHAPTER EIGHT

The grizzled old-timers who frequented Malley's called it the Drink Dungeon, and it didn't take a genius to understand why. It lacked even a single window and had such poor ventilation that the air tasted stale. Little more than a hole in the wall, it was dimly lit, with fourteen stools running the length of a scarred wooden bar. There were no tables, no booths—just a CD jukebox in the far corner and a cramped bathroom that probably hadn't seen a thorough cleaning since the Reagan administration.

Jay sat on a stool near the door, one arm curled around a pint of Sam Adams, the other resting on the edge of the bar, his sleeve still soaked from a spill three beers ago. He stared at the bottles lining a mirrored shelf and listened to the disembodied voice of Jim Morrison singing about the faces that come out of the rain.

Look at you, sitting there like a loser. Is this how you want to live? No wonder Crystal walked out on you. You're no good for her. You're not even good for yourself. Nothing but a lousy drunk ... just like your dear old dad.

Jay drowned the voice out with a frat boy chug and turned his attention to Steve's camera, which sat on the bar before him. The Puritan boy gazed up at him from the digital display, his eyes dark and intense, a nebulous blue surrounding his body.

He had shown Crystal this exact picture. So why couldn't she see him?

"Because he's a ghost. And he's haunting me. Just me."

He tapped the display and cackled.

"I think you've had enough, Jay."

63

Jay glanced up to find Bill Malley looming over him, a towel draped over his hairy forearm. "I called a cab. You been babbling to yourself for half an hour."

"Come on, Bill. One more beer."

Malley shook his head. "Not tonight." He wrapped an arm around Jay and steered him outside where a taxi idled by the curb. "Don't come back here. For your own good." He stuffed a leaflet into Jay's hand. "Read this, get some help."

Jay crumpled the paper into a ball and pitched it into the gutter. "You think it's so easy. You *all* think it's so easy. Maybe I don't want ... your help. Ever think of ... of that?"

CHAPTER NINE

Tim's eyes fluttered open, sensing a change in the light. From the window at his bedside, he detected the pale blue of the glow-in-the-dark necklaces that Randy had draped around the kid's shoulders.

He rolled out of bed and stood slowly, cocking an ear toward his parent's bedroom where the warning growl of a German Shepherd and the haunting moan of a dying goose suggested that his parents were once again trying to outsnore one another.

He slipped into a pair of Nikes and crept toward the window. The boy loomed near the tree line, his pale skin and gaunt features accentuated by a blue phosphorescence. Standing there in the darkness, the boy could easily have passed for a vampire.

Don't freak, Tim thought. *Take a deep breath, remember the plan.*

He focused on opening the window without making a sound. Once he slid the screen up, he leaned outside and grabbed hold of the stone chimney that ran up the wall past his window. He wriggled outside and gazed down at the darkened backyard.

Probably just Randy's kid brother. So just chill.

Thirty seconds later, he dropped to the ground and stood in a low crouch. Dewdrops clung to the grass and shimmered in the moonlight. He scanned the shadows, but could see no sign of the boy. No sign of Randy or his goons.

His plan was simple—lure them to the side of the house, soak them with the hose, and then climb up the tree at the end of the driveway. When they ran after him, he'd grab the ropes he had tied into ready-made slipknots, lasso them like cattle, and tie them to the tree for the night.

The only thing his plan lacked was eggs. With any luck maybe his Mom had some rotten ones in the fridge. He'd give anything to pelt Randy right between the eyes, cover his face in a slimy film of yolk.

But first he had to find the boy.

A pale blue arc of light illuminated the grass near the edge of the yard, just beyond the garage. Somewhere around that corner, standing just out of sight, was the boy.

Maybe he should just grab the kid and drag him back to the coil of hose. Draw Randy and his goons out of hiding. He drew a deep breath.

Here goes nothing!

Tim sprinted toward the garage, ready to pounce on the boy. But when he rounded the corner, the boy was gone.

How did—

He spotted the boy standing at the fringe of trees. Watching him.

So much for the element of surprise, Tim thought, and bounded across the yard after him.

The boy disappeared into the trees, and Tim crashed through the thick underbrush, vines smacking wet against his legs.

A crescent moon shone through the canopy of trees, its pale light fading in and out with the shifting cloud cover. Tim didn't dare run faster than a jog. He hadn't lived here long enough to be familiar with the terrain in the daytime, let alone at night.

He glanced ahead and saw that he had lost sight of the boy. He drew to a halt and turned in a slow circle, searching the darkness for any trace of the boy or that pale blue glow. He couldn't believe it when he saw how far away his house was. The outline of the roof was barely perceptible through the trees.

What if this was a trap? What if Randy expected him to follow? What if he and his goons were behind those trees right now, ready to jump him?

He listened to his surroundings—hands on his hips, head cocked to one side—but all he could hear was the sound of his own labored breathing.

The moon passed behind the scudding clouds, and the forest dissolved into darkness.

Why don't I hear any crickets? Why don't I hear even a single sound?

But he forced the thoughts away.

At last the moon emerged from behind the clouds and the trees could again be seen apart from the shadows.

Four kids missing. What if Randy is the one doing it? What if this is how he does it—using the boy to lure people into the woods.

No. It didn't make sense. It was too crazy. Wasn't it?

The boy appeared again. Fifty yards ahead.

Tim raced after him, more determined than ever to catch this kid, to expose Randy, to confront his fears for good.

The boy dropped out of sight, only to reappear again half a minute later.

A strange thought suddenly occurred to Tim. He couldn't hear the boy running. In fact, he hadn't even seen the boy run. It was as if the boy were disappearing and reappearing like some kind of ghost or something.

That was only an illusion, of course. He didn't see the boy running because the boy was abandoning the path and stealing tree to tree. But the noise—he should be able to hear something, shouldn't he?

A sense of dread began to steal over him. What if Randy hadn't put the boy up to this? What if this was something totally different?

He thought again of the boy's milk-white complexion, his dark, sunken eyes and pale blue glow, and suddenly his heart froze in his chest and the hairs on his neck tingled as if electrified.

What if the boy ... what if I've been chasing ...

He turned in the direction that his house should be in, but it was nowhere in sight. He clenched his hands into fists and fought to slow down his racing heart.

Okay, get a hold of yourself. The path must have split off. You can find it, you can do it again.

He retraced his steps, his thoughts of catching the boy now whole-heartedly abandoned. All he wanted now was to get home, and to get there fast.

Several minutes passed before he saw something that drew him to a halt. The boy was now ahead of him. Somehow the boy had backtracked past him, unseen, unheard, and was now blocking the path that would lead him home.

Tim shook his head. It wasn't possible.

He shuffled backward, inching away from the grim-faced boy.

No—not a boy. Not anymore…not for centuries.

The boy stepped toward him.

Tim whirled around and dashed through the forest, tearing through the underbrush, dodging around boulders, and leaping over fallen logs. He glanced over his shoulder, but the boy was nowhere to be seen. He was aware that he was running further and further away from home, but he knew that if he could elude the boy until daybreak he would be okay.

The boy materialized on his right.

Tim screamed and hooked a left into the underbrush. He realized with dawning horror that the boy was steering him. But to where? And why?

He charged through the forest, heedless of the twigs and branches that snapped back into his face. He glanced backward. Where was the boy?

His foot caught beneath a root and he went flying through the air, arms outstretched like Superman. He came down hard, smacking his stomach against a rock, his palms raking the ground. He rolled onto his side, gasping for breath.

The boy. Where's the boy?

And then he saw the foot. It was planted on the ground just a few inches from his face—old Reebok's splotched with mud. Size ten. Maybe eleven.

He scrambled to his feet.

The man in the Reeboks lurched toward him, arms stretched wide. "See? Did you see?"

Tim stumbled against the rough bark of a pine, a scream lodged in his throat.

Just ahead, something came rifling through the underbrush. Tim and the man glanced at one another ... and then at the little girl who emerged into the clearing. For a long moment, the three of them stood gazing at one another.

No one moved. No one spoke.

And then the boy appeared between them, materializing out of the ether. An aura of blue framed his body, his skin so white it was almost translucent. He was dressed in tattered Puritan clothing, his eyes black and sunken beneath the brim of his hat.

Tim's brain screamed for him to run, but his feet remained cemented to the ground. It was a bizarre feeling, like being caught in a dream from which he couldn't awaken.

An unexpected threat of laughter bubbled in his chest, but he quickly choked it back, fearing he might lose his grip on reality, that his mind might simply become untethered.

He could feel the boy's gaze upon him, so unearthly it made his skin crawl.

The boy's lips parted to reveal crooked yellow teeth. "At last," he said, "we have gathered in this moonlit glen."

The girl stepped toward the glowing apparition. "What's your name?" she asked.

The man seized her by the shoulder. "Careful," he whispered. His dark hair stood in sleepy corkscrews, his face dirt-streaked and covered with stubble. A moment ago Tim had pegged him as a lunatic. Now he wasn't so sure. The fear in the man's eyes suggested that he'd been lured here too. But why? And why did he look so familiar?

The boy shifted his gaze to the girl. "I am Samuel."

"What do you want from us?" the man asked.

"Are you a friend?" the girl asked. "You are, aren't you?"

What's wrong with her? Why isn't she afraid?

"I bear a message from the world of the lost. The beast of old hath returned, awakened from a slumber of centuries, stirred to life by the blood of the new. It lurks in the shadow of the forest and hunts in the world of man, this demon whose hunger knows no bounds."

"Who are you?" the man asked. "Are you...a ghost?"

The boy nodded almost imperceptibly.

This isn't happening. This can't be real. There is no way I'm standing in the woods in the middle of the night talking to a boy who's been dead for three centuries.

"Why are you telling this to *us*?" Tim asked.

The boy's eyes narrowed. "It is not I who sought you, but you who sought me."

"What?" the man cried.

The sound startled a bird from its perch and sent it shrieking into the sky.

"You have the vision," the boy said. "You see what others cannot. That is why you must be the ones to destroy it."

***

Most alcoholics know there's only one way to sober up quickly. Not coffee, not water, but fear. You want to sober someone up, you scare the bejesus out of him.

Jay could see clearly now. No longer was the boy a pale blue smear against the night. Now he had features, substance, definition.

70

It was a chilling sight—the boy standing there among the graveyard of pines, pallid face draped in shadows, dark eyes at once solemn and desperate. The only thing keeping Jay from bolting through the woods in a blind panic was the fact that he was drunk enough to have what his dad called barroom bravery. Just what was keeping the little girl and the other kid from tearing away like spooked cattle was beyond him.

The boy's words swam through the murky waters of his mind.

A beast ... awakened ...

He glanced at the violet sky and traced the flight of the bird he had startled. When he lowered his gaze, the boy's eyes found his. "You have the vision. You see what others cannot. That is why you must be the ones to destroy it."

For a moment his mind was so clear he could see everything at once: the boy, the trees, the probing fingers of a ground fog.

Destroy the beast.

"What beast?" Jay asked. "Is it a man, some lunatic? Or is it something else?" He clenched his hands into fists. "It has those kids, though. Doesn't it? This man, this beast. It killed them?"

The boy nodded.

"And you want us to kill it?" It was the kid who spoke.

"Yes."

"And how are we supposed to do that?" The kid again. "Which is it, a beast or a man?"

"It is both beast and man. A creature whose cunning is matched only by its hunger, its insatiable thirst for blood and death."

The little girl wrinkled her nose and looked up at Jay. "He talks funny."

Jay patted her shoulder. "Who sent you, Samuel?"

The boy frowned. "I do not know." Then suddenly: "You must go! Quickly! The beast—it has sensed us!"

71

"What? Wait!" Jay said. But the boy pointed into the night and disappeared.

"We've got to get out of here," the kid said.

"Look," the girl said. "He left a trail."

A thread of light—pale blue and as gossamer as razor wire—extended through the forest in the direction the boy had pointed.

Jay took the girl's hand. "Come on."

"But what about Samuel?"

"Samuel can fend for himself."

"But the beast ..."

A howl pierced the night.

A dog? A wolf? The beast? Jay didn't know and didn't want to find out.

"Let's move!" the kid said, and bounded into the woods.

Jay and the girl exchanged a glance and then chased after him.

They ran together, tearing through the underbrush, following the thread of light that pulsed like a plucked guitar string.

The effects of alcohol had vanished, leaving Jay with a strange exhilaration. He felt as if he had just taken part in some elaborate college prank and had barely escaped getting caught. For the first time in years, he felt free.

There really is a boy...and they saw him.

The light of the boy's trail was fading fast. After a minute, it vanished altogether, leaving only the afterglow imprinted on Jay's retinas.

Time passed without calibration. It could have been ten seconds, ten minutes, or ten hours. They ran through the shadows and half-light, navigating through a maze of trees, a forest of cobalt and gray.

Soon a light filtered through the darkness, and they found themselves standing at the edge of Elm Street Park.

"Is it safe now?" The little girl gazed up at him, her eyes wide and curious.

Jay struggled to catch his breath. "Yeah," he said. "We're safe."

The girl smiled, clearly relieved. "My name is Sarah."

"I'm Jay."

"What about you?" She glanced at the older boy with dirty blond hair.

"Tim." His eyes wandered back to the trees. "I don't mean to break up the party, but can we get the hell out of here?"

Jay led them past a gazebo and a tiny frog pond. "Where do you guys live?"

"Pennybrook Road," Sarah said.

It was a moment before Tim answered. "South Maple."

Jay raised an eyebrow. "South Maple? I live on eleven South Maple. You new in town?"

Tim nodded. "Can't say I'm loving it, though." His eyes strayed back to Washaka Woods. "Did we really just see a ghost back there?"

"I think we did," Jay said. "Crazy as that sounds."

"What are we going to do?" Tim asked. "Do you think it could be right about there being some kind of creature in there?"

Jay shrugged. "Could be. But who knows if Samuel was even telling the truth...or knew what he was talking about. Maybe he was just a scared little boy who died in the woods."

"Or a scared little boy murdered by a beast in the woods," Tim said.

"I think it's important not to let it get into our heads. Maybe it's best if we just forgot about what happened tonight."

"But what if the beast takes more kids?" Sarah asked. "What if they're really scared? What if they're hurt."

Jay didn't answer.

"We should tell the police," Sarah said.

Jay glanced at Tim, but Tim didn't offer any help. "Sarah, the police wouldn't believe us. They'd lock us up if we told them what we saw." He laid a hand on her shoulder. "But I'll do everything I can to find the kids."

"You promise?"

"I promise," he said, and felt a twinge of guilt. It wasn't easy to lie to her. But hey, he was a pro, right? The guilt would fade after awhile. It always did.

He drew a deep breath, and for the first time since spotting the boy that night, he thought about how good it would feel to knock back a cold bottle of Sam.

CHAPTER TEN

Tim sat in a secluded corner of the Glenwood library, a pile of books spread on the table before him. It was quieter here on the second floor. Less people, less distractions. The perfect conditions to focus on his history essay.

God knew, he needed all the help he could get. Ever since his ordeal in Washaka Woods, he found it hard to concentrate on anything. His mind kept circling back to that terrifying confrontation in the clearing and fleeing through the dark from something he knew only as "the beast".

It seemed crazy now, here in the daytime, surrounded by books in a suburban library, listening to the rustling of turning pages. This was normal, this was real. Not what he'd seen in the woods the night before last. A ghost? Really?

It had to be a dream. Between Randy's bullying, Glenwood's missing kids, and adjusting to a new school, he was under a lot of stress. If that wasn't a recipe for nightmares, he didn't know what was.

He glanced at his assignment and sighed. It was due tomorrow, and he hadn't even started it yet.

Compare and contrast the US government as it functions today with how it was intended to function at the time of the Constitution's ratification. How would Hamilton and Jefferson feel about the role of today's lobbyists and Political Action Committees (PACs)?

Tim opened his laptop and typed: *Since both of those guys are dead, I don't think they really care about lobbyists or PACs.*

There—short, sweet, and to the point. Not to mention, rooted in scientific fact.

COLONY OF THE LOST

Unfortunately, there were two problems with this response. First, the essay had to be six pages long. And second, it had recently come to his attention that the dead sometimes *did* take an interest in current affairs.

Tim glanced up at the sound of shuffling pages and saw a cute blond in yoga pants gathering her things at the next table. He turned to watch, but got caught staring as she bent over to retrieve her purse. When their eyes met, he shrugged and made a "call me" gesture with his thumb and pinky finger. She shook her head, but smiled before tossing her hair and walking away.

It was the best advice he'd ever gotten—if a girl catches you staring, make a joke out of it. Better to come across confident and funny than shy and creepy.

It was just one of the many teachings from the Great Bill Dexler, a sophomore from Tim's last school, who, ironically, seemed incapable of following his own brilliant advice. He'd have to shoot Bill an e-mail once he finished this paper.

Crap. This paper.

Come on, focus. No more fooling around.

Time slipped by as it always did, one hour, two hours, like water dripping from a faucet. Sounds of life in the library grew scattered and faint until all he could hear was the low hum of the fluorescent lights above his table.

Somehow he had managed to scrape together a rough draft of the essay. Once he added an introduction and conclusion and elaborated on a couple of points he could probably get five pages. And if he used Courier 12 point and a custom spacing of about 2.2, he would get the six pages he needed.

He glanced at his watch: 7:15. Hadn't the sign downstairs said the library closed at 7:00? Maybe this town had the only laid back librarian in the country. He shut his laptop and slipped it into his backpack. The finishing touches could wait until after dinner.

76

He glanced up at the sound of footsteps. A single pair echoed against the stone tile, drew close, and faded away. The pattern repeated itself a number of times—the sound of someone walking up and down the stacks, checking to see if everyone had gone home.

Tim zipped up his bag and slung it over his shoulder. He turned to leave and almost crashed into the man standing behind him.

Tim stumbled against the table and swore. "Are you *trying* to give me a heart attack?"

The man offered no apology. Didn't even change his expression.

Crazy old janitor.

The man glared at him. "Sit."

"What? I can't, I've got to get home."

"Sit!

"Look, I'd love to stay for a lecture—and I'm sure it would be a great one—but I lost track of time so I'm just gonna go now."

The man forced Tim into the chair. "Hey, come on!"

The man loomed over him, his face sun-browned and covered in stubble. "What did he tell you?"

"What did who tell me?"

"The boy."

A ripple of fear coursed through him. "I don't know what you're talking about."

"The boy. *Samuel.* What did he say?"

Tim stammered, his mouth so dry he couldn't make a sound. Which was just as well, seeing as he had no idea what to say to this lunatic. The guy looked like a drug addict—dark circles beneath his eyes, salt-and-pepper hair knotted and unkempt. His pupils were so dilated, you could barely see the whites.

And the longer Tim stared, the harder he found it to look away. In fact, if he tilted his head just right, he could see a gleam of red radiating from the center of the man's eyes.

77

That got him moving—he jumped out of the chair and dodged around the table, leaving his backpack on the floor.

"What did he say, Tim?"

The man was tall—at least six foot two—and had the shuffling gait of a zombie.

Tim retreated into the stacks, his heart hammering. Had he really just seen that guy's eyes turn red?

"You're going the wrong way," the man said, a teasing lilt to his voice.

Tim swore, realizing that he *had* run the wrong way. He turned down the next aisle and cocked his head to listen. The echo of the man's footsteps suggested that he was only an aisle or two over.

"Be careful where you step, Tim. You might encounter something…unsavory."

Tim peered through a gap in the shelves, but he couldn't see his stalker. How was he supposed to double back to the stairs without getting caught?

A hinge creaked somewhere to Tim's right. Something clicked, and he had time only to swing his head toward the sound before the lights went out and the library plunged into darkness.

"I do hope you're not afraid of the dark, Tim. That would be…*unfortunate*." He spoke the word tentatively—as if English was not his first language.

Tim held his breath and concentrated on not making a sound. He had an absurd fear that the man would hear his heart pounding. He gazed in the direction of the circuit breaker, but he couldn't even see the books that he knew were right in front of his face.

What was this psycho planning? He wasn't the janitor. He certainly wasn't the librarian. So who was he, and how did he know about Samuel? And even still, how did he know Tim's name?

It is both beast and man.

Samuel's words prickled his skin with gooseflesh. Crazy or not, this was happening. And it was serious. Life or death serious. He tiptoed further into the stacks, his elbow brushing a book that some kid had lazily propped on the shelf. It fell to the floor with a reverberating smack.

Laughter pierced the darkness. The sound was completely mirthless, like a machine grinding gravel. "Clumsy, aren't we?"

Tim turned in a slow circle, trying to pinpoint the direction of the sound. It seemed to be coming from everywhere and nowhere at once. Either the man was lightning-fast or he could throw his voice.

Tim suddenly wished Randy and his goons were responsible for this. He would get his beating, they would have their laughs, and then he could go home. He'd be bloodied and bruised, but at least he'd be alive.

"What do you want from me?"

"You know what I want. Tell me about the boy."

Tim held his breath. Maybe the man would leave him alone if he told him what he knew. "He warned of a beast."

"Oh my, how terrifying." The man sounded closer now. "What else did he say?"

"Nothing."

"Do you really expect me to believe that, Tim?"

Tim shuffled backward. "I'm leaving now."

"I'm afraid I can't let you do that."

A hand seized him by the throat and slammed him against the stacks. The man's face pressed close to Tim's, the red of his eyes shining bright enough to reveal the outline of his features, the madness of his grin. "The hunt is finished, Tim. But the killing ... the killing is just begun."

A squirt of urine escaped into Tim's pants as he flailed his arms and groped for something, anything with which to defend himself. His hand closed around the thick spine of a book—a dictionary, maybe, or a thesaurus. He brought it down like a hatchet, driving the corner into the man's eye.

The man roared, his grip slackening.

Tim dropped the book and sprinted toward the stairs. After a few steps, he slipped in something wet and his feet flew out from underneath him. His tailbone smashed against the floor, sending a white-hot jolt of pain radiating up his spine. He rolled over and tried to get up, but his hand got tangled in what felt like hair.

Wet, sticky hair.

By now, his eyes had begun to adjust to the darkness, and he could discern the jackknifed form of an older woman lying in a pool of blood, her mouth frozen in a silent scream.

Somewhere, the man chuckled. "I see you've found the librarian."

Tim scrambled to his feet and raced down the aisle. He rounded the corner at full speed, his sneakers squealing against the tile as he broke into the straightaway. He risked a backward glance and spotted the man in close pursuit. He grabbed a cart of books and rolled it into the man's path.

The man leaped over it, landed on his hands and knees, and bounded after Tim on all fours like some kind of animal. Tim turned another corner and noticed a faint light illuminating the tiles at the end of the corridor. A streetlight filtering through the blinds? But why would it have a reddish tint?

Exit! *It's an Exit sign.*

Somehow he'd missed the stairs to the lobby and stumbled upon the emergency exit at the rear of the building. He burst through the door and raced down the stairs on the balls of his feet, his momentum threatening to send him tumbling head over heels.

The man caught the door on its closing arc and slammed it into the wall so hard that chips of concrete rained onto the stairs.

Tim reached the landing and dove to his left just as the man vaulted off the steps like a jungle cat pouncing on its prey. The man collided with the wall and fell onto his back, momentarily stunned.

Tim jumped over him and lunged for the door. He pushed it open and charged out into the night where a sliver of a moon gleamed in the darkening sky. His eyes locked on the brick building opposite the library, and he darted across the street and flung himself through the doors to the Glenwood Police Department.

CHAPTER ELEVEN

Jay squinted against the bright sunlight and sipped a glass of lemonade. A beer would've been a hell of a lot better, a hell of a lot more satisfying, but Steve hadn't offered him one and he thought it best not to ask.

"Find a job yet?"

Jay chomped on an ice cube and shrugged. "Haven't really been looking."

"What have you been up to?"

"Not much. Just trying to adjust. How's work?"

"It's not the same without you. We all miss your jokes about Hoffman. Did I tell you someone slashed his tires?"

"Really?" Jay couldn't help but grin.

"Yeah, all four."

"Serves him right. Any idea who did it?" He imagined himself stumbling around the parking lot with his Swiss Army knife. A daydream ... or perhaps the foggy memory of a bender? These days, who could say for sure?

"Hoffman thinks it was someone from your geometry class."

Jay shrugged. "I could see Brian Mossler joking about it, but I don't think he'd actually do it." He set his glass on the patio table and gazed into the woods beyond Steve's property line. "Glenwood was settled in the 1700's, right?"

"Yeah. 1709."

"Did people still dress like Puritans back then—you know, the black and white suits and all that?"

"Well, maybe on Sundays or formal occasions. Why?"

"Just wondering."

"You know there was a settlement here in the 1640's, one that predated Glenwood?"

"There was?"

"Yeah, it was an offshoot of the Puritans in Boston. I wrote an article about it last summer in the Item."

Jay shrugged. "I must have missed it. Sorry."

Steve waved him off. "It's actually pretty fascinating." His voice took on the same scholarly tone he normally reserved for his lectures. "In the summer of 1643, a hundred and five people abandoned Boston and headed west to start their own lives away from the strictness of Puritan society. They formed their own settlement under the leadership of a man named William Johnston—a place they called Freetown. But the settlement didn't last long…three or four years, five at the most. No one's really sure."

"Why? What happened?"

Steve adjusted his glasses. "A band of French fur trappers passed through the settlement in 1648 and found it deserted. Not a soul around. No dead bodies, no remains of any sort, nothing to suggest that they had died of starvation, cold, or disease. It was as if the whole town had vanished in an instant. They left behind all their supplies, all their food and earthenware. In a few cabins they even found place settings on the tables, crock pots hanging over fires that were long dead." He shrugged. "Whatever happened, happened fast. These people left in a hurry."

"Sounds almost like what happened at Roanoke Island," Jay said.

"Yes, except there were no markings found here. At Roanoke, they found the word Croatoan carved into a tree."

Jay nodded. He remembered reading about that years ago in history class. "What do you think happened?"

Steve laced his fingers behind his head and leaned back. "It's possible they went to live with the Washaka tribe. King Philip's War

83

was still thirty years away, so the Washakas might have been friendly toward them. But I don't know. Sometimes I think that maybe the Washakas led them away from the settlement and killed them."

"You're kidding, right?"

"Think about it. Every day, the white man cut down more of their forests, pushed the Indians further and further from the coast, spread smallpox like wildfire. They had their reasons."

"Did you put that in your article?"

"Are you crazy? It's just a theory. When I was doing my research, I spoke to Chief Skatchawa, the Washaka leader who's building that casino in Gilway. He knew something that he wasn't telling me. I could see it in his eyes. So what else could it be?"

Jay tilted the glass to his lips and chomped on the last ice cube. *You wouldn't believe it, Steve. Not in a million years.*

***

Jay watched the sun slip behind Mount Greylock, sending shadows stalking into the valley to smother the last vestiges of daylight. Centuries ago, a colony vanished from these lands, an entire settlement lost. And now all these years later, three children had disappeared without a trace. It couldn't be a coincidence. Not after what Samuel revealed to them in Washaka Woods.

The sudden blare of a horn startled him as a car roared past, sending sand spiraling up into his windshield. Jay swerved back onto his side of the double yellow line and swore. In the rearview mirror, he caught a glimpse of an irate driver flipping him off.

Christ, I drive better when I'm drunk.

By the time his heart had resumed a normal rhythm, he was steering the LeBaron into his driveway. Darkness greeted him as he stepped into the foyer, a waft of musty air reaching his nostrils. He wrinkled his nose at the stench and cracked a window, then kicked off his shoes and collapsed onto the couch.

Even with his eyes closed, it seemed he could still see the refrigerator looming over the kitchen counter. A beer would taste great right now. A nice, cold bottle of Sam. Or maybe a Jack and Coke to take the edge off.

With Crystal gone and no job to tie him down, he could have a drink whenever he wanted. Drunk without the guilt...now that was living!

The first step in AA was to admit that you were powerless against alcohol, and at least a dozen times he had spoken those very words in the smoke-filled church basement on Summer Street, staring out into a crowd of strangers. But not once had he ever believed it. He wasn't powerless against alcohol. He didn't drink because he had to— he drank because he *wanted* to.

But what if that wasn't true? What if he'd been lying to himself all these years?

He felt a sudden twinge of empathy for his father. It was the first time he'd felt anything but loathing since the bastard walked out of his life twenty years ago. He could always count on Dad to get wasted at every family gathering. No matter how drunk, Dad was always quick with a backhand—especially where Mom was concerned.

But it wasn't like that in the beginning. The hitting only began after the drinking had spiraled out of control, a spiral he felt himself drawn into now...a great sucking vortex like a black hole. First drinking leads to unemployment, then unemployment leads to more drinking, then the attainment of another job becomes impossible, and there's nothing left to do but die.

He didn't want it to happen that way, didn't want to die a drunk.

But the call of the bottles in the kitchen mocked him.

Just a sip, Jay. What're you afraid of? You know you want it.

He made a fist and punched himself in the thigh, angry at the voices, angry at himself because he was salivating. He snatched the morning paper off the coffee table and tried to drown out his inner voices.

GLENWOOD LIBRARIAN SAVAGELY MURDERED!

Glenwood- A startling new development in the Glenwood missing persons case occurred here last night while most citizens were returning home from work. A local youth, whose name police would not disclose, was seen fleeing from the library just after 7:00 P.M. Bystanders reported that as the boy ran into the police station across the street, a shadowy figure emerged from the library and slipped away toward Salem Street and Washaka Woods.

A grisly scene awaited police in the library, where the body of long-time librarian Jane Maclaren was found nearly decapitated on the second floor.

Police speculate that the suspect was involved in the recent disappearances of four other Glenwood youths: ten-year-old Ryan Brakowski, thirteen-year-old Tanya Anderson, seven-year-old Billy Deegan, and, most recently, eleven-year-old Ben Wesley. With the exception of a small shred of Ryan Brakowski's blood-spattered shirt, which was found by joggers on a trail in Washaka Woods, police have found no traces of any of the victims. Police, in conjunction with the federal agents now working on the case, called this latest incident a tragic breakthrough.

Police have released a sketch of the assailant. He is described as a tall white male in his early to mid forties, 185-205 pounds, with dark skin, dark eyes, and graying hair. Police are asking residents to notify them immediately of anyone resembling the man in the sketch.

The disappearances of the four youths in this historically quiet town have seriously shaken residents. A curfew went into effect early this week and school officials are now considering a suspension of classes until the suspect is caught. Police hope that information from the public will lead to the eventual capture of the suspect and the discovery of the whereabouts of the missing children. Residents say they are optimistic, but will continue to take careful precautions while the man in the sketch remains at large.

Jay felt a sinking sensation in the pit of his stomach. He stared at the charcoal sketch of the mystery assailant. Was that really who the boy had seen in the library, or had he seen some hideous beast and then lied about it so people wouldn't think he was crazy?

He chewed a fingernail. Tim. He could see the kid's face clearly, a portrait of terror burned into his memory like a scar. They had almost run into each other in the midnight woods, both of them scared senseless, tearing through a forest shrouded in darkness, searching for an escape from the phantom child born out of some half-forgotten nightmare.

He'd seen a police car parked outside of Tim's house around nine o'clock last night. It had pulled up alongside the white Colonial, flashers off, siren silent, tires grinding pebbles. A pair of cops got out—a fat one and a skinny one. Both hitched their pants like TV repairmen and headed up the walkway. They disappeared inside and emerged onto the porch a few minutes later. The fat cop said something to Tim's dad, patted him on the back, and then waddled back to the cruiser.

The cruiser remained there throughout the night—he had woken up repeatedly and checked. He tried telling himself not to worry, that maybe the kid's father was a witness to a crime and needed to be guarded until the trial. It was a stupid theory. But in the dead of the night, it was a more comforting thought than the alternative—that Tim had been attacked by the beast Samuel had warned them about and had barely escaped with his life.

How much had Tim left out of the story? What kind of terror had the boy faced? He thought suddenly of the little girl—of Sarah—

87

and felt ashamed. He'd promised to find out all he could about the warning Samuel bestowed upon them, had said in so many words that he would protect them, that he would stop any more kids from disappearing. And what had he done? Nothing. Not a damn thing.

And what about the suitcase sitting packed on his bed? Was he really just planning to get away for the weekend, or was he trying to skip town while Tim and Sarah remained behind to face an almost certain death?

It's coming for you, Jay. It's coming to kill you. And you deserve it. The pain, the suffering ... you deserve it all.

"Shut up."

Yelling at the voices in your head? People might think you're going crazy. I think maybe you already are. So why not have a drink? Throw back a cold one with your dear old dad.

"Go to hell."

Been there, Jay. Too hot for my liking. But I think you'll enjoy it.

He wiped his mouth.

Getting thirsty?

Jay drew a deep breath and promised himself he wouldn't give in to the temptation.

Why fight it, boy? You know you can't beat it.

He got up from the couch and decided that he needed to walk around, to clear his head. After his third lap around the living room, he found himself standing before the refrigerator, arms folded across his chest. His throat felt constricted, his breathing too shallow. He definitely needed a drink. A glass of Coke, maybe ... or some orange juice.

He licked his lips, opened the door, and groped inside for a bottle. When he got to the counter, he realized that he had grabbed a bottle of Sam instead of the two-liter of Coke. He shook his head and shrugged. Honest mistake.

He slid his finger along the glass, cutting a slick track through the condensation.

Don't do it.

He glanced at the refrigerator. He could put it back. It wouldn't be too hard. Just three steps, a quick tug, and voila! It would've been a good plan except that the Coke looked a little flat. How long had it sat there on the shelf, the cap barely tightened? Flat Coke gave him indigestion, always had. If he drank it, he'd be up all night with that awful burning in his chest.

Better to have a couple swigs of beer than to make himself sick. He supposed he could have water, but the tap didn't get very cold. Besides, there probably weren't any ice cubes in the freezer, at least not any fresh ones.

He cradled the bottle of Sam, stroking its shapely neck. Three sips. That's all he wanted. He could do it, he had the willpower.

A test, then! That was it! A way to prove if he really did have a drinking problem. He would have three sips and then dump the rest down the sink.

He grinned fiercely at the challenge.

Somewhere in the back of his mind, the voice of his father cackled.

He tilted the bottle to his lips. Beer poured into his mouth in an icy rush, expanding the pinhole of his throat. After the third gulp, he set the bottle down and wiped his hand across his mouth.

There! That wasn't so hard. Still a quarter of a bottle left, and he didn't even want it.

He strutted into the living room and clicked on the TV. When a commercial interrupted the program five minutes later, he returned to the kitchen. He held the bottle over the sink and hesitated. Why throw it out? He proved he could resist the urge to drink it, so he obviously wasn't an alcoholic. Any normal, sober person wouldn't waste the last few sips of a beer if he was thirsty. So if he was, in fact, normal he should probably finish it. It only made sense, after all.

Stop it, Jay. For God's sake, are you listening to yourself?

But the voice held no power over him. He brushed it aside and downed the last few swallows. For a long moment, he stared at the empty bottle, at the delicate web of foam clinging to the bottom. Then he heaved it into the sink, shattering the glass into a thousand glittering shards.

"Why can't I help it? Why can't I just... *stop?*" And then he was sobbing. But it was too late. The damage had been done.

Why couldn't Crystal be here? Her presence would force him to stay sober. He lowered his face into his hands. The house was so empty without her, so utterly devoid of life. Alcohol had ruined him, had cost him his fiancée, his job, his future. So why was he reaching into the fridge for another drink?

Because there's nothing left for me to do.

He hoisted the bottle of Sam to his lips.

***

Fingers of light flickered across the room, muted grays and blues producing a host of lurking shadows. Jay sat slouched on the sofa, a half empty bottle of Sam cradled in his lap. The ghostly glow of the TV illuminated his face. In the kitchen, the refrigerator hummed softly to itself, the noise cycling in and out every ten minutes or so.

Alcohol numbed his body, beginning with his lips and branching out to consume his head, chest, and legs. He stared at the TV in a daze. The room orbited him every time he closed his eyes. Jimmy Fallon shook hands with his guests—two actors and a leggy blond model—while the credits rolled across the screen. With the volume turned low, the words had difficulty penetrating the fog that enveloped his mind.

For once the voices remained quiet; none seemed to have anything to say. He sat back, enjoyed the buzz, and let the alcohol

COLONY OF THE LOST

carry him away. Two or three hours must have passed before he came awake with a start.

A crash emanated from somewhere in the house. He blinked sleepily and pulled himself into a sitting position.

The house was utterly still. He waited a moment longer, shrugged, and closed his eyes. *Must have been—*

Glass tinkled to the floor in the kitchen, followed by a grunt and a heavy thud.

"Looks like I've got company." He took a swig of beer and set the bottle on the coffee table. It missed its mark and tumbled to the floor.

The refrigerator awoke with a purring hum. The door swung shut with a click. Footfalls approached, the sound interspersed with the clinking of glass. "Sorry about the window, Jay, but you didn't leave me a key."

Jay turned toward the voice and saw a tall man crossing into the den. He carried a bottle of Sam in each gloved hand. His face was a mask of shadows, and Jay had to close one eye to keep from seeing two men instead of one.

The man placed the bottles on the table and seated himself in the recliner opposite Jay.

Jay reached for the opener and popped off the cap.

"That a boy," the man said. "Drink up." He propped his feet up and spread his arms over the back of the chair. "Nice place you got here." His eyes swept the room. "Dark. Just the way I like it."

Jay tipped his head back and took a long pull of beer. He glanced at the newspaper on the table, at the charcoal sketch on the center of page one.

The man leaned forward and grabbed the paper. He spread it open on his lap and shook his head. "The resemblance is rather striking, wouldn't you say?" His dark eyes were humorless.

"Have another sip, Jay. I'd like to let you finish, but I've got to kill you soon." He reached for a bottle and angled it into his mouth, twisting the cap against his teeth. It tore free with a squealing pop. The man grinned, then spat the cap onto the floor.

Jay watched the cap roll underneath the sofa before shifting his gaze back to the tall stranger. Blood stained the man's teeth and trickled from the corners of his mouth in dark rivulets.

There was something oddly familiar about the man, something he could see even through the screen of alcohol, a screen that was dissolving as his fear intensified.

The man licked his lips and closed his eyes briefly, as if savoring the taste of blood. "Tell me about the boy, Jay. Tell me about Samuel."

Jay finished his beer and stared at the TV. "Why should I tell you anything?"

"Is that any way to treat a guest?"

"Try bringing your own beer next time."

"I'm afraid there's not going to be a next time."

Jay set his empty on the coffee table. "I know who you are."

The man flashed him a leering grin. "No Jay, I don't think you do."

"You're a kidnapper. And a murderer. And my mailman."

"Is that so?"

"It's a small town. Did you really think you wouldn't get caught?"

"You see, Jay, I am he... and yet I am not he. I am the One and the Many, the Hunter and the Hunted...and all things in between. I bring Death to Life and Life to Death."

Jay could feel himself sobering up fast. "Why don't you bring yourself to the front door?"

"Just as soon as I kill you." The man's eyes flickered. Red light winked in the depths of his pupils.

Just an illusion. Didn't really see that.

The thing sitting opposite Jay laughed, but what came out sounded more like a growl.

Something cold and unyielding pressed into Jay's back. At first he had no idea what it could be, but then his mind retrieved the answer—his dad's .45. He had taken it out this morning, digging it out of the shoebox at the top of his bedroom closet. He'd carried it around the house ever since, afraid something like this might happen.

He reached behind his back and drew the gun from the waistband of his jeans.

The thing that looked like a man brandished a hunting knife. The blade gleamed in the TV's flickering light.

Jay rolled off the couch and clicked off the safety.

The thing's grin faltered. It inched forward, rotating its wrist, cutting tiny circles into the air with the point of the knife.

"Don't come any closer," Jay said.

"You can't kill me. You can't even hurt me. All you can do is ruin my disguise."

Outside, his neighbor's bamboo wind chime echoed its eerie tune. The sound it made was low and hollow, like the ratting of bones.

It's not even scared, Jay thought. *I've got a gun pointed right at it, and the son-of-a-bitch isn't even afraid.*

Blood pounded in his ears, a sound like soldiers at march. Sweat seeped from his pores, threatening to loosen his grip on the gun.

The thing snarled, spittle flying from its lower lip. It dropped into a crouch, bloody mouth curling into a grin. And then it sprang at him, knife poised to strike.

The trigger was slippery, oiled with a sheen of sweat. Jay's finger slipped once, twice. And then the gun fired—a deafening report like August thunder. A brief flash illuminated the room, followed by the acrid stench of gun smoke.

The thing jerked back. The force of the bullet tore the knife from its hand, sending it clattering to the floor. Its face twisted into a mask of agony. It clutched its shoulder. Blood seeped through its fingers and dripped onto the hardwood in thick, red drops. The thing met his gaze, the red light gone from its eyes. It staggered back, looking human again—a he rather than an it.

Jay cocked the hammer, took aim.

The man glanced down at the knife. Confusion clouded his face. He glanced up at Jay and saw the gun as if for the first time. "Oh God. Not again. "

Kill him!

But something in the man's face gave him pause.

It's playing you—don't you see? It's not human.

A warble of sirens rose in the distance. Jay stole a glance out the window, at the flashing lights reflected in the trees.

The man made a break for the door.

Jay had a clear shot to his back. He took aim, but didn't fire. He lowered the gun and shook his head.

The man slipped outside into the waiting embrace of darkness.

CHAPTER TWELVE

Sarah sat on her bed and doodled in her notebook. Outside, the rain poured down in fat drops, drumming against the roof and fogging up her window. Mr. Whiskers lay curled by her side, his fluffy head nuzzled against her thigh. She scratched him beneath his chin and gazed out the window.

She hated the rain. It was gray and gloomy and made everything look so ugly. At least it was Thursday. Just one more day of school before the weekend.

She glanced at the clock on the nightstand: 3:05. Her parents wouldn't be home from work for another two hours, so for now she was all alone with Jenny and Mr. Whiskers. Mom didn't like leaving her home all alone, but Daddy said they needed the money, and for once Mom agreed with him.

Sarah liked staying home by herself. It felt grown up to be in an empty house. Plus, she got to do whatever she wanted. She could play out in the woods without being yelled at, she could play dress up with Jenny. That was her favorite game—putting on Mom's make up and jewelry and walking around the house in high heels and dresses.

But today she didn't feel like playing games. Another kid had gone missing, this time an eleven-year-old boy who went to private school. She didn't know him, but from the picture they showed on TV he looked nice enough. Not a big, mean jerk like Joey Cobb or Bobby Peterman. This boy looked like someone she could have been friends with. "Ben Wesley," she told Jenny. "That was his name."

Jenny twirled her hair around her finger and nodded. "Do you think the monster killed him?"

Sarah shrugged. "I don't know. I need to talk to Samuel."

Mr. Whiskers stretched his paws and spread his toes. "Sarah, I hope you don't plan on searching for Samuel in the woods. You remember what he said, don't you?"

Sarah frowned. "He said we had to go because the monster sensed us."

Mr. Whiskers nodded. "Exactly." He licked a paw and scrubbed his face. "If you go into the woods, it may find you."

"And then it would kill you," Jenny said.

Sarah nodded. "And then we'd all die. Well, except for you Mr. Whiskers, but you wouldn't be able to talk anymore."

Mr. Whiskers scratched behind his ear and sneezed. "That's okay. No one understands me besides you two anyway." He sneezed again. "I hate this new flea powder."

Sarah and Jenny giggled. "Sorry," Sarah said. "It was probably on sale."

Mr. Whiskers flipped his tail. "That certainly figures."

Sarah went back to her notebook and drew a dark shadow lurking in the trees. There were four kids missing now. And if someone didn't stop the monster, there would be a lot more than that soon. She wondered what the man—what Jay—had found out. Did he know where the kids were? Had he told the police?

She would have to talk to him soon.

***

"Could you pass the butter?"

"Sure, Daddy." Sarah handed him the tub of margarine. He was sitting across from her, his tie loosened, his shirt untucked. When he hadn't come home by 6:30, she began to worry that he might never come home, that maybe the monster had gotten him.

"How was school today?"

Sarah forced a smile. "Great."

"How was your day, Margaret?"

96

But Mom didn't answer. She was staring off into space and looked confused, almost lost. And that was strange because Mom was always in control.

"Margaret?"

"Huh?"

"How was your day?"

"Oh, okay. Same old story." She smiled, but it looked fake.

They finished dinner in silence. Sarah wondered if her parents had been fighting again. Sometimes they didn't talk after a fight. She frowned at her plate and ate her mashed potatoes with her head down, the only sound the clinking of silverware.

When dinner ended, Sarah helped with the dishes. As she rinsed the plates and stacked them beside the sink, she noticed Mom glancing out the window, her eyes scanning the edge of Washaka Woods.

Does she see Samuel? Is that why she's acting funny?

Mom whirled around. "What did you say?"

Dad wiped his hands on the dishtowel. "No one said anything. Are you sure you're feeling okay?"

Mom glanced at the floor and massaged her forehead. "Yeah. Uh-huh. I'm fine." But she didn't look fine.

He put the towel down and gave her a hug. "Maybe you should lie down. You don't look so good."

She glanced left, then right, frowning. "Maybe you're right. I think I'll go upstairs."

***

By nine o'clock the rain had stopped, leaving behind a soupy gray fog that clung to the treetops. In the sky, a fuzzy yellow moon seeped through the clouds. Sarah watched TV to pass the time, the volume turned low so her parents wouldn't know she was still awake. Every few minutes, she glanced out the window, keeping watch for Samuel.

97

All her life her parents insisted there were no such things as ghosts, no such things as monsters. Whenever she couldn't sleep because she saw a scary movie or heard a strange noise coming from the closet, Daddy would sit on her bed and tell her there was nothing to be afraid of, that monsters didn't exist.

I saw that movie last year, he'd say, *and no monster ever ate me.*

But he was wrong. Monsters did exist. And ghosts too. All those nights she had listened to his comforting words, there really could've been a monster hiding in her room. Eyes watching from the closet...arms reaching from underneath the bed.

Until a few days ago, she'd never doubted anything he said. Now she doubted everything. What else was he wrong about? Death? God? Santa Claus?

Maybe she was overreacting. Maybe Dad was right about there being no such thing as ghosts. She could have dreamed it, could have imagined Samuel the way she imagined Jenny. Was it possible to imagine something so clearly that you couldn't tell if it was real or not?

It's not my imagination. Samuel is a ghost. I saw him—and so did Jay and that boy, Tim.

She knew she was right. She'd seen Jay a couple times in the neighborhood. One of those times, Dad was with her and he had waved to Jay as he walked by. So if Dad had seen Jay, that meant Jay was real. And if Jay had seen Samuel, then that meant Samuel was real.

It was a circle of logic she couldn't deny. Samuel was real. And so was the monster he'd warned them about. It lived in the woods somewhere and had already killed a bunch of kids. Who would be next? Her? Tim?

It made sense—they knew about the monster, and if it had really sensed them in the woods, then it might know who they were. Maybe it had even followed them home that night, creeping behind them in the dark. Or maybe it had picked up their scent and could follow it to them at any time.

You're being silly. Daddy would laugh if he heard the way you're thinking. He'd give you a hug and tell you it's time to start acting like a big girl.

She glanced at the clock awhile later: 12:03, and still no Samuel. Maybe she'd imagined him after all. It was probably best if she had. Sure she might be crazy, sure Mom might be right, but at least it would mean there were no monsters out there.

A breeze blew through the open window, puffing out the curtains and blowing back her hair. The air smelled of moss and wildflowers, the scent of the woods after a rain. When the wind stilled, the night fell silent, and all Sarah could hear was her blinds knocking against the window frame.

A few moments passed before she heard another noise. It sounded like it came from out back. She sat up straight and waited for the sound to repeat itself. It wasn't until she heard the creak of stairs that she realized it had been the back door.

Her heart raced. Had someone come in?

Maybe Daddy let Mr. Whiskers out. Or maybe it's—

Take it easy. Don't jump to conclusions. It was Dad's voice, but it didn't give her any comfort.

She drew a deep breath and peered over the side of her bed. Mr. Whiskers sat crouched on the floor, his ears spinning round on his head.

She squeezed her eyes shut and listened to the approaching footfalls.

Please be Mommy. Please be Daddy.

Whoever it was paused in the hallway, then continued toward her parents' bedroom.

99

She clenched the sheets in her hands. A minute passed. It felt like a year. She held her breath. What if the monster was in the house? What if it had sneaked into her parents' bedroom?

She imagined a monster standing over her parents, something that was all claws, scales, and teeth. She had to know what was going on, had to prove to herself that everything was okay.

She slipped out of bed and crept to her bedroom door, which stood open a crack. A slant of light from the hallway filtered into her room. She opened the door wider and peered out, glancing in both directions.

But the hallway was deserted.

She stole a glance at Mr. Whiskers, then stepped into the hall. A railing overlooked the darkened living room below. She crept alongside it, walking on tiptoes.

A floorboard creaked. She stopped short, one foot suspended in the air. Over her shoulder, she could see the stairs as they wound up to the second floor. A trail of muddy footprints led up them, the color a deep, glistening brown. The trail veered right at the top of the stairs and ended at her parents' doorstep.

Sarah drew a deep breath and tried to calm herself. *Maybe there's a good reason for it. Maybe Daddy took out the trash and forgot to wipe his feet.*

That got her going again... but just barely. As her hand folded around the doorknob to her parents' room, her mind screamed for her to run away. But she couldn't leave without knowing what happened.

The knob turned in her hand, and the door swung in with a groan.

Mom sat Indian-style on the bed, her hair wet and tangled, her face streaked with mud. Her nightgown was filthy, the sheets too, everything covered in mud.

Her head jerked up as the door opened and she glared at Sarah. "What're you doing? Go back to bed!"

Sarah scanned the room. She didn't see any monsters. But something was wrong, just the same. "Mom, are you okay?"

"Yes, fine. Everything's just ... fine. Now go back to bed."

Sarah lingered for a moment longer. "Okay," she said. "Goodnight." But as she turned to leave, she could see Mom watching her, and maybe it was just her imagination, or maybe just a trick of the light, but she could have sworn that for just one second Mom's eyes blazed a brilliant red.

CHAPTER THIRTEEN

For a moment Tim just sat there and stared at the paper Mr. Tuscardi placed face down on his desk. Everything swam out of focus and suddenly he was no longer looking at the paper, but through it.

He imagined himself back at the library, hunched over his laptop on the second floor, pecking at the keys while the other kids packed up and went home, leaving him alone to face a man who wasn't really a man at all.

He leaned back in his chair and drew a deep breath.

Try to forget it.

He sighed, wishing he could, and flipped the paper over.

Scrawled across the top in a looping red script was a C-. It would've been a B-, but Tuscardi dropped him a full letter grade for turning the paper in late. He probably could've avoided the penalty if he'd told Tuscardi that his laptop was locked overnight in a building roped off by yellow police tape. But instead he opted to keep a low profile. Students weren't the only ones who gossiped.

Talk at the school had already shifted from the murder in the library to the shooting late last night. It hadn't even been twelve hours and already the whole school seemed to know everything about it. Of course, part of that had to do with the fact that the guy whose house was broken into used to teach here.

Mr. G—that's what the kids called him. But to Tim, he was Jay Gallagher—the drunk guy from Washaka Woods. No wonder the guy looked so familiar—he'd probably walked past him in the halls a dozen times since transferring here.

According to the rumors, Jay was drunk when the man broke in. Big surprise there. The guy's breath had reeked of alcohol that night in the woods. What he found most surprising was that the students loved him and had protested his firing. But they'd never seen him drunk, never seen him make promises to a little girl that he couldn't keep.

I promise I'll find the kids.

Sure you will, Tim thought. *You'll search every liquor store in the county, poke your head around the toilet when you're puking, see if maybe they'd accidentally flushed themselves.*

Like the guy or not, he needed to talk to him. They had to figure out what to do, how to protect Sarah. He was certain that she was its next target. But why was it so eager to learn what Samuel had told them? Did it think Samuel knew how to kill it?

The bell signaled the end of class. He grabbed his paper and headed into the hall.

"Hi Tim."

Maria stood just outside the door. God, she was sexy.

"Hi, Maria." He was suddenly very conscious of how he was standing, where his hands were. Was he smiling too much?

God, I'm such a dork.

He shoved his hands into his pockets and glanced over his shoulder. How many of his classmates were friends with Randy? Was it too soon for another beating? Maybe he could work something out with Randy, perhaps schedule the pummeling for some time later in the week.

"So how'd you do?" She brushed a lock of wavy brown hair behind one ear.

"What?"

"On the paper."

"Oh. All right. I passed it in a day late, got a C-."

"That's pretty good. Tuscardi's a tough grader."

"How about you?"

"B+."

Wow, smart and sexy. Very nice. So what was she doing with Randy? "Not bad," he said. "Not as good as an A, I guess, but ... um ... better than a C."

Not exactly a smooth talker, are you?

Maria grinned, one eyebrow lifting in what he hoped was amusement. She inched closer, put her hand on his shoulder. "You've been avoiding me, Tim. Why?"

"Well, for starters, your boyfriend is a psychopath."

"He's not my boyfriend anymore. I broke up with him yesterday. I was so sick of his jealousy."

"To tell you the truth, I wasn't too fond of it either."

Maria caressed his cheek. "Your bruises are healing. I'm so sorry about what he did to you."

"It's okay. It's nice to get beat up every once in awhile. The body produces new blood; it's very invigorating."

She laughed. "I like you, Tim. You're funny."

"Thanks. I like you too. It hurts, but I like you."

She pressed a button on her iPhone and glanced at the display. "Uh-oh, I'd better get to Chemistry. I've got to do some last minute cramming for a quiz."

"Sure, go ahead."

"Thanks," she said, and kissed him on the lips.

He stood there, too stunned to speak, and watched her hurry down the hall.

"It's official," he muttered. "I'm a dead man."

***

Jay leaned against the headrest and massaged his temples. He'd had his share of hangover headaches before, but this one seemed destined for the history books. The pressure was so intense he thought his eyes might pop right out of his skull. He wondered briefly if he'd be able to pop them back in like they did in the Tom and Jerry cartoons he used to watch as a kid.

"You okay over there?" Steve asked.

"Don't worry. I'm not going to puke on your leather seats."

"That's not what I meant…though I am relieved to hear it."

Jay glanced out the window. "Thanks for bailing me out."

"No problem."

But Jay knew it was a lie. Steve and Gloria probably fought over it. And bitterly, at that. Poor guy would probably be sleeping on the couch for the rest of the week.

"I can't believe they arrested me. Guy breaks into my house, pulls a knife on me, and I'm the one who spends the night in jail."

"You fired an unlicensed weapon."

"It was licensed to my father."

"Yes, but he's dead now and you don't have a permit." He hesitated, as if considering whether to continue. "Besides, I don't think your being drunk helped matters any."

Jay shook his head. "I knew that was coming." He rubbed his lower back. "God, I've slept on curbstones more comfortable than that bunk."

"Just be happy you didn't share a cell with anyone—your back wouldn't be the only thing that's sore."

Jay groaned. "I can always count on you to see the bright side." He settled back into the seat and closed his eyes. His thoughts drifted back to last night.

The first cop to arrive at the scene barged into Jay's living room with his gun drawn, his face backlit by the stroboscopic blue of the police flashers. It took the cop a moment to register Jay sitting on the couch, and when Jay tipped him a wave, the cop nearly pumped him full of lead.

When the second cop arrived, they ushered Jay into the back of a cruiser and drove him to the station. For the first hour, he sat in a cracked plastic chair while a plainclothes detective with a bad hairpiece typed a report at the desk next to him.

The questioning didn't commence until his interrogators strode into the station dressed in expensive suits. Even in his drunken state, Jay knew they weren't cops. They steered him into the interrogation room and introduced themselves as Special Agents Calhoun and Murdock. FBI.

A wiry man in his mid-thirties, Calhoun had pale skin and angular features, and wore his hair slicked back like he'd watched one too many reruns of Miami Vice. Murdock seemed a few years older and had the athletic build of a guy who might have played football in college. They got right to business, peppering Jay with questions, barely giving him time enough time to respond before firing off the next question.

Did he know the man who broke in? Was there anything missing from his house? What was the man wearing? Where did he shoot the man? Which direction did the man run? Did the man say anything about the recent disappearances or the librarian's murder? Whose gun was it? Who was it licensed to? Why did he have a packed suitcase on his bed?

He answered the questions as best as he could, but he must have been slurring his words because they gave him an impromptu sobriety test. Surprisingly, it was the first time he'd ever been put through the routine.

"Congratulations," Murdock said, "You're drunk."

Instead of letting him go, they charged him with discharging an unlicensed weapon and possession of a firearm without a permit. They read him his rights, printed him, stripped him of his belongings—keys, wallet, gum—and then threw him into a tiny cell.

Just before dawn, they woke him for another round of questioning. When he asked if he should have an attorney present, Murdock shrugged and said he could if he wanted to, but he wasn't a suspect in any crime other than the weapons charge. The agent told him he could go home once they were through with their questions and he paid a fine for the gun violation. There would be no court date, no bail set, no further time served.

That should have eased his mind, but the agents wouldn't allow him the luxury to relax. They kept grilling him with the same questions over and over, firing from different angles, trying to get him to contradict himself. They knew there was something he wasn't telling them, something important to their investigation. They didn't seem to believe him when he said he didn't know the man who attacked him.

"Tell me something, Gallagher. Here we have this guy who preys on little children, a guy who most likely rapes and kills them. You don't know him. In fact, you've never seen him before in your life. But tonight, out of the blue, he decides that children are too easy to kill, so he breaks into a house at random and attacks a man half his age and probably a good deal stronger. Now, does that make any sense to you?"

"No, but rape and murder don't make sense to me either. The guy's a psycho. Why should he be expected to behave rationally?"

Calhoun leaned across the table, his ski slope of a nose just inches from Jay's face. "Here's what I think, Gallagher. I think you know the guy who did it, but he's got something on you. And you think if you give him up, he'll tell us all about your dirty little secrets."

Jay glanced out the car window and sighed. Why had he lied? Why hadn't he just said the guy looked a lot like his mailman? What if the guy killed another kid by the time someone recognized him in the sketch? How would he live with himself?

He rubbed his temples and gazed at the distant peaks of the Berkshires, the green hills shrouded in an early morning mist. He shook his head. "How did my life get to be so screwed up?"

"I think we both know the answer to that," Steve said. "But it doesn't have to be that way. You can beat this thing, take your life back. But you can't do it on your own."

"I know."

"There's a place in Lenox, a rehab, probably the best in the state. You think about it. We've known each other our whole lives, so I'm not going to lie to you. You've got a problem. And I don't want to watch you turn into your father. But I'm afraid that if you don't do this soon, that's exactly what will happen."

Steve steered the car into Jay's driveway.

"All right," Jay said. "I'll think about it. But there's something I've got to do first."

***

As soon as Jay got inside, he swallowed three Advil and sank into the sofa. He wondered if Crystal had heard about what happened. In all likelihood, she had. Word traveled fast in Glenwood. Even with the feds on the case, the news would leak and people would talk and his name would take another dragging through the mud.

Why had he allowed himself to get drunk last night? Whatever chance he had of getting Crystal back was gone now. Pissed away like last night's beer. But he couldn't blame her. She'd given him more chances than he deserved, and all he ever did was take advantage of her. He never thought she'd actually follow through on her threats, especially not after he'd bought her that diamond.

He chewed a fingernail. *All right. Got to think. Got to figure a way out of this.* He concentrated hard, but all he could see in his mind was a frosty bottle of Sam.

He paced through the house, circling through the living room, into the kitchen, and back again. He poured himself a glass of ice water and sucked it down.

There. Not thirsty anymore.

He returned to the sofa and sat awhile in silence.

Got to keep the thoughts flowing. No time for distractions.

His eyes wandered to the crimson splotches on the hardwood floor, and his mind brought him back to the moment the bullet ripped into the man's shoulder. The guy had just stood there, clutching his

108

wounded arm, his eyes clouded in confusion. Like he'd just woken up from a dream. There was something strange about the guy, something more than just the crazy way his eyes had changed color ... or *seemed* to change color.

I am the One and the Many, the Hunter and the Hunted... and all things in between.

It didn't make sense. Still, he couldn't shake the feeling that the man who cowered from him after being shot was somehow different from the man who had broken into his house and brought him a beer.

Maybe he's schizophrenic.

Jay reached for his cell phone and looked up the number for the Post Office.

A man's voice picked up on the fourth ring.

"I was wondering if you could help me," Jay said. "Yesterday, my son choked on a piece of candy in front of the house and my mailman gave him the Heimlich maneuver. Saved his life. I tried to give him a reward, but he wouldn't take anything. Please, if you would just tell me his name ..."

"I'd be glad to," the man said. "Where do you live?"

"Eleven South Maple."

Paper rustled in the background. "Okay. That'd be Ted Richardson. He worked your route yesterday."

Jay nodded and wrote the name down on the back of an envelope. "Is Ted the guy who normally delivers my mail?"

Another pause. More paper rustling. "Ah, no. That would be Frank Patterson. He's been out sick the past couple days."

"Oh. Okay. Thanks."

"My pleasure."

Jay hung up the phone and grinned. *Sick, huh?*

***

Jay stood in front of the 7-Eleven on Main Street and fumbled open a blister pack of Trident. From his vantage point, he could see number 352—a small colonial with black shutters and a dilapidated picket fence. He shielded his eyes from the sun and stared across the street at the flagstone walkway choked with weeds. Three windows ran the length of the porch, the blinds drawn tight against all of them.

He popped a piece of gum into his mouth.

This is crazy. I should turn back.

But he ignored the thought and adjusted his BU sweatshirt, pulling it down to conceal the gun tucked into the waistband of his jeans. The police had confiscated the .45 he fired last night, but he had another one just like it. His dad had always been a big advocate of self-defense. Who else would protect his beer from the enemy?

He glanced at the telephone pole to his right with its mosaic of missing persons flyers flapping in the breeze. He leaned against the pole and pretended to text on his cell phone, his eyes staring beyond the screen at Frank Patterson's house.

A few minutes passed with no sign of activity. He knew he should probably watch for a bit longer, but that required more patience than he was willing to spare. Dangerous or not, it was time to make a move.

Worst case scenario, Patterson would just put him out of his misery.

Jay crossed the street and mounted the steps to the porch. He knocked on the door, then dropped back and waited. A faint shuffling emanated from inside. From the corner of his eye, he detected one of the slats lifting on the blinds.

Jay drew a deep breath. *Now or never*, he thought, and banged on the door even harder.

"I know you're in there, Frank. Let me in or I'll call the cops. I just want to talk to you."

Jay's heart pounded. What was he doing here? What kind of idiot stalked a psychopath and threatened him at his own home?

He was about to walk away when the door swung open. He expected Frank to lunge at him with a butcher knife, but instead, Frank simply held the door open, his face worn and haggard. "Please," he said. "Come inside."

CHAPTER FOURTEEN

"So where are you and Chuck going tonight?"

Denise leaned toward the mirror and brushed mascara into her lashes. "Dinner and a movie. You know Chuck, not a creative bone in his body."

"Well, at least he's got his life together," Crystal said. "You're lucky, you know." Denise had been dating Chuck ever since graduating from college three years earlier, and he'd already promised her a ring by the end of the summer.

Crystal frowned. She'd never imagined her kid sister would beat her to the alter. Why couldn't Jay just admit he had a problem and take control of his life? She glanced at Denise. "Do you think I should call him?"

Denise lowered her lipstick and looked at Crystal as if she'd gone insane. "I don't believe this. You're not seriously considering calling that bum?"

Crystal averted her gaze. She should've kept her mouth shut. Now she'd have to suffer through a lecture from her kid sister. *Bring it on, Denise. I deserve it.*

"He was drunk, Crystal. Don't you remember what Chuck said? They found him sitting on the couch with a gun, drunker than a skunk. They don't even know for sure who he shot. You're just lucky it wasn't you."

"Jay would never hurt me."

"Why are you defending him? Please tell me you're not still in love with him."

A tear slid down Crystal's cheek.

112

"I don't understand," Denise said. He treated you like crap, and you still love him?"

"He didn't treat me like crap. He just broke some of his promises." She knew she was making excuses for him, and it made her angry.

Denise joined her on the bed and draped an arm around her shoulders. "You did the right thing. He was no good for you. You can't be with a guy who can't take care of himself. What kind of father would he make? He'd end up stealing from you to feed his habits." She sighed. "You gave him more chances than he deserved. I'm sorry, Crystal. I really am. But it's time you moved on. Why don't you come out with us tonight? I'll ask Chuck to bring Joey along. I think he likes you."

Crystal sniffled. "No, you go. I'll be alright. I'm a little tired anyway."

After Denise left for her date, Crystal went downstairs to watch TV. As usual, there was nothing on. She surfed the channels for twenty minutes before settling on a Discovery channel special on prairie dogs.

She ran her fingers through her hair and sighed. Here she was, twenty-nine years old, single, and all alone on a Friday night. Pretty depressing when you thought of it like that. Maybe she should have gone with Denise after all.

She'd wasted seven years of her life on a doomed relationship. And now she had to move on, start all over again. God, she was almost thirty. How had she let this happen?

When Jay was sober, he was sweet, charming, and funny—the kind of man she always wanted. But ever since their engagement ten months ago, it seemed he was sober less and less...almost as if he thought the ring gave him some sort of free pass to booze it up.

If they got back together, it would only get worse. He had a problem that was certain to spiral out of control. And if he couldn't stop now, how was he going to stop a year or five years from now when he finally realized that he did have a problem?

It was hard to hate him. Alcoholism was a disease. She just wished he could find the strength to beat it. If you believed the studies, only about a third of those in rehab ever remain sober. But Jay refused to give rehab a chance. He insisted that he didn't have a problem, that he could stop anytime he wanted to.

His excuses were so pathetic. But he couldn't see it. He believed every word of his own lies. Like that time he swore there was a boy in the backyard, a boy who appeared to be glowing like a ghost. Then, a few days later, he showed her a picture of some shadowy trees and claimed that the boy was in it. The funny thing was, he was sober when he brought over the camera. And somehow that made it all worse. He was so desperate to convince her that he wasn't drunk that night, that he actually tricked himself into seeing something in the picture.

It was sad. The whole situation was tragic. At least she'd given back the ring. If she'd gone through with it, if they'd gotten married and had kids, it could've been a whole family that got ruined. She supposed Denise was right. She did the right thing in leaving him. He was no good for her, could never make her truly happy.

She lowered her head until the tears ran their course. Then she sat up straight and drew a deep breath. It was time to put him out of her life forever.

CHAPTER FIFTEEN

Tim plodded along Pennybrook Road and thought about the hard ironies of life. For as long as he could remember, he'd fantasized about meeting a girl like Maria, a girl who was smart, sweet, and sexy. And now, after a move he thought he'd never forgive his parents for, he had finally met the girl of his dreams, and by some amazing stroke of luck she actually seemed to like him too.

I can't believe she kissed me. Right there in the hall.

He'd never kissed a girl so pretty before, never met a girl so outgoing. She knew exactly what she wanted and went after it.

But even as he relished in his excitement over Maria, the phantom of his other problem darkened his mood. It wasn't fair. Why couldn't he be allowed happiness for just one week? There were no such things as ghosts, no such things as creatures that were part man and part beast. And yet, since coming to Glenwood, he had seen both.

If Sarah and Jay hadn't admitted to seeing Samuel, he would have thought himself crazy. But what was this beast and where had it come from? What did it want, and why had it come to Glenwood? It didn't make any sense. And no matter how hard he wracked his brain, he couldn't come up with any answers.

From somewhere up ahead came the squeal of brakes. He shielded his eyes and stared down the tree-lined street. A school bus from Glenwood Elementary idled a hundred yards away, its stop sign extended, red lights flashing.

A group of kids poured off the bus, shouting and laughing, jockeying for position on the sidewalk. Tim spotted Sarah after the bus pulled away, walking alone with her head down, a purple Little

Mermaid backpack slung over one shoulder. She looked lonely and dejected, as if she didn't have a friend in the world.

Tim cut a path through the crowd of kids and positioned himself between Sarah and the front walk for which she was headed. She nearly bumped into him before looking up and stopping short.

"Tim! Hi. What are you doing here?"

"Just wanted to talk. Hope I didn't scare you."

Sarah smiled. "It's okay. I wasn't really scared. Just surprised."

Tim grinned. She was so sweet. He couldn't imagine why she wouldn't have any friends.

"What do you want to talk about? Is it about Samuel?"

He nodded. "A few things have happened since that night in Washaka Woods. I don't want to scare you, but I think I should tell you what's going on." He watched the smile fade from her face, transforming her back into the sad little girl he'd seen get off the bus.

"We can talk inside. I'll make you some lemonade and introduce you to Mr. Whiskers."

"Are your parents home?"

"Not until after five."

He scratched his head and glanced over his shoulder. A couple of moms stood on the sidewalk a few houses down, eyeing him suspiciously. "Is there somewhere else we can meet?"

She mulled the question over before responding with an excited clap of her hands. "We can meet by the stream. It's my favorite place!"

"Do you mean that little brook in the woods?"

She nodded. "Uh-huh. It runs right by my backyard. If you go into the woods you can follow it right to me."

He nodded. "See you in a few minutes."

***

As Tim entered the woods at the edge of his yard, he glanced at the trees and noticed that tiny leaves had recently sprouted, shiny and

116

delicate like the feet of newborn frogs. He recalled how tall and foreboding the trees had seemed the other night, looming over him like gray specters, reaching for him with skeletal arms.

He glanced back at his house and gauged the direction of Sarah's street. The stream weaved through the trees ahead, sunlight glistening on its rippling water. As tranquil as the woods seemed in daylight, he had to remind himself of the evil that lurked here after dark.

There were eight kids missing now, four of them reported just this morning. He couldn't believe it. They had to stop this thing, had to prevent it from striking again. But how they were going to do that, he hadn't a clue.

He spotted Sarah through a screen of birch, sitting on a rock by the water's edge. "So this is your favorite place?" he asked.

A grin lit up her face. She motioned to a bed of moss beside her. "Do you want to sit?"

Tim plopped down beside her, folding his legs beneath his body Indian-style.

"Aren't you going to put your feet in?" she asked, swirling her toes in the water.

"I don't know if that's such a good idea. My feet are so stinky they might kill the fish. Besides, I don't want to scare you, but I've got fourteen toes."

"No sir! Nobody has fourteen toes!"

Tim shrugged and dipped his hand into the stream. "Ah, that's freezing! How can you stand to keep your feet in there?"

Sarah giggled. "You get used to it."

They sat in silence for awhile and listened to the gurgling water. Tim stared off into the trees and watched dust motes swirl through a sunbeam. "Did you hear about what happened at the library?"

She nodded. "Some kids were talking about it at lunch, but I didn't hear everything."

Tim filled her in on the details she had missed, skipping over the part about stumbling into the librarian's mutilated body. He told her how the man's eyes had changed from brown to red and how the man had chased him through the library on all fours. When he finished, Sarah shook her head. Tim tried to read her expression, but couldn't.

"What did the police say when you told them about how his eyes changed color?"

"Well... I didn't tell them about that part. They never would have believed me. They would've thought I was crazy or that I made it up. But I told them everything else and gave them a good description of what he looked like."

Sarah nodded, but Tim could tell she wished he'd told the police everything. It was something he'd noticed about little kids. They thought every authority figure was perfect—their parents, the police, the government. They were in for a rude awakening one day, but he supposed it was part of growing up.

He tossed a stone into the water. "The other night, the same man broke into Jay's house. Jay shot him in the shoulder and then spent the night in jail because he was ... because he had too much to drink."

He shook his head. "This thing, it looks like a man, but it's really some sort of monster. And I'm afraid that if it knows who Jay and I are, then it knows who you are too. It thinks Samuel told us something that could hurt it. That's why it's coming after us. So you have to be careful. If you see a strange man, yell for your parents. Then call me or Jay." He handed her a slip of paper with their phone numbers on it. "I haven't talked to Jay yet, but when I do, we'll try to figure a way out of this, okay?"

Sarah nodded. "Are you scared?"

Tim knew it wouldn't do any good to lie to her. He took her hand. "Yeah, I'm scared. But at least we don't have to be scared alone."

CHAPTER SIXTEEN

Jay stood within the shadows of Frank Patterson's foyer. A rancid smell wafted out of the kitchen and tugged at his gag reflex. He followed Frank into the living room and sat down in a tattered gray recliner. It smelled even worse in here, a noxious mixture of sweat, urine, and wet dog.

He watched Frank ease himself onto the couch, his shoulder wrapped in a bloodied bandage. Frank's face strained with the effort of this simple task, sweat glistening on his forehead.

He met Jay's gaze. "I can't decide if your coming here was brave or foolish."

"Neither can I. But I need to know what's going on. I thought you might be able to tell me."

Frank mopped sweat from his brow and studied Jay for a long moment. "I can tell you a great deal. More than you bargained for, I imagine." His eyes gleamed in the lamplight, narrowing slightly as his forehead wrinkled and the corners of his mouth curled into a grin. At that moment he looked utterly insane, and just as Jay began to question the wisdom of coming here, Frank began to speak.

"It started about two weeks ago, shortly before the disappearance of Ryan Brakowski. I was on my nightly walk in the woods, a ritual I started ever since the passing of my wife. It always seemed to ease my pain, to put me at peace. Somehow in nature I felt close to Mary. Almost as if I could sense her presence. At times I thought if I just concentrated hard enough I could hear her voice in the wind." A ghost of a smile touched his lips. "I know how it must sound, but after the cancer took her, I withdrew from the world. I let my imagination run wild, because in the end that's all I had left. A

119

warehouse filled with years and years of memories that I could sometimes bring to life.

"So when one night I heard a voice in the wind, a voice drawing me toward some secret destination, I allowed myself to believe that it was Mary, that somehow she had broken through the boundary of death and had come back to me. I followed the voice through the woods, a voice that I seemed to be hearing with my mind rather than with my ears.

"I don't know how much time passed before I found the cave. All I know for sure is that I never would have found it at all if the voice hadn't told me where to look. To me it seemed like an ordinary boulder concealed by a tangle of thorns. But the voice was right; it was a cave. The opening faced away from the path, a dark crevice barely wide enough for a grown man to pass through sideways. But even that was partially obscured by a growth of ivy clinging to the rock.

"I remember wading through the bramble and tearing away the ivy with my bare hands. I can't recall there being any pain, but I imagine there must have been because when I got home later that evening my pants were bloodied and I had scratches all over my arms and legs. I squeezed into the cave and walked along the main passageway. It was pitch black and I couldn't see a thing, so I just closed my eyes and followed the sound of the voice. I think a part of me might have been scared, maybe even terrified, but for some reason I couldn't turn back. It was like being in a trance. Like a sleepwalker who can't wake up.

"I walked for a long time, winding further and further into the dark. I could hear water dripping all around me, echoing in muted plops. I could hear the voice growing stronger, getting louder. I wanted to turn and run away, but I couldn't. I was drawn toward the voice. Mesmerized by it.

"After awhile I detected light. At first I thought my eyes were playing tricks on me, but then I realized there really was light up ahead.

It had a strange bluish tint to it, more of a glow than a light. Phosphorescent—I guess that's the word for it.

"The pathway led into a cavern that ended at a pool of water. The pool appeared to stretch back about a hundred feet or so, the water so smooth and black that, at first, I mistook it for glass. I figured some lava flow must have caused it thousands of years ago. But when I walked out to the edge, I stared down at my reflection and saw it ripple.

"I knew then that it was water, but I couldn't imagine what would have disturbed it because there wasn't any wind in the cavern and I hadn't kicked any pebbles into it. After awhile, I began to feel like I wasn't alone in the cave, that somewhere someone was watching me. But even so, I couldn't take my eyes off the pool.

"Then a weird thing started happening—my reflection began to contort as if I were gazing into a funhouse mirror. It was a few seconds before I realized that my reflection wasn't changing shape at all, that instead another image was being superimposed onto mine. At first I didn't see how that was possible, but then it occurred to me that it was something on the other side of the water, something drawing nearer to the surface every second."

"The water broke as I stared down at it, sending an icy spray into my eyes. I stumbled back and wiped my face, and when I opened my eyes, I saw a creature standing in the pool. Staring right at me. It was massive, covered with scales, and gave off a swampy stench that nearly made me vomit.

"I wanted to turn and run, but its eyes held me captive, its pupils glowing like the embers of dying fire. It growled at me, deep and loud ... almost sounded like a laugh. And then its lips parted with a kind of sickening slurp and revealed a jaw full of razor-sharp fangs. I staggered back a step, but even then I knew it was too late. The creature made an awful shrieking sound, and a jet of liquid shot from its mouth and hit me straight in the eyes.

"I fell back and smacked my head against the ground, rolling around while that stuff burned into my eyes and the creature laughed in the rippling water. When I pulled my hands away, I saw a sticky black goo dripping from my fingers like tar. I could feel it in my eyes, warm, wet clumps of it caught in my lashes and stuck behind my eyelids. I remember lying there, screaming, sure that I would go blind. But after awhile the burning stopped and I felt my eyes soaking up the goo like a sponge.

"And that's all I remember. I don't even know how I got out of there, how I made it home. But all that night ... I felt strange. Like I wasn't completely with it, like I had somehow become detached from my body. Even my dog Buster noticed it. He shied away from me all night and just stared at me from across the room, cocking his head and whimpering. When I tried to approach him, his back bristled and he darted into the living room. I found him cowering on the couch, and when I went closer to him, he peed all over the cushions. He was shaking all over. You would have thought he was a Chihuahua instead of a one hundred and twenty-pound Rottweiler.

"I should have been concerned or even confused, but instead I found myself laughing. A part of me wanted to scream at that because the laugh I was hearing belonged to the creature in the cave—that deep laugh-growl. It scared Buster so bad he let out a kind of whining bark and leaped off the couch.

"He never made it to the floor. I sprang after him with reflexes I never knew I possessed and caught his throat in my teeth. I bit down as hard as I could, tearing into fur and flesh until I tasted his blood pouring into my throat and running down my chin.

"After that, I lost consciousness. I'm not sure how long. When I woke up, Buster was gone, but the carpet was stained with his blood." He motioned to the floor with one hand, and Jay looked down to see a large maroon stain like some sinister inkblot stretching from the couch to the coffee table.

"I never did find Buster, and I think it's best that I never do. I killed Ryan Brakowski too. Only I didn't remember it until afterwards. I had another one of those blackouts, and when I woke up my shirt was smeared with blood. It wasn't until a few hours later while lying in bed that I remembered pulling Ryan from the street and dragging him into the woods. When I got to the pool, the creature was waiting.

"The boy kicked and squirmed and tried to wriggle away, but the creature just sat there and watched. When the boy's voice finally gave out, it slit his throat with a hooked claw. I dropped him into the water after that, and the creature pulled the body beneath the surface. The water churned, and I could only imagine what was happening. After awhile the water went still, and I could sense that somehow the creature had grown stronger."

Frank shifted in his seat and grimaced. "Ryan wasn't the first. There was another boy before him, a seventh grade runaway from Albany. He had flagged me down to ask for a ride to Boston. I picked him up, intending to take him to the police station, but before I got there, I began to feel strange, like I was about to faint. The next thing I knew, I lost consciousness. When I finally came to hours later, sitting where you are now, covered in dirt and soaked with blood, I knew I must have done something terrible.

"But the amnesia didn't last very long. After a few hours I remembered taking the boy into the cave, remembered every detail of what... transpired, even though I wasn't conscious of it at the time." He shook his head. "It was the same with the others."

Jay bit a fingernail. "You're saying the creature was controlling you? You're sure it didn't order you to kill those kids and you obeyed out of fear?"

"It happened just like I said. I can't stop what I don't know about. Believe me, I would give anything to take back that night in the woods. Anything." He folded a hand over his wounded shoulder.

"Would you believe me if I told you this thing has a name?" When Jay didn't respond, he leaned forward and whispered. "It calls itself Trell."

"Trell?" He wondered how Frank would have known such a thing. "What is it?"

Frank shook his head. "A vampire? A demon? I don't know. Maybe a little of both. What scares me most is its intelligence. I told you before that I wasn't conscious when it seized control of me. That was true ... but only at first. The last couple of times I managed to stay awake, but I don't think Trell knows it.

"When it's inside me, it uses my brain as well as its own. I can feel it sifting through my memories and picking my mind of the knowledge it needs to survive in our world. It knows to be wary of policemen, it knows how to look up an address, it knows that a gun can harm it. As soon as you pulled that gun on me last night, Trell withdrew from my body. If I had died, Trell wouldn't have died with me. Not as long as it escaped before my death."

He sighed. "And Trell is getting stronger. It used me in the beginning to nurture it, to build its strength. It was barely alive when it first summoned me, so weak it couldn't even venture out of its pool. But now ..." He shook his head. "It won't need me much longer. Soon it will emerge from its cave and begin hunting on its own."

"But what does it want?"

"The same as you or I—to live, to eat ... to breed."

Jay shook his head. "This is crazy."

Nothing a little alcohol won't fix.

But he brushed the thought aside. "Where exactly is this cave?"

Frank shrugged.

"What do you mean, you don't know? I thought you said that recently you've been able to remain conscious."

"Yes, but not the entire time. When I tried to map the journey, Trell sensed what I was doing and pushed me into unconsciousness." He surprised Jay with a grin. "But what I don't think Trell knows is that during those times when it's mining my brain for information, I can do the same thing to it. With enough time, enough practice, I might be able to discover something to help us destroy it. It's the only reason I haven't killed myself."

Jay folded his arms and sat back. "We've got to do something to stop Trell from using you. We've got to stop it from killing again."

"You've got to lock me up, keep me..." His words trailed off into an incoherent garble.

"Frank? You okay?"

Convulsions jerked Frank's body, his eyes rolling back to the whites.

"Oh Christ," Jay muttered. He sprang to his feet just as Frank slid onto the floor and thrashed on the carpet. He was fighting Trell. But the question was... could he win?

"Cellar," Frank moaned. "Through ... the ... kitchen ... Quick!"

Jay glanced into the kitchen and choked back a wave of panic. Could he get him into the cellar before Trell seized control?

Move! Before it's too late.

He grabbed Frank by the wrists and dragged him into the kitchen where a tower of dirty dishes rose from the sink. The kitchen had three doors—two against the opposite wall and one against the wall to his left.

But which one led into the cellar?

He dropped Frank onto the cracked linoleum and yanked open the first door: a bathroom. The second door had both a slide bolt and an eyehook lock. It had to be the cellar.

On the floor behind him, Frank kicked his legs and uttered a menacing growl.

Jay unlatched the eyehook with jittery fingers, but the slide bolt refused to budge. "Come on, come on!" He smacked the door with the heel of his hand, striking the jamb just below the lock. That seemed to loosen the bolt enough to enable him to wriggle it free. He flung the door open and exposed a rickety flight of stairs descending into darkness.

Behind him, the thing that was either Frank or Trell lurched across the floor and groped for the edge of the kitchen table.

Jay drew his gun with one hand and helped Frank to his feet with the other. As Jay steered him toward the cellar door, Frank spun around and belted him across the face with a right hook.

The blow caught Jay by surprise and sent him stumbling into the table. He tripped over a chair and fell, the impact knocking the gun from his hand. He lunged to retrieve it, but Frank's work boot stomped on the back of his hand and pinned him to the floor.

Luminous red eyes glared down at him. "You were a fool to come here."

Jay struggled to free his hand, but Trell pressed down with all of Frank's weight.

Trell eyed the gun. "Looking for this?" it asked, keeping its foot anchored on Jay's hand as it stooped for the gun.

Jay knew he wouldn't get another chance. He curled his legs to his chest and kicked upward with all the force he could muster. His feet struck Trell in the groin and drove it into the sink where it collided with the tower of dishes and sent them crashing to the floor.

Jay snatched up the gun and scrambled to his feet, leveling the barrel at Trell. "Into the cellar! Now!"

Trell grinned. "Why don't you just pull the trigger?"

"I will if I have to."

"Why not have a drink first? Some beer? A bottle of whiskey, perhaps?"

"Shut up! I'll blow your head off. I swear to God I will."

"God? You think God cares what happens to you? I'm the one who controls whether you live or die. You should be praying to me. The people of Freetown didn't understand that—I think you can guess what happened to them."

"This isn't the 17th century anymore. Technology has come a long way since Freetown. So get ready, because we're going to find you. And kill you."

"The town drunk and a couple of kids? I'd say the odds are against you."

Jay waved the gun. "Last warning: get into the cellar."

"Go on and shoot. I'll be out of this body long before the walls are splattered with Frank's brains. And I'll come back for you. You and those you seek to protect. Tim, Sarah ... your lady friend." Trell grinned. "That's right, Jay. I know all about Crystal. Where she lives, what she looks like. Perhaps I'll even pay her a visit in my true form. Show her what a real fuck feels like."

"You stay away from her! Do you hear me?" He almost pulled the trigger. Almost destroyed any chance he had of discovering a way to kill Trell.

He shoved the gun into the waistband of his jeans, grabbed a kitchen chair, and rushed Trell like a linebacker on a blitz. Trell's lips formed a tiny "O" of surprise as the legs of the chair caught it in the chest and sent it staggering back toward the open cellar door.

With a final thrust, Jay drove the beast over the threshold and into the darkness where its screams mingled with the sound of its body thudding down the stairs.

CHAPTER SEVENTEEN

Dusk settled over Washaka Woods in a blaze of orange and gold. Shadows stole in at the passing of the light, gathering between the trees and weaving a blue-gray cloak about the land.

Margaret Connelly watched it all through her kitchen window, a dishtowel draped over her shoulder. In the past, she never paid the woods much heed—it was just a bunch of close-knit pines, a breeding ground for fat mosquitoes and poison ivy—but lately she couldn't focus on anything else.

Although it was now pitch black and impossible to see more than the shadowy outline of the trees against the night sky, she felt that somewhere deep in the woods where even the brightest moonlight failed to penetrate, something was watching her.

Trell, her mind whispered. *Its name is Trell.*

And with that came a haunting image of an eerily lit chamber, an image which surely had to be a shred of memory from some half-forgotten nightmare.

***

She lay on her back beneath a ceiling of stalactites. Her head rocked rhythmically, thumping against cold, wet stone. Her view of the cavern swam in and out of focus with each thrust. Water dripped from the hulking form that loomed over her. Icy droplets spattered her stomach and thighs, prickling her flesh with goose bumps.

Beneath her waist, it burned. The whole region radiated an icy hot numbness.

The thing on top of her growled. She could feel its hot breath brushing against her face, could hear its guttural voice inside her mind. "Worship me, Margaret. Speak my name."

128

And then she heard herself screaming as loud as she could, screaming until her voice was hoarse, until her vision was blurred by a veil of tears. "Trell! Trell! Trell! Trell!"

***

She wiped away her tears with a trembling hand and stared out into the darkness of night. It was hard to believe that the mere memory of a nightmare could dredge up so much terror.

It wasn't a nightmare, she told herself. *It really happened ... and you know it.*

But she shook her head. Huh-uh. No way. It was a bad dream; no more, no less.

So how do you explain the mud? You tracked it all through the house. And what about the cuts on your legs? The scratches on your back?

I was sleepwalking.

Oh really? So why can't you find your panties? Why are you so sore down there? Why can't you even sit without wincing?

Shut up! Please, just shut up. I don't know what happened, okay? People do crazy things when they're sleepwalking. Maybe I caught my panties on a branch and it tore them off. Maybe I tripped and fell, and a rock hit me there.

A hand clamped down on her shoulder, and she nearly screamed. She whirled around to find her husband standing there, and not some terrible beast with lurid red eyes. "You scared me half to death, Nick."

"I'm sorry," he said, his eyes blinking behind his glasses.

Margaret smiled in spite of herself. The expression he wore made him look like a confused little boy—a far cry from the cool, collected attorney on the rise. But the smile didn't last. Something was happening to her, something so terrible she refused to even think about it.

129

Nick slid his hands over her shoulders. "Margaret? Are you okay? You've seemed out of it the past couple days. You know, off in your own little world. What's wrong?"

She drew a deep breath. How was she going to explain it to him? She stared down at her hands. "It's the nightmares. They haven't stopped."

"The same one from the other night?"

"Not exactly. It changes all the time, but it's always similar. It's just that—" She shook her head. "It seems so real. Even hours after waking, it's still with me. I can't ever get it out of my mind. And the strange thing, the scary thing, is that sometimes it seems less like the memory of a nightmare and more like a plain old memory."

"You haven't been sleepwalking again, have you?"

She shook her head. "I don't know." But in her mind's eye she saw herself standing over the sink and rinsing blood from her hands. She couldn't bear to tell him the truth. Partly because she didn't want to upset him, and partly because she wasn't sure she knew the difference between dreaming and waking anymore.

He stroked her hair and hugged her. "Maybe you should see a doctor. Or a psychiatrist. I'm sure there's nothing to worry about, but I think it will help to put your mind at ease. And mine too."

She wrapped her arms around the small of his back and was saddened to find that his embrace failed to evoke its usual sense of security. *Why can't I shake this feeling that something terrible is going to happen?*

She squeezed him tight. "I love you, Nick." But in the back of her mind she heard a deep, mocking laugh.

Oh God, what's happening to me?

CHAPTER EIGHTEEN

Jay walked home in the failing light, his mind reeling at the revelation of Frank's dark secrets. Samuel was right about the beast, about Trell. It wasn't some mindless animal. It was cunning. It was evil. And it liked to play games.

Thank God he'd listened to his instincts and withheld Frank's identity from the feds. They would have locked Frank away in an insane asylum, along with the truth about what was happening in this town.

Jay had a hard enough time believing it himself. If the back of his hand didn't display a pattern of clover-shaped welts from Frank's work boot, he probably would have dismissed what he'd just witnessed as a hallucination.

He hoped Frank wasn't seriously hurt from the fall down the stairs. For the first half hour of being locked down there, Trell had shouted at him until Frank's voice was hoarse. After that, nothing but silence. He wished he knew whether Frank had slipped into unconsciousness or whether Trell had simply grown tired of making threats.

When Jay got home he noticed that he had a missed call from Tim. After what he learned today he wasn't sure he should get the kids involved any more than they already were. In fact, what he needed to do was get them uninvolved, find a way to get them out of town because, in the end, whoever stood in Trell's way would likely die. And if anyone had to die, it might as well be Jay. No one would mourn his passing anyway.

As he walked through the living room, he took notice of his surroundings and stopped dead in his tracks. The place had been

131

ransacked—drawers pulled open, books stripped off the shelves, papers strewn about ... everything coated in a fine, white powder.

Come on, he thought, his arms flopping to his sides.

He'd told the feds that Frank had worn gloves ... so what did they expect to find? But then he remembered the way agents Calhoun and Murdock had studied him during questioning and how Calhoun had accused him of knowing the man who did it.

Cleaning up was the last thing he felt like doing, but he set about the task anyway. When he finished, he called Crystal. Denise answered instead and cheerfully told him that Crystal didn't want to speak with him. He was about to argue with her when he heard Crystal in the background saying she'd take the call.

"Fine. Here you go. Talk to the loser all you want."

He heard a brief rustling as the phone changed hands. "What do you want, Jay?"

"Uh, hi Crystal. I just...it's been a rough couple of days. I wanted to hear your voice. And Denise's too. I think she misses me."

The sound of Crystal's laughter made him grin. "I knew I could surprise a giggle out of you."

"Don't flatter yourself. Denise just gave you the finger."

"She can hear me?"

"Not anymore. You're lucky she didn't hang up on you."

"I hope that means my luck is changing for the better because, frankly, I don't see how it could get any worse."

"I heard about what happened the other night. Are you okay?"

"Yes. I'm fine. It's actually you that I'm worried about."

"Me? Why?"

"It's a long story, but it has to do with what's been happening in town. Twelve kids have been murdered. And I'm afraid it's going to be more than that soon. Probably adults too." He paused. "I think you should leave town. Take Denise and go on vacation for awhile. Please. The last thing I want is for you to get hurt."

It was a long moment before Crystal answered. "You haven't gotten yourself involved in anything dangerous, have you?"

Her tone said it all. "Don't you mean am I the one killing those kids?"

"I didn't say that. It just seems odd that you'd think they're all dead. The cops haven't found any bodies. Does this have anything to do with the boy you insisted was in that picture? Don't tell me the boy is responsible for the missing kids."

"Actually, it's not a who that's responsible. It's more like a what."

Judging from the awkward silence, he was pretty sure he'd crossed the line.

"I've got to go, Jay. I don't have time for this."

"Wait, Crystal. Please. Just hear me out. I'm not crazy. That man tried to kill me because I know too much. And now he's threatened to go after you. Look, I know you probably don't believe me, but please just humor me. Get out of town for a week or two. I'll pay for it. Wherever you want to go."

"Goodbye, Jay," she said, and hung up.

***

With a runner on first in the bottom of the ninth with two outs and six runs in the hole, the Red Sox didn't stand a chance. The Yankees had attacked early with a five run lead and posted another eight by the seventh inning stretch.

The camera panned out on the stands and Tim saw that only a few die-hard fans remained in all of Red Sox Nation.

"Come on!" his dad shouted. "What's that idiot swinging at?"

Tim sat on the sofa next to his mom, who was leafing through a Woman's Day magazine and glancing up every so often to see if the game was over yet. Just as the umpire called the batter out on a cutter over the inside corner of the plate, the phone rang.

Tim leaped off the sofa. "I'll get it!" He bounded up the stairs to his room and snatched the receiver from his bedside. His parents refused to provide him with even a basic cell phone, so he was forced to suffer the indignity of sharing a landline.

"Hello?" he said, making his voice an octave deeper than normal.

"Tim, it's Jay."

"Oh." He was hoping for Maria. "I take it you got my message."

"Yeah. What's going on?"

Tim recounted his ordeal at the library, including how the man's eyes had changed from brown to red and how he'd stalked Tim through the maze of stacks. When he finished, he said, "I heard that someone broke into your house. I thought it might've been the same guy."

"It was."

"You're sure?"

"Positive. And believe me, I've spoken to both of them twice."

"Both of who?"

"Frank Patterson, my mailman, and a thing that calls itself Trell."

Tim pictured Jay spread-eagled on his couch, surrounded by a pile of crumpled beer cans. But the thing was, he didn't sound drunk. Didn't sound like he was joking, either. "Why do I get the feeling that your story will be a lot more interesting than mine?" He swung his legs over the side of his bed and leaned forward. "Go ahead, tell me what happened."

When Jay finished speaking, Tim sat for a moment in stunned silence. "Where is Frank now?"

"Still in the cellar. I think I might have hurt him when I pushed him down the stairs."

"You think he can tell us how to kill this thing?"

"Maybe. But I probably shouldn't even be telling you this. You should get out of town before you get hurt. Sarah too."

"How am I supposed to do that? I can't leave without my parents."

"Take them with you."

"Yeah, right. And tell them what? *'Guess what, Mom, there's a monster in the woods, and apparently it LOVES the taste of children! So what do you say we get out of here before it feasts on our flesh?'* I'm sure she'll march right into her bedroom to start packing our bags."

"So make up some other excuse."

"Like what? You don't know my dad. He just started this job. He's not going anywhere."

Jay sighed. "All right, I guess that's not going to work."

"So what do we do now?" Like it or not, Tim would have to take an active role in stopping Trell. He couldn't trust Jay to do it on his own. The guy had good intentions, but he was a drunk, and Tim refused to put his life in the hands of a guy who drank first and asked questions later.

"You're sure you want to be a part of this?"

"Yes," Tim said, and pictured Jay on his knees, hugging the toilet while Trell killed several children in the next room. "I'm positive."

"All right," Jay said. "Here's what I need you to do."

***

Jay stood in the kitchen with his arms folded across his chest. He'd earned a drink, and not even the holier-than-thou voice could argue with that. He grabbed the Jack Daniels off the counter and took a swig from the bottle.

Later, when the empty slipped from his hand and thumped onto the floor, he closed his eyes and let the alcohol work its magic. And as the moon rose above the trees outside, hoisting itself into a violet canopy of stars, he felt himself drifting away on a sea of alcohol.

Sometime later, the phone rang. It could have been ten minutes, it could have been ten hours. The sound was muted and low, miles distant. A part of him knew he should get it, knew it might be something important. But that part was no longer in control.

He closed his eyes and slipped into the welcoming arms of sleep.

CHAPTER NINETEEN

Helen Winthrop stood at the intersection of Elm and Main streets and hummed softly to herself. A warm breeze fluttered her dress about her legs, the tickle of the silky fabric sending a pleasurable tingle coursing through her body. An image flashed through her mind—a deeply tanned man lifting her onto the bed and sliding off her panties. The man wasn't Bill, her husband. In fact, she'd never even asked his name.

He had come to her house one day to repair her hot water heater, muscles flexing beneath his too-small brown uniform, and she had found herself instantly aroused. Bill was out of town as usual on business, probably boring the hell out of a room full of executives in an attempt to win a consulting bid. And six-year-old William Jr. was still at school where he would remain for another two hours.

The repairman went to work in the utility room, and she retreated into her bedroom to slip on a negligee. When she emerged from the bedroom, she walked slowly over to him, enjoying the way his eyes crawled all over her.

"Have you ever made love to a married woman?" she had asked, and pressed her body against his. What followed was the hottest, most satisfying hour of unbridled passion she had ever experienced. She was pregnant now, and poor, stupid Bill thought it was his. It served him right. He was such a bore and always unsatisfying as a lover. Not like her mystery man, who had made her feel so good she thought she might explode.

Trell grinned at Helen's memory and watched the approaching school bus through her eyes. The doors folded open and the kids filed off the bus, backpacks and lunch boxes swaying among a sea of little bodies. Trell wondered if Billy knew his mother was a self-serving whore. Not that it cared, of course; human life was meaningless to it, but occasionally it found itself amused by their antics.

"Hey there, kiddo," Trell said, using the pet name Helen reserved for Billy. "How was school today?"

Billy, who turned out to be a brown-haired boy with bright green eyes and a toothy smile, looked up at his mother and said, "It was great! Ms. Hurley let us make paper animals in art class." He dropped his backpack at his feet and unzipped it. "Look!" He pulled out a neatly folded piece of Origami resembling a big dog. "I made a dinosaur! It's a T-Rex!"

In Helen's sultry voice, Trell said, "That's wonderful! It looks just like a T-Rex."

Billy smiled.

"Come on, big guy. I've got something I want to show you."

"A surprise?"

"Why yes," Trell said. "A surprise."

Billy switched the T-Rex to his left hand and folded his right into his mother's. Together, they walked along the sun-dappled sidewalk. Billy hummed a Disney song and swung his arm back and forth, the T-Rex chasing imaginary prey. A few minutes later, they arrived at a sprawling field spotted with giant elms. Wooden benches lined the side of a brick path, the only occupants a pair of elderly men hunched over a chessboard. Trell rifled quickly through Helen's memory and learned that this was Elm Street Park.

Billy glanced around the near-empty park. "Where are we going?"

Trell drew the boy to a halt. "Can you keep a secret, kiddo?"

Billy nodded. "You bet!"

Trell grinned at the child's stupidity. "I'm taking you to a cave. There's something there I want to show you."

"Is it the Bat Cave? Are we going to meet Batman?"

"Better than Batman. Come on. You'll see." It led the way through the woods, Billy's tiny fingers curled around Helen's.

Upon entering the cave, Billy's excitement began to wane. "It's really dark in here. Do you think it's safe? What if there's a bear in here?"

Billy tightened his grip, his fingers moist with sweat. "Not a bear, Billy. Better than a bear." It was pitch black now, but Trell could see just fine. Its luminous red eyes swept back and forth across the snaking passageways.

Billy glanced up at his mother. "Where are we going? Why are we—" He stopped dead in his tracks. "What happened to your eyes? They're ... glowing."

Trell answered the boy in a guttural voice. "Your mother's gone, Billy."

The boy let out a whining gasp—the kind of sound Trell would have expected from a cornered fox. Trell squeezed until the boy's fingers snapped, and then laughed over the boy's wailing sobs as it dragged him through the tunnel.

"Mommy! Help!" His high-pitched shrieks echoed off the walls.

"Your mother is mine, Billy. She can't help you now." It stroked the boy's cheek, caressing the baby soft skin with Helen's manicured nails. "It'll be over soon."

Tears streaked down the boy's face. "What are you gonna do to me?"

Fear rolled off the boy in waves, the scent strong and sweet. Trell could hear his heart pumping, could hear blood coursing through his veins. "You are going to yield your life to me, Billy. You are going to die so that I may grow stronger."

It steered Billy to the pool and the surface came alive with movement. Phosphorescent light gleamed on the rippling water, rings of dazzling blue dancing among the shadows.

Billy struggled to break free. "Mommy!"

But his mother didn't respond. Instead, she pushed him closer to the pool.

It *was* his mother now—Trell had withdrawn from her body—but she was still under its command.

Billy stared down at his feet and watched the roiling water. Helen gripped the boy's shoulders and watched the Dark One reveal itself to her. She offered it the boy and admired its stark beauty, the fluid grace with which it lifted a clawed limb and slit the boy's throat.

Billy let out a garbled scream, clutching his neck with frantic hands. His lifeblood seeped into the pool, dripping into the swirling black waters ... death begetting life.

***

Helen awoke slowly, climbing through staggered levels of consciousness. At first she was aware only of darkness. But gradually, a sound filtered through her muddled thoughts, a sound like the thrashing of water.

Soon the sound subsided, and all she could hear was the lapping of tiny waves. Wetness seeped across her cheek and formed a seal between her face and the floor. She sensed that she was lying down, one arm curled between her breasts, her bare legs pressed against cold stone. Pale light filtered in through her fluttering lids and revealed the inside of a monstrous cavern. The ceiling and floor were lined with stalactites and stalagmites, like a lion's jaw frozen in a snarl.

She struggled to her feet and rubbed her eyes. A Lightning McQueen backpack lay on the ground before her. Beyond that, a few feet further into the shadows, stood a massive beast.

Helen screamed, and all at once her mind was flooded with a memory only days old.

***

She stood in the darkness of her kitchen, checking the lock on the sliding glass door. A noise emanated from outside—a hollow bang followed by a rolling thud.

For a moment, the sound paralyzed her with fear. But then she realized it was only the barrels falling over. Fear dissolved into anger. Those damn raccoons were into the trash again. She grabbed the nearest thing she could find—a plastic kitchen broom—and stormed outside, weapon in hand. She kicked a barrel aside, flinging trash into the air. She expected to see a whale of a raccoon.

But nothing was there.

She turned around, aware suddenly of a presence, a strong sense that she was being watched. She swung the broom like a hatchet, eyes shut tight, and smacked the raccoon. But the broom connected with its target long before it should have—no raccoon was that tall.

When she opened her eyes, the broom slipped from her fingers and dropped to the ground. She staggered back in silent terror, pressing her body against the chain link fence.

A creature stood motionless before her, crouched down on all fours, its mottled gray-green skin ridged and scaly. Its eyes bored into her as its lips peeled away from its fangs. It uttered an awful shriek and propelled a jet of sticky goo into her face.

And then, later, came the nightmares, the horrible images of knocking children unconscious with a rolling pin, dragging them through the woods to ... to a cave.

***

It was then that she burst through the final level of consciousness, then that she realized it was never a dream, never a nightmare.

The lips of the creature spread apart with a sickening slurp and revealed the jagged yellow of its fangs. It seemed to be smiling at her, its head cocked to one side, blackened tongue slipping out over its jaws.

Its name is Trell, she thought, and then it was on her.

Its fangs tore into the soft flesh of her throat, and she was vaguely aware of a medallion around its neck smacking against her cheek. The beast mounted her, forcing its bulk deep inside of her. She screamed with the last of her strength, blood bubbling out of the wounds in her neck. As she breathed her dying breath, she thought of poor, stupid Bill, and how he would never learn the truth of her unfaithfulness ... or of the fitting way in which she died.

CHAPTER TWENTY

Tim sat on the first floor of the library and leafed through a book on the history of Glenwood and Washaka Woods. According to the bio, the author taught at Glenwood High, although Tim didn't think that was true anymore. The book was written in 1982 and the small black and white photo above the bio could easily have been an obituary picture, snapped on the old man's deathbed.

It was printed in large type, accompanied by a number of crude sketches that depicted scenes from the 1600's to the 1980's. He flipped past the drawings of the Washaka Indians dressed in loincloths and hunting deer, and turned to the chapter entitled: *Local Attractions, Landmarks, and Points of Interest.*

He read the chapter closely, looking for any mention of a cave, but it was silent on the subject. He snapped the book shut and tossed it onto the pile with the others. After two hours in the library, all he'd managed to find was a trail map of Washaka Woods. Talk about wasting a Saturday.

He leaned back in his chair and laced his fingers behind his head. There had to be some caves in the woods. The kids at school probably partied in them on Friday nights, probably sat around a bonfire and drank beer. But then again, if that was true then the first kids to disappear would have been teenagers rather than fifth and sixth graders.

Somewhere behind him, a book crashed to the floor. He slammed his knees against the underside of the table and whirled around, expecting to see a man standing over him with luminous red eyes. But it was only a girl in tight jeans and a concert tee shirt stooping to pick up a book.

143

He made a copy of the trail map and tucked it into the front pocket of his backpack. A glance at his watch told him it was 4:30, a couple of hours before closing. He wasn't going to make that mistake again.

He slung the backpack over his shoulder and exited the library. The temperature had dropped ten or fifteen degrees since he'd arrived, the sun obscured by a swollen mass of storm clouds.

He zipped up his windbreaker and glanced into the sky. Maybe the rain would hold off until after he got home. He started toward his house, walking along the route he'd only recently memorized, and thought about Trell. They had to stop it before it killed again. Four more kids had disappeared today and it wasn't even nightfall yet.

He kicked a stone, sending it rifling through the grass. It was only a matter of time before Trell killed him. It knew where he lived, it knew where he went to school. It probably even knew where he was right now. And if Jay was right about the way it could seize control of a person's mind and body, then that meant any one of the people passing by on the street could be Trell's assassin.

It was crazy. And the scary thing was, there was no way to tell who Trell was controlling. Jay had said that Frank was himself except for when Trell needed him for something. Then he fell into a trance and Trell took over. If that was true, then his own parents could be used against him and he wouldn't even know it until it was too late, until he saw the gleam of red in their eyes.

The thought of his parents hunting him brought up another question—could Trell be inside two people at once? It didn't seem likely. The key had to be the black stuff it sprayed into Frank's eyes. That had to be what allowed it to control people. Frank said that the stuff had seeped beneath his eyelids and had been absorbed into ... into what? His blood? His brain?

What if that black goo was a living extension of Trell, a piece of its brain that fused into the brains of its victims? If that was true, then

Trell could probably command a group of people to do its bidding simultaneously, provided they had all been sprayed with the goo. And then, as it had done with Frank, it could fully transfer its consciousness into the mind of whoever it chose so that instead of simply telling that person what to do and the person being forced to obey, it would be physically inside that person's body, seeing through his eyes and using his body as its own.

But where would its own body be in that situation? Would it be catatonic whenever it transferred its consciousness into a single individual? If so, wouldn't it be vulnerable? Wouldn't someone near its body be able to approach it and kill it before it even knew what was happening?

He shook his head. *What have I been smoking?*

But he brushed the thought aside ... because in a weird sort of way, it made sense.

It was growing darker by the minute. Tim glanced into the sky, into the heart of the approaching storm, and felt dwarfed by the raw power of nature. Above him, the sky groaned. And behind him ... voices.

He glanced over his shoulder.

Three guys were walking in a close knit group behind him, all of them his age or older and coming up fast.

Randy?

He didn't dare steal another glance. If it was Randy, there was a chance he and his goons hadn't spotted him yet. He turned left at the next intersection, strolling casually, trying to project the image of a kid with nothing to fear. Maples lined the street, their trunks gnarled and gray and bent over the road. He held his breath and continued walking. Then came the sound of sand grating beneath shuffling feet, and Tim knew that they had turned the corner too.

Maybe it's just a coincidence. Maybe they live on this street.

But his gut told him it wasn't a coincidence.

145

"Get him!" someone shouted.

I hate it when I'm right, Tim thought, and darted across the street.

Randy and his goons were gaining fast. Tim could hear their feet pounding the pavement, their breath hissing as they closed the gap. His backpack was slowing him down. If he didn't do something quick, they were going to catch him.

He summoned a burst of speed and made a sharp left into someone's backyard. Randy and his goons continued past him for several strides before skidding to a halt and changing direction.

Tim grinned and cut through one yard after another.

Somehow Randy and his goons made up for lost ground.

He broke left, tore through a gap in the hedges, and sprinted across another yard. Randy and his goons followed. One of them caught his foot beneath a branch and fell headlong into the grass.

Randy jumped over him. "Gonna kill you..."

But Tim barely heard him. He dashed through the yard at full speed, skirting the edge of an inground pool, and weaving around a maze of plastic patio furniture. He knocked the chairs down one by one, flinging them into the path of Randy and his goons.

But it didn't work.

He headed toward the house. Sweat trickled down his face and stung his eyes.

Randy almost had him.

Tim faked left, then spun right.

Randy stumbled past him.

Tim scrambled up the stairs to the deck. He yanked open the door and stormed into the house. Randy and his goons were there a moment later. They plowed through the door and raced down the hall toward the front of the house.

In the kitchen, a middle-aged woman in a bathrobe dropped a glass and screamed.

Tim ducked into the living room, then backtracked toward the door he originally came through. He crept down the stairs and ran across the lawn. Out front, Randy and his goons crashed through the door and flew down the porch steps.

Tim made it three quarters of the way to the next yard before they spotted him. He glanced over his shoulder and tripped over a patio chair. He jumped to his feet an instant later, kicked aside the chair, and headed toward the next yard. He plunged through the bushes, emerged onto an unfamiliar street, and darted into traffic.

A van screeched to a halt and swerved onto the shoulder. The driver leaned on the horn.

Randy and his goons stepped into the street.

Ahead, Tim spotted a dirt road running through a gate. It looked like a business property, some sort of storage lot. He hurried toward it.

Maybe he could find some help. Maybe he could find a place to hide.

He charged through the gate, then skidded to a halt ... and swore.

He was trapped.

CHAPTER TWENTY-ONE

Jay awoke to bright sunlight and rolled over with a moan. He peeled away the crust from his eyes and blinked curiously at his surroundings. Sometime in the middle of the night, he'd rolled off the sofa and passed out under the coffee table.

He crawled out like a wounded animal and stretched his back before trying to stand. His gorge rose as he straightened, and he barely made it into the bathroom before he dropped to his knees and vomited. When he was through, he rinsed his mouth and shuddered.

He caught a glimpse of himself in the mirror and frowned. His dark hair stood in spiky tangles, his face bearded and swollen. A one-inch gash marred his cheek, set against an impressive fist-sized bruise where Frank had clocked him.

God, he looked like hell. But worse than that, he looked like his dad ... like the wasted shell of a man who had died in a garbage-strewn gutter, face down in a pool of his own vomit.

You're on your way, my friend. Another few years of drinking like this and you won't need Trell to kill you.

After a shower and a shave, he felt a little better. He dressed, drank a cup of coffee, and leafed through the morning paper. It was the same old story—more disappearances in Glenwood, no arrests made by police.

If he didn't figure out how to kill Trell soon, the whole town would be wiped out, just as it had been over three centuries before. And unfortunately for the residents of Glenwood, the fate of the town rested in the hands of a worthless drunk.

You have the vision, Samuel had said. *You can see what others cannot. That is why you must be the ones to destroy it.*

148

Jay laughed. *I've got news for you, Samuel. I think the only reason I saw you was because I was drunk off my rocker. The part of my brain that knows there's no such thing as ghosts was fermenting in a pool of alcohol. You should have given your message to someone else, someone who could stand up to Trell, someone who could deal with the situation without getting plastered every night.*

His cell phone caught his eye. It showed a voicemail waiting for him. But when had it rung? And then he remembered. Last night as he sat on the sofa, drinking himself into oblivion.

What if it was Tim? Or Sarah? What if they'd needed help? He pictured them tangled together in some dark corner, bloodied and mangled beyond recognition, arms and legs bent at ghastly angles.

A cold feeling settled over him as he retrieved the message. There was a slow hiss, followed by a crackle of static. And then a voice.

"Jay, it's Frank. Call me as soon as you can. I think I found a way to kill it."

***

From the street, Frank's house appeared dark and foreboding. Jay stood before the picket fence and bit his lip. Exactly who would be there to greet him when he walked through the front door?

He drew a deep breath. *How lucky do I feel?*

He pushed through the gate and stepped onto the weed-choked walkway. The gate swung shut behind him, struck its frame, and bounced back open. He glanced at the darkened windows set on either side of the door like a pair of watchful eyes.

Maybe this wasn't such a good idea.

He climbed the stairs and fumbled for the key he'd swiped from Frank's house yesterday afternoon. The smell hit him as soon as he opened the door, a noxious mix of spoiled meat and wet dog. He drew his gun and waited for his eyes to adjust to the darkness.

149

An oppressive silence permeated the house, and he wondered if that was a good sign or a bad sign. He crept through the living room and into the kitchen, his muscles tensed like piano wire. The door to the cellar was just as he'd left it, both the eyehook and the slide bolt still engaged. He glanced at the floor. A smear of blood gleamed on the linoleum. He crouched down and dabbed it with his fingertip.

Still wet.

That's not possible.

He stood up, his heart pounding. If it wasn't his blood from yesterday's struggle, then whose was it?

Had Frank escaped from the cellar? And if so, how? He'd checked the perimeter of the house last night. There was no way out of the cellar, not a single door or window.

Could Trell have sent someone to let Frank out?

He raised the .45 and tiptoed to the cellar door. A spatter of blood glistened on the frame.

Don't go in there. It's a trap.

But he had to go in, had to talk to Frank. He pressed his ear against the door.

Silence.

"Frank? You down there?"

No answer.

Jay uttered a silent prayer and yanked open the door. A stairway descended into darkness. He aimed his gun toward the bottom and probed the wall for a light switch. His finger happened upon one and flicked it up ... but nothing happened.

He fished his cell phone from his back pocket and angled it before him. The display cast a faint, silvery light that failed to penetrate more than a three foot radius.

This is stupid. Really stupid.

The stairs creaked beneath his weight. When he reached the bottom step, he glanced up at the white light glowing through the doorframe. What if someone closed the door and sealed off the only exit? What if he got trapped down here, imprisoned in the dark?

Or worse—what if Trell was down here? Crouched in the dark, watching ... waiting.

He turned in a slow circle. His cell phone illuminated a desk and a brass banker's lamp. He pulled the chain to the lamp, and the room flooded with light.

Frank lay on the floor a few paces away, his mouth frozen in a silent scream. One of his eyes hung from the socket; the bloody sphere rested on his cheek, still attached to the optic nerve. Blood pooled around his body, most of it concentrated around the ruined stumps where his legs should have been. Both were gone, torn off at the thighs in a ragged, crimson mess.

"Oh God," Jay muttered, backing away. His foot kicked a cordless phone and sent it spinning under the desk. The battery compartment yawned open, the battery severed from the wires.

Jay glanced back at Frank and noticed a sliver of paper protruding from the front pocket of his jeans. He bent over the body, careful not to step in any blood, and pinched the paper between his thumb and forefinger. He unfolded the note beneath the greenish glow of the banker's lamp.

Scrawled in blood in the center of the page were the words: *Trell Arrow Wol—* The last letter ran off the page in a sharp streak. Below these words, Frank had drawn three strange symbols, like runes from a Tolkien map. On the back, he'd drawn an obelisk with a key at its center.

Jay stared at the paper for a long time, trying to make sense of it. Then he shook his head and frowned.

What were you going to say Frank, what were you planning to tell me?

CHAPTER TWENTY-TWO

Murdock paced about the cramped office and ran his hands through his hair. He paused to sip his coffee, winced at its bitterness, and then resumed pacing. What the hell was happening in this town? Fifteen kids missing. Fifteen goddamned kids!

He'd never seen anything like it in his eighteen years at the bureau. How did fifteen kids disappear in a town this small without anyone seeing or hearing anything? Even the half dozen search parties had turned up nothing. It was the strangest damned thing. The hounds seemed hot on the trail of something, but then stopped in the middle of the woods and started whimpering.

He drummed his fingers against the desk and glanced at his watch. He was expecting a guy named Wayne Gillespi, had, in fact, been expecting him for more than twenty minutes.

Probably just a low life looking to score a reward.

His ex was right—he had to stop being so cynical. Maybe this guy would turn out to be kosher. Maybe he'd provide a tip that would enable them to ID the bastard.

There was nothing worse than a psycho who preyed on children. Monsters like that didn't deserve to live. If one of them ever laid a hand on his Nathan, he'd hunt the scumbag day and night until he found him. And when he did, the badge would come off and he'd beat the dirtbag to death. Scum like that didn't have any rights, didn't deserve a trial.

He rubbed his eyes, bloodshot and itchy from lack of sleep. This was the most frustrating case he'd ever worked. The town was so small, and yet these kids were vanishing right under his nose. It didn't bode well for his career, that was for sure. His boss was already on his ass, threatening to replace him with someone more competent.

More competent. What a load of crap. He was good at his job, damned good. Better than anyone his superiors could get to replace him.

He sipped his coffee, cold now, and glanced again at his watch. Thirty minutes late. Where the hell was this Wayne character? He scratched his head and wished they had more to go on. Right now all they knew was that the blood from the knife in Gallagher's living room didn't match Gallagher's or the blood on the rug. Didn't match the librarian's either. DNA testing would probably confirm that it belonged to one of the fifteen kids, but that would take weeks to run.

He collapsed into the desk chair. Gallagher knew something. But what? The question had nagged him for days. Was he protecting someone? Was he in on it?

A thorough search of his house had turned up nothing, not one iota of incriminating evidence. So why had the guy gone after Gallagher? Had Gallagher seen something? Or maybe Gallagher knew the guy, but was too scared to spill his guts.

It was something. He just wished he knew what. A wiretap might come in handy, but no judge would authorize a bug with so little evidence.

Maybe I'll put a watch on him, have Calhoun coordinate it when he gets back.

One of the local cops knocked on the door. "Wayne Gillespi here to see you, sir."

He could see the man standing behind the local. He appeared to be thirty-five or so, balding, overweight. He wore a blue golf shirt with a US Postal Service logo embroidered above the left breast. Murdock glanced at his watch and sighed. "Send him in."

CHAPTER TWENTY-THREE

Tim turned in a slow circle, glanced left and right, but what he saw left him little hope. He had trapped himself in the town's compost dump. Mounds of twigs and leaves rose from a vast area of trampled dirt, and green signs planted at the base of the piles indicated what could be dumped where. A chain link fence sealed off the entire area. It was at least eight feet high and topped with sharp ribbons of gleaming barbed wire.

Tim hadn't noticed the barbed wire when he first ran in. He had hoped to lose them among the maze of piles, sneak away into a wooded corner and hop the fence, unseen. But he had panicked. And in his panic he had missed that very important detail.

Randy and his goons—Lenny and Brett—stormed through the gate, their heels coughing up plumes of dust. Randy drew to a halt and motioned for his goons to follow suit. They obeyed the gesture like well-trained dogs.

Randy's eyes blazed with the promise of violence. He looked more than mean—he looked crazy. Stark, raving mad.

Lightning parted the sky—a forked blue tongue followed by a peal of thunder. For a moment, Randy was silhouetted against the sky, his body framed in a seemingly angelic halo. The contrast between that and his sadistic grin was hideous.

Tim slid off his backpack and let it drop to the ground. Could he lose them among the piles, circle back to the gate somehow, and trap them inside? It didn't seem likely, but he had to try.

He darted down a path that wound through the compost heaps and zigzagged through mountains of decaying leaves. Randy and his goons split up, coming after him from three different directions. They cornered him a minute later, trapping him against a tower of branches.

Wood snapped beneath his weight as he scrambled up the nearest pile. He made it less than halfway before he began sliding down, riding on an avalanche of deadfall.

Lenny—the smaller of the two goons—snatched a hold of Tim's pant leg and dragged him to the ground. He shoved Tim into the open, herding him to where Randy stood waiting, arms folded in smug satisfaction.

Thunder rumbled in the distance, and the first droplets of rain spattered the earth.

Lenny and Brett grabbed Tim's arms and twisted them behind his back. Randy clamped his hands on Tim's shoulders and squeezed hard enough to make him wince.

"Timmy, Timmy, Timmy ... what *am* I going to do with you?" He glanced at the goons. "Do you believe this punk? He comes into my town, steals my woman ... punches me in the fucking eye." He leaned in close to Tim. "Didn't I tell you that Maria was mine? Did you think I wouldn't find out that you kissed her, that you put your filthy lips on my girlfriend? I warned you, Tim. But you didn't listen. And now you're gonna pay."

And then Tim felt something cold against his wrists, heard a series of metallic clicks ... and realized he'd been handcuffed. Randy nodded to his goons, and Brett—the huge hockey player with the Mohawk—ran through the gate and disappeared around the corner.

"Are you scared, Tim? Because you should be. You thought you could mess with me. You thought you could stand up to me and win. But guess what? You lost ... and now I'm gonna kill you. What do you think about that?"

But Tim didn't answer.

"What's the matter? Can't think of any wiseass remarks? Go on, say something funny. I dare you."

155

Don't you think you should return the handcuffs before your mom and the dog miss them?

But he bit his tongue. He couldn't risk insulting Randy. Not with his hands cuffed behind his back, not with Randy and Lenny blocking the only exit.

Rain pelted his head and slicked back his hair. "Someone's going to see you, Randy. One of the workers here will call the police. So why don't you let me go? You've had your fun. Let's just end it, okay?"

"No one will see anything in this rain. Whoever's working will stay inside until it's time to close the gate and go home." He motioned to the corrugated metal shed in the distance. "And they won't hear anything, either. Not with the rain pounding against the roof and all the thunder outside." He glanced at Lenny. "Let's take him back between those piles just to be safe."

Randy pushed him forward.

A minute later, a rust-colored Chevy lurched to a halt beyond the gate.

Tim was about to yell for help, but then Brett hopped out of the car and opened the trunk. He reached inside with his whole upper body, stooping low as if attempting to lift something heavy.

Tim narrowed his eyes. What was he getting?

Brett slung a dark-haired girl over his shoulder and carried her across the dump with one arm locked behind her knees. "Special delivery," he said, and dropped her at Randy's feet.

Maria rolled onto her back, her lips sealed with silver duct tape. Tim started toward her, but Brett kicked him in the stomach.

He dropped to his knees and pitched forward into the mud. Maria wriggled over to him, her hands also cuffed behind her back. She mumbled something unintelligible and touched her forehead against his. Tim tried to speak, but all he could manage was a wheezy gasp.

156

Randy and his goons howled with laughter.

A thunderclap sent a shudder through the earth, and the rain poured down as if the sky had torn open.

Randy elbowed Brett. "Now for some real fun."

Tim struggled into a sitting position and fought to catch his breath. "Leave us alone," he gasped. "You'll get ... in trouble."

Randy laughed. "Why would *I* get into trouble? The cops will think it was that crazy kidnapper who got you. And they'll never find out the truth. Do you know why? Because dead people don't talk."

"Don't be so sure."

"What's that supposed to mean?"

"Let us go and I'll tell you."

"I don't think so. I like you right where you are. I told you I'd cut your tongue out if you ever talked to her again. Did you think I was kidding? And you ..." He prodded Maria with a muddy foot. "You went behind my back like a filthy whore." He ripped the tape off her lips and unzipped her pants. "You like being a whore? You wanna do other guys? Huh?" He yanked her jeans down to her ankles, exposing the sleek curve of her hips.

Tim gaped at the sight of her bare flesh. Water beaded on her thighs and rolled like mercury across her black bikini briefs.

"Hey Tim, wanna watch us take turns with this bitch? I bet she'll like it. Won't you?"

"Get away!" she yelled, thrashing her legs.

"She's a feisty one," Brett said. "You getting wet for me, honey?"

The three of them burst out laughing.

"Leave her alone!" Tim shouted. "You hear me?"

Randy reached into his jacket and pulled out the biggest handgun Tim had ever seen. "You like this, Tim? It's a .357 Magnum. One shot will tear your head off, blow your brains into a million little pieces. But don't worry, I'm not gonna shoot you in the head. That would be too quick … and I really want to savor this."

"I'm sorry, Randy. Please … don't do this."

"Oh, so now you show some respect? Well, it's too late, Tim. We're way past that now. In fact, now we're at the part where I shove this gun up your ass and pull the trigger. I'm not sure how long you'll live after that, but I'm hoping it's like ten or twenty minutes, cause then I can sit back and watch you die. And while you're dying you can watch us gangbang this cheating little bitch over here. What do you say to that?"

"Don't do it," Tim said, and glanced at the two goons. "You've got to stop this. Please!"

But Brett wasn't even listening. He was too busy patting Randy on the back and laughing like a hyena. But with Lenny, it was hard to tell. A minute ago he seemed to be as excited about the prospect of a double rape homicide as any self-respecting lunatic would be. But now he appeared subdued, almost as if he'd undergone a change of heart. He stared off into the woods beyond the fence, his eyes wide, but distant.

Randy didn't seem to notice. He kicked Tim in the small of the back and knocked him into a puddle. Tim turned his head to the side and locked gazes with Maria. Even in the rain, he could tell that she was sobbing.

Randy unbuckled Tim's belt and tried to force his pants down. "Get away from me!" Tim yelled.

Lenny placed a hand on Randy's shoulder. "Stop."

Randy smacked his hand away. "What did you say?"

Lenny's face was expressionless. "You are not to hurt him."

"Why the hell not?"

"Because he belongs to Trell."

"Who the hell is Trell?"

158

Tim studied Lenny's eyes. They had a wide, vacant look, but they weren't red. Could his theory be right?

He crawled over to Maria. "We've got to get out of here. Right now."

A low rumbling reached his ears.

Thunder. Just thunder.

But it didn't sound like thunder. It seemed to be coming from somewhere behind them, somewhere beyond the pile of branches.

Tim positioned himself so that his back was pressed against Maria's. "On three, try to stand."

Maria nodded.

"One..."

The rumbling sounded again. Closer this time.

Not rumbling. Growling.

"Two..."

"Hand over the gun," Lenny said. "Don't make Trell angry."

"Three!"

They got to their feet just as Randy shoved Lenny to the ground.

Maria managed to hike up her pants before Randy turned toward them. "Where do you think you're going?" he asked.

Lenny grinned up at them. "Now you'll answer to Trell."

A blur of movement caught Tim's eyes. He glanced past Randy, his eyes directed at the top of a soggy leaf pile. "Oh God," he muttered.

Randy leveled the gun at Tim, and Tim stepped backward ... but not because of Randy. He motioned with his head. "Behind you."

The thing standing atop the leaf mound was a nightmare fusion of claws, scales, and teeth. Even crouched on all fours, it stood over six feet tall, its thick forepaws buried into the muck. It glared down at them, its eyes blood red and luminescent.

Randy's face transformed into a mask of terror. He raised the gun and squeezed off a wild shot.

Tim and Maria raced for the gate. Behind them, twin shots pealed like cannon fire. Tim glanced over his shoulder and saw Trell stumble back, growling in pain. Then it leaped into the air and pounced on Randy, knocking him to the ground.

Randy let out a series of bloodcurdling shrieks, and then Brett began screaming too. A few moments later, the screaming ceased, and Tim and Maria were more than halfway to the gate.

Tim spotted his backpack on the ground near the entrance. He stooped awkwardly—still running—and snatched it up with his hands cuffed behind his back. He glanced over his shoulder in time to see Trell leap off Randy's mangled corpse and come bounding after them on all fours. Behind it, Lenny jumped up and down, shouting, "Kill them! Kill them!"

Tim swore under his breath. *I hate it when I'm right.*

Trell was fast. Scary fast.

"To the car!" Tim yelled. "Hurry!"

As they charged through the gate, Tim skidded to a halt and dropped his backpack. He had to close the gate behind them, had to buy enough time to allow for their escape.

Trell was almost on top of him, twenty feet and closing.

The gate was the kind that rolled closed on a track. Tim grabbed hold of the chain link and began to pull, but it was heavier than it looked.

Come on, come on!

He dug his feet into the mud. It wasn't easy with his hands cuffed behind his back. The grip was all wrong, his footing reversed. Trell was close enough now that Tim could see into its massive jaws. Its razor sharp fangs gleamed in the rain.

The gate began to move, rolling horizontally on the track. It gained momentum quickly and was almost fully closed when Trell leaped into the air. The beast flung itself against the gate, swiping at Tim through the gaps in the chain link. Tim jumped back and sucked in his stomach as a hooked claw sliced within an inch of his chest.

The gate hit the rubber stopper and bounced back open. Trell retracted its claws, dropped to the ground, and bounded toward the gap.

Tim lunged for the gate and slammed it shut. A padlock hung from a link by the post. He lifted a foot, tried to kick it toward him.

Trell crashed against the fence, and the padlock flew into the air. Tim used all his weight to hold the gate shut.

Behind him, the Chevy roared to life.

"Maria!"

She was by his side a moment later, her cuffs gone. She plucked the padlock from the ground, slipped it through the latch, and set it.

Trell threw itself against the fence and snarled in rage, the chain link ballooning outward.

Maria grabbed his backpack and hopped into the car. "Hurry!"

Tim darted for the passenger side and saw Trell backing away from the fence, preparing itself for a running jump.

"Oh my God Tim, what is that?"

"I'll explain later." He pulled the door shut. "Let's go. Hurry!"

"I ... I've never driven before!"

"You've got about three seconds to learn."

Trell leaped into the air.

"It's gonna make it!" Tim said.

Maria hit the gas and the car slammed into the fence.

"Reverse! Put it in reverse!"

The ground shuddered with the force of Trell's landing. A surge of mud splattered the windshield.

Maria jerked back, flicked on the wipers. And there was Trell, crouched on all fours beside the hood of the car. Maria stomped on the gas and the car shot backwards. She cut the wheel and straightened the car, slamming on the brakes so she could shift into drive.

Trell stepped into their path, its alien eyes glaring at them through the windshield.

"Gun it!" Tim yelled.

Maria pinned the pedal to the floor. At first the Chevy went nowhere, its rear wheels spewing mud. And then it screamed forward and slammed into Trell with a bone-snapping crunch of metal.

The car raced down the driveway and lurched into the street. Tim glanced out the rear window and saw Trell stagger to its feet and lumber off toward the woods. He was about to yell for Maria to hit it again, but it was too late. The compost dump loomed a hundred yards behind them.

He glanced at Maria and saw tears coursing down her cheeks. "Are you okay?" he asked.

She drew a shuddering breath. "How can I be okay? That thing tore them apart. Right in front of our eyes."

Tim frowned. "I know."

"It was horrible. I can't get their screams out of my head."

"I'm sorry."

"It's not your fault."

"But it came there to get *me*."

"Why do you say that?"

"It's a long story. I'll tell you everything soon, I promise."

"What do we do now?"

"We've got to ditch the car. But first I need out of these cuffs. How did you manage to get free?"

"Pull your arms down over your butt, then bend your knees and bring your hands over your feet. The keys are in the console."

Tim struggled to lower his arms further than a few inches. He sank back into the seat and sighed. "I think my butt's too big. I'm gonna need your help."

Ten minutes later, Tim stood at a pay phone in a 7-Eleven parking lot. He shifted his weight from foot to foot and listened to the static-choked ring. He was surprised the thing even worked. Who used payphones anymore?

Finally, someone picked up, and a woman with a gruff smoker's voice identified herself as the Glenwood police. Tim turned his back to the gusting wind and cupped his hands around the receiver. "There's been an accident at the compost dump. Two people might be dead." And then he hung up and glanced at Maria. "Did you wipe the prints off the inside of the car?"

She nodded. "What do we do now?"

Tim slung the backpack over his shoulder. "Ever hear of a Geometry teacher named Mr. G?"

CHAPTER TWENTY-FOUR

When Murdock arrived at the small house on Main Street, he squeezed his unmarked Impala between the squad cars parked haphazardly out front. He climbed out of the car and cut a path through the cruisers, the rain reflecting the stroboscopic blue of the police flashers.

A local stopped him as he ducked beneath the crime scene tape and headed up the walkway. Murdock flashed his FBI credentials and the officer stepped aside with a mumbled apology. Murdock entered the house to find a swarm of locals watching as the CSI unit dusted for prints, snapped pictures, and swabbed blood samples.

"What is this, amateur hour?" he bellowed. "Let's go, everybody out! Before you contaminate my crime scene!" After banishing the locals to the porch, he motioned to one of the CSI techs. "Where's the body?"

"In the cellar. Only access point is through the kitchen."

Murdock nodded and crossed into the kitchen. A CSI tech finished lifting prints from the cellar door and stepped aside to let Murdock through. Murdock descended a narrow staircase and spotted Calhoun talking to a woman from the Medical Examiner's office. "What's with all the people upstairs? Place is like Grand Freaking Central."

Calhoun seemed surprised. "I left Andrews in charge up there."

"Hell of a job he's doing. Next time, I want you working the door until I get here. Understand?"

Calhoun nodded. "I didn't—"

"I don't care. Just don't let it happen again."

"It won't," Calhoun said. "Body's over here." He stepped aside to reveal a Caucasian male in his late forties lying face up in a pool of blood. The man's right eye hung from its socket and his legs were severed above the knees, ending at two mangled stumps that looked disturbingly similar to raw hamburger.

"Jesus," Murdock said. "Is that Patterson?"

Calhoun nodded. "We got a positive ID from his driver's license. He also looks a lot like the guy from the sketch."

Calhoun was right. The kid had given the artist a good description, right down to the exaggerated arc of the man's eyebrows. Murdock motioned to the woman from the M.E.'s office. She was a tough looking blond who might have been pretty once. "What do you think?" he asked.

The woman glanced down at the body. "At this stage, it's hard to say. We won't know anything for sure until we run a number of tests."

"Best guess," Murdock said.

"The wounds appear to be consistent with the bite marks of a large animal."

"You're saying something chewed this guy's legs off."

"Best guess," she said.

"So what are we talking? Pit bull? Doberman?"

The woman raised an eyebrow. "Ever see a dog chew through bone and carry away a pair of legs without leaving a trail of blood?"

Murdock peered at the body. There didn't appear to be any bruising of the wrists. "Hands weren't bound. Guy was probably alive while whatever it was tore his legs off. Christ, I bet he was screaming his head off. Did any of the neighbors hear anything?"

Calhoun shook his head. "The cellar door was closed. Front door too." He gestured around the room. "No windows or doors down here, either. But we found this phone. Looks like he tried to make a call."

"Get the phone records."

"Already put in the request."

Murdock drew a deep breath and leaned against the wall. This case got stranger every day. Christ, every hour. What the hell could have ripped the guy's legs off?

"That Gillespi guy said Frank was a mailman, right?"

Murdock glanced up at his partner. "Yeah."

"Ten bucks says his route includes Gallagher's house."

"Worth looking into." Murdock turned to the M.E. official, who had just sealed the bloody phone inside a plastic evidence bag. "When you get back to the lab, have your people run Frank's blood against the samples found in Gallagher's living room."

The woman nodded. "I'll pass it along to the M.E."

Murdock watched the rest of the M.E. staff prepare the body for transport. They bagged Patterson's hands as well as what remained of his legs so that any flesh, saliva, or hair samples wouldn't be contaminated. He turned back to Calhoun. "Make sure we get some of our forensics people to oversee the lab work, and expand the watch on Gallagher to 24-7. I don't want him so much as taking a dump without us knowing what shade of brown it is."

"Got it. You ready for some more bad news?"

Murdock sighed. "No, but go ahead."

"I just got word that a twenty-man search party disappeared."

"What are you talking about? We never authorized a search party."

"It was civilian-organized. The mother of a missing kid said she was tired of sitting around while all the town's children disappeared." He paused. "I can't say I blame them."

"How long have they been missing?"

"About six hours. They set up base at one of the local's houses. The searchers were communicating with walkie-talkies, checking in with base every half hour. No one's heard from them since noon."

166

Murdock glanced at his watch. It would be fully dark in a few minutes. "Send a dozen patrolmen into the woods. I want everyone in pairs. If nothing turns up by midnight, call it off until morning. I want you leading the search."

Calhoun nodded. "You got it."

There was commotion upstairs, followed by the sound of pounding footfalls. Detective Andrews charged into the basement. "We just got a report of a double homicide at the compost dump."

"Christ," Murdock said. He glanced at Calhoun. "Finish things here, organize the search, and check back with me at nine." And then he mounted the stairs—taking them two at a time—and stormed through the house and into the rain.

CHAPTER TWENTY-FIVE

Chief Skatchawa's office overlooked Washaka Woods and a meandering tributary of the Housatonic River. In the distance, the hulking form of Mt. Greylock rose above the trees, its outline obscured by a rolling gray fog. The office was sparsely furnished, decorated with Native American art, clay-potted plants, and tribal artifacts displayed in glass cases.

The Chief sat tall in his chair, his leathery hands folded atop a mahogany desk. He appeared to be in his early sixties, his long, silvery hair pulled back into a loose ponytail. He wore faded blue jeans and steel-tipped boots, and when he met Jay's gaze, his dark eyes glinted in his weathered face.

"Thanks for meeting with us," Jay said, and glanced over at Steve, who fidgeted in his chair. "As Steve mentioned on the phone, we were hoping to learn more about the settlement at Freetown and anything that might have led to the disappearance of its people…anything that you might have overlooked the last time you met with Steve."

For a moment, the Chief remained silent. Then he shrugged, his long hair brushing his shoulders. "Starvation. Desertion. Disease. It could have been anything."

"But what did your ancestors believe? Are there any histories?"

The Chief shook his head. "Nothing written. But there are legends, of course. Folklore passed on from generation to generation. But what is fact and what is fiction, I cannot say."

Jay leaned forward in his chair. "Could you tell us about the legends?"

The Chief studied his face for a long moment, perhaps deciding whether he could be trusted, or perhaps deciding whether he would take the story too seriously. Then he lifted his right hand and motioned to the window behind him, gesturing to the vast expanse of forest.

"This land. It is the land of my people—our home, our sanctuary—for centuries. But understand, we do not own this land, for land belongs to no man. Land is the gift of the Earth Mother, a gift to all of her creatures. It does not belong to man alone, for man is no more significant than the blade of grass, the cloud in the sky, or the fish in the sea. My people know this, my people have always known this.

"But not the white man. The white man has always been greedy. He has always sought to make everything his own, to conquer, destroy, and bend the land to suit his needs. The white man did not respect my people, did not respect the land. He cleared the forest, spread disease, and drove us from our homes. And all across the land it was the same.

"When the white settlers began disappearing, my people believed it was the Earth Mother punishing them for their sins. And there was great rejoicing. But when my people began disappearing as well, we knew it could not be the Earth Mother, but rather a malevolent spirit. It was said by the tribal elders that this spirit dwelled deep in the bowels of the earth, an evil manifestation that hungered for human flesh.

"Within six months, nearly half my people had vanished. It was said that the spirit had drawn them into its lair. But my people would not be defeated so easily; our warriors fought back. They assembled before the cave where the spirit was believed to dwell, a place they called pontow wampaga, which is Washaka for, 'where the dark one sleeps'. Legend says there was a terrible battle that resulted in many deaths. But in the end, my people discovered a way to defeat the spirit."

"How?" Jay asked. "How did they do it?"

COLONY OF THE LOST

"By poisoning the wellspring of its life."

"What does that mean?"

But the Chief only shrugged.

"This spirit," Jay said. "Did it have a name?" He could feel Steve's eyes upon him and knew that Steve was afraid of what he might say next.

"The legend doesn't refer to a name."

"Was it Trell?"

The Chief flinched—ever so slightly. "I don't know. Where did you hear that name?"

"Your people didn't kill it, Chief. It's back, I've seen it. I know what it can do."

Steve grabbed his shoulder. "That's enough, Jay. He told us what he knows. Leave the man alone."

"Guns won't kill this thing. But your people managed to send it into hibernation for over three centuries. Tell me how."

Steve stood up. "I'm sorry Chief Skatchawa. I shouldn't have brought him."

"You've got to tell me what else you know. Before more people die!"

"I think you should leave," the Chief said.

"You don't understand. It's back! It's not going to stop until the whole town is destroyed, until we're all dead! Don't you get it? Don't either of you get it?"

The Chief stood, his face flushed. "Get out of my office."

* * *

They drove home in Steve's Lexus, cruising along the highway at just a hair above the legal limit. Jay stared out the window and watched the trees zip past in a blur of green. The tension inside the car was palpable.

"What the hell has gotten into you? And don't give me any crap about how drinking is ruining your life and clouding your thought

170

process because this goes way beyond drinking. This," he said, shaking his head, "this is insanity."

"I'm sorry if I got a little out of control back there, but if you knew the whole story you wouldn't blame me. Besides, if you were so concerned about your precious academic reputation, you shouldn't have insisted on being there."

"You wouldn't have gotten a meeting if I hadn't called him myself. The Chief and I have a mutual respect that we've built over the years. I agreed to arrange the meeting because I wanted to learn more about the disappearance of the settlement and because you agreed to keep your mouth shut. Now I'll probably never get the opportunity to speak to the man again and learn more about the history of his people and how they influenced the land. Christ, Jay, you were ranting and raving like some kind of doomsday prophet."

Jay stared at his friend in growing agitation. He was so naive. He and the rest of the townspeople. They'd allow themselves to be slaughtered before believing that a creature like Trell could exist. "Steve, in a few more weeks there may not be any history left for you to write about. I'm not drunk, and I know for a fact that this town will be systematically wiped out if something isn't done to stop this creature, this beast that calls itself Trell. I'm serious. I've got three people who will corroborate my story. So just listen to it all before you make a judgment, okay?"

"Fine," Steve said, his eyes never leaving the road.

When Jay finished telling the story, he drew a deep breath. "So what do you think?"

"Honestly?"

"Yeah, honestly."

"I think you're delusional."

They arrived at Jay's house. Steve pulled into the driveway, the car's headlights illuminating the forest beyond the backyard. "You don't even care that I've got people who can vouch for me?"

Steve didn't reply.

"I don't believe this," Jay said, and got out of the car. "You're so caught up in your own concept of reality that you won't even consider the possibility that I may be right. That's just the attitude Trell is hoping for ... just the attitude that will get you all killed."

CHAPTER TWENTY-SIX

Calhoun picked his way through the darkened forest—trees crouched on either side like spindly goblins—and began to entertain serious doubts about Murdock's decision to authorize the search. The odds of finding anyone in this were a hundred to one, Murdock's motives for calling the search purely political.

The whole town was caught in a panic. And who could blame them, really? Over two-dozen children were missing, not to mention twenty plus adults from today's search party. To say that the town was unhappy with the way the investigation had been conducted thus far would probably be the understatement of the century.

The people of Glenwood wanted their children back, a suspect in custody, and a tree to string him up on. And if he and Murdock didn't deliver one soon, the two of them would find themselves hanging from the nearest tree by their balls.

The townspeople had already disobeyed an order not to venture into the woods without police supervision. He had a feeling that if they didn't get results soon, the town would splinter into anarchy.

Calhoun swept the flashlight across the trail, illuminating silvery beads of water clinging to the underbrush. The rain had tapered off an hour ago, replaced by a steady wind that broke apart the clouds and sent them scudding across the sky.

Somewhere close, an owl hooted.

Calhoun's search partner—officer Adelson—jumped back and dropped his flashlight.

"Just an owl," Calhoun said, although it had made him jump a little too.

Adelson retrieved his flashlight from the dirt. "Place gives me the creeps."

Calhoun nodded and glanced at his radio. He and Adelson both carried one, but Calhoun's was tuned to the channel of the original search party rather than the police frequency. Although the police radio had sporadically cut in with a crackle of activity, the search radio had remained eerily silent.

It was almost eleven o'clock and they still hadn't found any trace of the lost search party. Calhoun couldn't understand it. They all had radios. Why hadn't someone called into base at the first sign of trouble?

At 11:05 the second to last team radioed in its report for the previous half hour. So far no one had seen or heard anything. Calhoun and Adelson continued through the darkness, following the trail signs nailed into the trees at every intersection.

A few minutes later the original search radio cut in with a crackle of static. Calhoun and Adelson glanced at one another and shook their heads—the last team was calling on the wrong channel. He spoke into the radio. "Search Command, go ahead."

Silence.

"Go ahead."

Static. And then a voice. Deep and gravelly. "Looking for me?"

Calhoun froze. "Who are you?"

"I am the Hunter and the Hunted."

Calhoun and Adelson exchanged a glance. "Where are the people from the search party?"

"Dead. Every … last … one."

"You killed them?" He fought to prevent the fear from creeping into his voice. He had to remain calm, had to ask this lunatic a bunch of questions, get him to slip up, reveal some clues that would allow them to discover his identity.

"They yielded their lives to me."

"Why?"

"So that I may grow stronger."

Calhoun surveyed the darkness. "Did you have help?"

"You have no idea what you're up against."

"Did you have help?" he repeated.

"Would you like to play a game?"

"Where are you?"

"That's not how you play, agent Calhoun."

Calhoun's arms crawled with gooseflesh. "How do you know my name?"

"Because I am the One and the Many."

Calhoun cocked his head to listen. Was that a rustling in the trees? He crept toward the sound.

"That's it," the voice said. "You're getting warmer."

Calhoun drew his weapon, and Adelson followed suit. They tiptoed to the junction ahead. Adelson looked petrified, sounded like he was on the verge of hyperventilating.

"You're getting closer," the voice said.

Calhoun turned right.

"Wrong way."

Turned left.

"That's it."

"Why the game?" Calhoun asked. "Why not tell me where you are?"

"And spoil all the fun?"

Calhoun peered between the trees, searching the shadows for movement.

"You've almost found me."

Something rustled in the underbrush.

Calhoun and his partner fired, the flash from the muzzles momentarily lighting up their faces.

A scream rang out from the trees. Something thudded to the ground and a hoarse voice croaked, "Friendly fire."

Adelson glanced at Calhoun, his eyes huge. "Oh my God!" He scrambled to reach the fallen officer.

Calhoun stood there, too stunned to move. And then he heard that same gravelly voice on the radio. Except, this time, he could hear it behind him as well.

"You missed me."

Calhoun whirled around, and what he saw there, crouched within the shadows, paralyzed him. For a moment, his gun was forgotten. But a moment was all it would take.

The blood-red light cast by its eyes shone upon him ... and Calhoun screamed.

CHAPTER TWENTY-SEVEN

Tim's mom passed a bowl of mashed potatoes to his dad. Afterward, Dad picked up a steak knife and waved it in the air, punctuating some point that Tim wasn't listening to. He could easily imagine Dad reaching across the table, grabbing him by the hair, and slicing the knife across his throat while Mom munched on a sliver of steak.

Sorry, Tim. Trell's orders. Hey Hon, could you pass me the broccoli?

The crazy thing was, it wasn't all that far-fetched. Trell wanted him dead, and what better way to kill him than by seizing control of his parents? Staying here definitely put them all at risk. But where else could he go?

We should've crashed into Trell again, killed it while we had the chance.

He stared down at his steak swimming in its juices and pictured Frank's mangled corpse lying in a pool of blood. Jay had told him about it on Saturday after he and Maria showed up at Jay's doorstep.

"Timmy, what's the matter? Aren't you hungry?"

Tim glanced up to find both of his parents staring at him, their faces wrinkled with concern. "Just got a little stomachache, that's all."

"Your father heard that the superintendent canceled school until this maniac is caught."

Tim nodded. He'd heard it too—on the radio at Maria's house. They called in sick to school and spent the day hanging out in her bedroom. They talked for hours about music and movies and their plans for the future. Maria wanted to travel the world, join the Peace Corps, and become a doctor. Tim wanted to become a writer or a journalist and was always up for playing doctor. Maria called him a perv and pushed him onto the bed, and they made out for what seemed like hours.

Neither spoke about the horrors they'd witnessed at the compost dump, though they both agreed to stay inside to avoid any chance of running into Randy's goon, Lenny.

He's not Randy's goon anymore. He belongs to Trell now.

"Well I sure hope they get this guy soon," Dad said. "I'm beginning to regret moving here."

"You just make sure you stay indoors, Timmy. And don't let in any strangers."

Tim rolled his eyes. "Yes, Mother."

When dinner ended, Tim retired to his room and locked the door. He lay in bed and watched TV, but his mind kept circling back to the day before yesterday when Randy and his goons chased him through the streets of Glenwood and cornered him in the compost dump. When Randy pulled out that gun, Tim thought for sure he was going to die right there in the mud.

He thought of Maria lying on the ground beside him, her legs glistening with rainwater, her black panties molded to the curves of her body like a second skin. Selfishly, he was glad she'd gotten dragged into this mess. She was smart, beautiful, and funny. And he could talk to her—really talk to her—about his hopes, his dreams, his fears.

The whole situation with Trell had brought them a lot closer than they would've been under normal circumstances. He just hoped she felt as strongly for him as he did for her. And more than anything, he hoped they'd live long enough to find out.

***

Night crept like death through Glenwood, smothering the last bastions of daylight. Maria lay on the couch and leafed through an issue of *Glamour* magazine. She flipped absently through the glossy pages and tried to focus her attention on the articles.

But it wasn't working.

Her mind kept looping back to when Randy showed up at her house on Saturday, begging for another chance. She couldn't believe she had actually agreed to go out with that loser in the first place. And to think she had let him talk her into having sex, not once, but twice. How could she have let that maniac touch her?

Outside, the wind gusted, rattling the shutters against the window frames. Maria hugged her knees and shivered, recalling how Randy had yanked her from her house and stuffed her into the trunk of his car while Lenny and Brett laughed like hyenas in the backseat.

She always knew Randy was a little crazy—and maybe at first she was attracted to the danger—but she never thought he was crazy enough to kill someone. But that was before he took her to the compost dump, before he whipped out a .357 Magnum.

She had a vivid recollection of Randy brandishing the gun in the rain. She had been more afraid for Tim than for herself, and whether that was because she really liked Tim or because she didn't believe Randy would actually kill her, she couldn't say for sure.

But then Randy threatened to gang rape her, and she could tell by the look in his eyes that he meant it. She tried not to imagine what that would've been like, but her mind betrayed her and she pictured them on top of her, one after the other, laughing and hollering as they forced themselves on her.

She wiped her eyes, not at all surprised to find that she was crying. Somehow, things had gotten even crazier from there. A creature born out of some half-forgotten nightmare appeared out of nowhere and killed Randy and Brett.

How could such a thing even exist? It was all scales, claws, and teeth. And if Tim and Mr. G were right, then this thing was responsible for the disappearances in town and wouldn't stop until it killed everyone. The police wouldn't believe a word of it. So that meant it was up to them to put a stop to it. But how were they going to do that?

The doorbell startled her out of her thoughts. She hopped off the sofa and ran into the hall. "I'll get it!" But when she opened the door, nobody was there.

She peered into the darkness. "Hello?"

The wind answered her with a moan, ripping the screen door from her hands. "Hello?" she called again. She was about to close the door when she heard a rustle emanate from somewhere beyond the porch.

"Tim?"

No answer.

Don't even think of going out there.

But a part of her wanted to go out, a part of her wanted to see, had to see, what was there. She had been scared enough over the past two days. And she hated it. Hated living in fear. Besides, it was probably just a cat.

Then who rang the bell?

She brushed the thought aside. She had to see for herself, had to prove to herself that she needn't be afraid. Trell was injured. Maybe even dead. She was getting herself all worked up over nothing.

The rustling sounded again.

Don't be stupid.

But she wouldn't be stupid. She'd be careful.

She stepped into the blustery night, the porch entrenched in shadows. She walked half the length of it and then stopped. What was she thinking? Putting herself at risk just to prove a point? Screw it. She was going back inside. Who cared what was out here?

Something moved in the dark, something just beyond her field of vision.

She heard a squealing shriek and turned toward the sound. Then she stumbled backward, staggered through the door, and sank to her knees in the foyer.

Thank God, she thought ... and then realized that there was something on her face, something dripping into her eyes.

Something sticky and black.

CHAPTER TWENTY-EIGHT

Sarah lay awake and stared into darkness. It was quarter of ten—way past her bed time—but with no school tomorrow, it didn't really matter. She knew she should be in a good mood because of it, but she wasn't in a good mood at all. She was worried about Mom.

I think she's sick, she'd told Jenny earlier. *She looks pale. Plus, she's acting kind of funny.*

Lately, Mom seemed really nervous, always reacting to things that Sarah and Daddy couldn't see. She jumped at every little noise and sometimes even talked to herself. Sarah didn't want to admit it, but it seemed like Mom might be going crazy.

She thought back to a few nights ago when Mom came into the house all covered in mud. When Sarah had peeked into her bedroom to see if everything was okay, Mom had yelled at her.

Maybe Mom and Dad are fighting again.

That might explain why she was so angry all the time, but not why she was wandering around the woods after dark, getting all muddy. Could Mom be pregnant? Didn't hormones make women crazy when they were having a baby? Maybe that's why Mom was rubbing her belly so often.

Or was it something else? When Mom yelled at her the other night, there was a moment when her eyes had almost looked red. Hadn't Tim said something like that about the bad man from the library—that his eyes had changed from brown to red?

She scratched Mr. Whiskers behind the ears. She'd probably imagined the thing with Mom's eyes. Dad always said she had an overactive imagination, and she guessed she couldn't argue with that.

But still, something was wrong with Mom. She just hoped it wasn't anything bad like cancer or AIDS because you could die from those.

After awhile her eyes grew heavy with the weight of sleep. In her dreams, a shadowy figure chased her through the woods, sometimes running upright like a man, sometimes dropping to all fours like an animal. But no matter how fast she ran, the figure was always a half step behind her, the slits of its eyes gleaming red.

Going to kill you, Sarah. Going to kill your whole family.

She raced through a darkened section of Washaka Woods, trees crowding her on either side, their knotted trunks transforming into ghoulish faces. Branches reached for her, smacking against her body. Wrapping around her legs. She lost her balance and crashed to the ground. A creature loomed over her, its lips parting to reveal a mouth full of razor sharp fangs.

Get up, Sarah! Before it's too late!

But the voice didn't belong to the creature; it belonged to Samuel. And it sounded like he wasn't in the woods at all. But if he wasn't in the woods, where could he be?

My room!

She awoke with a start, sitting bolt upright and throwing off the covers. Samuel appeared at the foot of her bed, a pale blue light pulsing around him. From far away, he'd seemed like a lost little boy, but up close ... up close, he looked scary. His eyes were black, without any whites, and his teeth were small and yellow and sharp. His skin was blotchy and bloated—like the flesh of a toadstool—and a purple gash flapped open at this throat.

"You must listen, Sarah. You are in grave danger. The beast I warned of controls the will of your mother. You must leave. You must escape at once!"

Sarah stared at him. What did he mean? Why would Mom want to hurt her? "Mom's just sick. That's all."

183

"The beast is the cause of her sickness. She is a slave to its will, a soldier to its dark intents. Only in its death can she be saved. That is why you must go to the others. Tell them what I have told you. Tell them that its strength is fueled by the blood of its victims, that the pool sustains its life."

Somewhere beyond the walls of her room came the stealthy creak of footfalls on the hardwood floor. Samuel jerked his head toward the door. "Go Sarah! Hurry!"

Samuel had to be wrong. Tim said that the beast was a gray-haired man with red eyes. How could he make her Mom do bad things?

Suddenly she heard a voice—Mom's voice—drifting through the house. "Oh Sarah. Wake up, darling. Mommy wants to talk to you."

Mr. Whiskers squatted at the foot of her bed and stared at the door, his back arched. Growling.

"The window, Sarah. Go!"

The urgency of Samuel's voice snapped her into action. She rolled out of bed and scrambled to the window.

Fingernails tapped against her bedroom door. "Open up, Sarah. Mommy's got a surprise for you."

Sarah slipped on her sneakers and opened the window, but she struggled with the locks to the screen. She glanced over her shoulder at the eyehook lock securing the bedroom door. Daddy had agreed to install it two years ago after her recurring nightmares about monsters creeping up from the basement to eat her. Once the lock was in place, the nightmares stopped. But now that she was older, she knew that no flimsy little lock could keep a monster out.

Mom rammed into the door, and the wood around the lock splintered.

"Daddy!" Sarah cried. "Help!"

Another crash.

This time the eyehook pulled free and the door slammed against the wall.

Sarah backed away from the window, a scream lodged in her throat.

Mom stepped through the doorway, her eyes glowing red. She wore a silky black nightgown and a crazed expression on her face.

"Daddy!"

Mom shook her head and pointed at Sarah with the blade of a butcher knife. "Mommy doesn't like tattle tales."

"Leave her be!" Samuel cried.

The Mom-thing sneered. "What are you doing here?" And then it grinned. "Do you recall the night you came to me in the forest? Ah, how the blood gushed from your throat, young Samuel. So rich, so sweet. Your family came looking for you, scouring the forest by torchlight. Such simpletons. They died because of you. And now, all these years later, you've done it again. How will it feel, Samuel, to witness her death, to know that you brought this fate upon her?"

"You would have killed her eventually. Whether she could see me or not."

The Mom-thing grinned. "So true," it said, waving the knife in the air. "Who's going to save you now, Sarah? Your imaginary friend?"

Sarah bit her lip to keep it from trembling. "You're not my mother," she said. "I don't know what you are, but you are NOT my mother."

From the hallway: "Sarah? Margaret? What's going on?"

The Mom-thing lunged for her, and Sarah tripped over a bundle of blankets and fell to the floor. Mr. Whiskers sprang off the bed and attacked, his claws ripping into the thing's cheeks.

The Mom-thing peeled Mr. Whiskers off its face and held him by the scruff of the neck.

Sarah jumped to her feet. "Don't you hurt him!" She grabbed the nearest thing she could find—a ceramic unicorn—and hurled it at the thing that wasn't her mother. The base of the figurine struck it in the temple and sent it stumbling into the wall.

Mr. Whiskers dropped to the floor and scurried underneath the bed.

Sarah dashed out of her room and into the hallway where she collided with Daddy. He caught her in his arms and held her by the shoulders. "Sarah, what is it? What's wrong?"

"It's Mommy! There's a ... a ..." Her brain screamed for her to spit it out.

"A what?" Daddy asked.

"A monster inside her!"

Daddy moved her aside. "It's all right, honey. She's probably just having another bad dream. I'll go talk to her."

"No, Daddy! Don't go in there!"

But Daddy just smiled and went into the bedroom.

Samuel floated right through Daddy's body. "Go, Sarah. "Save yourself. Trell wants you, not your father."

But Sarah just stood there with her back pressed against the railing, one hand curled into her mouth.

"Go, Sarah! I cannot remain here much longer. My time in this world grows short."

And then he faded before her eyes and dissolved back into the night.

The monster disguised as Mom lurched into the hallway, its eyes fixed upon Sarah. Daddy held the Mom-thing back. "Margaret, honey. Relax. It's just a dream." He tapped her on the cheek, then paused to examine the blood that seeped onto his fingers. "You can wake up now. It's alright."

But Sarah could tell from his voice that he wasn't so sure anymore. "Be careful, Daddy."

The Mom-thing smacked Daddy's hands away.

"Honey, stop." Then Daddy glanced down at the knife. "Margaret? What are you doing?"

"Daddy, no!"

The knife disappeared into his stomach, and he fell against the wall, his mouth locked in a silent scream.

The Mom-thing pulled the blade free, and blood spattered the wall in a glistening arc.

"Margaret?" he croaked.

"So stupid," the Mom-thing said. "But then, you always were."

"Daddy!"

"Run Sarah!"

Sarah hurried toward the stairs.

"Nowhere to run, Sarah. No one to save you now."

Tears blurred her vision as she scrambled down the stairs and stumbled into the foyer. She turned the corner and charged out the front door and into the darkness of night. The cold air prickled her flesh with goose bumps and turned her breath into rolling puffs of white vapor.

She had to find help for Daddy. But where could she go? Who could she tell?

She crept across the lawn and passed through the trees marking the entrance to Washaka Woods.

The Mom-thing stormed outside and stood on the front lawn. "Sarah?" she called in a sing-song voice. "Come out, come out, wherever you are."

Sarah held her breath and hid behind a giant oak.

Come back, Samuel. I need you!

But if Samuel heard, he didn't answer.

She pictured Daddy all alone in the house, lying on the floor. Bleeding.

Don't die, Daddy. Please don't die.

187

She stared into the woods where the trees grew thick enough to shut out the moonlight. What if there was a monster in there? Waiting for her? A monster with glowing red eyes and razor sharp teeth.

Got to be brave. Got to be a big girl now. Daddy needs me.

She drew a deep breath, said a silent prayer, and tiptoed into the woods.

CHAPTER TWENTY-NINE

Chaos reigned over the Glenwood police station. Distraught parents paced through the cramped waiting area, some sobbing, some wringing their hands, all of them talking at once, pleading with officers to get out on the streets and find their children.

Plainclothes detectives sat hunched over metal desks piled with paperwork, sleeves rolled to the elbows, ties loosened. They clacked away at keyboards, documenting case after case, detail after detail in hopes of finding some similarities, some clues that might have escaped them before, small shreds of evidence that might serve to profile a killer or killers. The phones rang incessantly, crying out in a dozen different tones, the calls fielded by volunteers and by officers on loan from neighboring communities.

Murdock watched it all through the blinds in his office, an office that had once belonged to a police captain in the long ago days before the Devil came to Glenwood. Nineteen children—vanished. A twenty man search party—gone. And now he had three bodies lying in the morgue, mauled beyond recognition.

It couldn't be one man. One man couldn't take out a twenty person search party without at least one of the victims radioing for help.

Maybe it's not human.

The thought conjured up an image of Frank Patterson's mangled corpse, his eyeball hanging out of its socket like a bloody yo-yo.

He brushed the thought aside. Whatever animal tore Frank's legs off couldn't possibly have ... have what? Swallowed three dozen people whole? No, it wasn't possible.

Maybe it didn't swallow his legs. Maybe it chewed them off and the thing's owner put them in a plastic bag. Or maybe there wasn't an

189

animal at all. Maybe somebody sawed Patterson's legs off and then dropped them in a bag.

Both scenarios would explain the lack of blood beyond the immediate vicinity of Patterson's body. But even assuming one of these theories was correct, it still didn't explain everything. In fact, it only muddied the waters further.

All the evidence pointed to Patterson. The kid in the library had described a man who looked exactly like Patterson. A print lifted from the knife in Gallagher's house matched Patterson's. And Wayne Gillespi confirmed that Patterson had called in sick every day for nearly three weeks, beginning shortly after the disappearance of Ryan Brakowski.

But Patterson was dead now, murdered under mysterious circumstances, and yet just hours after his death an entire search party vanished. It certainly couldn't have been Patterson—not unless you were willing to believe that dead people could commit crimes—so he must have had an accomplice.

But who? Gallagher? It didn't quite add up.

If you asked him yesterday, he would've said Gallagher did it. Hell, he had a motive—he just got canned from his job, his fiancée split on him, and he had a drinking problem. Too much strain on a guy like that and he's bound to snap. And maybe Patterson snapped with him—the guy had been a loner ever since his wife died. Maybe they teamed up and went on a rampage, each of them trying to get even with the world in his own way. Then maybe Gallagher came to his senses, sobered up a bit, and threatened to turn them both in. Patterson tried to stop him, broke into his house when Gallagher was on a bender, tried to stab him, but Gallagher was more alert than he let on. Gallagher shot him—grazed him on the shoulder—but Patterson managed to get away. Then, after Gallagher got out of jail, he headed over to Patterson's house to finish the job. Killed him by sawing his legs off or sicking some sort of animal on him. The murder made Gallagher realize that he really did enjoy killing, so then he continued on the rampage alone.

The theory made a little sense until you added the latest catch—the voice on the search radio didn't belong to Gallagher. In fact, while the voice taunted Calhoun in the woods, baiting him and his partner into killing a Glenwood cop, Gallagher was snoozing on the couch in his living room.

The voice on the radio had sounded like pure evil. It was clear they were dealing with a real psychopath. And then there was Calhoun's scream. Listening to it was like having a sliver of glass jabbed into your brain. You would have thought he'd seen the Devil himself instead of the bear he mentioned in his report.

Maybe it wasn't a bear. Maybe it was ... something worse.

Murdock dismissed the thought. While some folks in town were whispering of vampires, zombies, and demons, he wouldn't allow himself to be lured in by that kind of hokum. Better to stick to the facts, no matter how senseless or inconsistent they seemed. The truth was out there somewhere, and he damn well was going to find it.

The phone rang. It was Martinez from the CSI lab with the results from Patterson's house. "What've you got? And don't tell me you've got nothing."

"We're lucky to have anything. The perp wiped away his prints before he left. But there were a couple he missed, pretty good ones too—a thumb on the cellar door and an index finger on the desk in the basement."

"You get a match?"

"It was Gallagher."

Murdock clapped his hands. "I knew it! Any traces of blood in the prints?"

"Negative."

Murdock sighed. That would've been too easy. Now Gallagher could argue he was a guest in Patterson's house days before the murder. "What about the blood itself? All of it Patterson's?"

"We won't know until the DNA tests come back."

"Anything else?"

"Not from my end. But the M.E. wants to see you. Said he found something strange."

Murdock grabbed his sports coat from the back of the chair. "Tell him I'm on my way."

***

Dr. Weisman was a wiry man in his late fifties with bushy gray eyebrows and thick glasses. He greeted Murdock and Calhoun with a firm handshake and motioned to a pair of chairs opposite his desk. "Please. Have a seat."

Murdock leaned forward and rested his elbows on the edge of the desk. "What did you find?"

"Well, first off, Mr. Patterson died from blood loss related to the injuries sustained to his legs. Based on the characteristic messiness of the wounds—the uneven and variable punctures and tears—it appears that the severing of Mr. Patterson's legs was accomplished by chewing and tearing, rather than by sawing."

"You're saying an animal did this?"

Dr. Weisman nodded. "And judging by the splintered bones, whatever animal did this had phenomenally strong jaws."

"But you don't know what kind of animal did it?"

"Not for certain. I've made a number of comparisons to documented cases of animal attacks, but none even comes close to what I would consider a match."

"What came closest?"

"The profile was nearest to a grizzly, but, as I said before, it certainly wasn't a match. However, it appeared to be the most consistent in terms of bite width and jaw length, but some of the

192

puncture wounds near the top suggest that the teeth of this particular animal were barbed."

Murdock stole a glance at Calhoun, who was sitting uncharacteristically straight in his chair, an almost vacant look in his eyes. "You mean it had teeth growing out of the side of other teeth?"

The doctor nodded. "It appears that way. I've never seen anything like it."

"So it's definitely not a bear?"

"Definitely not."

"What about traces of saliva? Would DNA testing identify it?"

"It should, yes. But it's going to take some time."

"Anything else?"

"Mr. Patterson had bruises and chafing on his back, shoulders, and sides. You said he was found in the basement?"

Murdock nodded.

"Well, then I'd venture to guess that either Mr. Patterson fell backward down the stairs before his death ..."

"Or he was pushed."

"Precisely."

"Did you establish the time of death?"

"Between eleven fifteen and eleven thirty P.M. on the night before last."

Murdock sighed. He had hoped the doctor would clear things up for him, but that last bit of information made things even hairier. The phone records proved that Patterson had called Gallagher the night he was killed—at 10:52 to be precise. Patterson must have said something to piss Gallagher off, so Gallagher headed over to his house and killed him in the basement. The time of death meshed with the theory, but the problem was that Gallagher never left his house that night. The local staking out the place swore Gallagher had passed out piss drunk around 10:00.

Maybe the local fell asleep. Maybe he's just trying to cover his own ass.

He drew a deep breath. Christ, he had such a headache. "That it?"

Dr. Weisman shook his head. "There is one more thing. When I sectioned Mr. Patterson's brain, I discovered a rather peculiar growth."

"A growth? You mean like a tumor?"

"No. Not like a tumor. I don't quite know how to explain it. This was a substance unlike anything I've ever seen. It appeared to be some kind of black protoplasm concentrated in the frontal lobe. Did Mr. Patterson exhibit any problems with his fine motor skills?"

Murdock shrugged. "Not that I know of, why?"

"Whatever this stuff was, it was attached to the motor control centers of Mr. Patterson's brain. I can't be sure at this point, but I believe it may have been some kind of parasite." His eyes narrowed. "Now for the strangest part. Whatever it was—parasite, tumor, what have you—it was still alive when I performed the autopsy."

"I take it that's not normal?"

"No. Tumors, parasites—they feed off the afflicted tissue. When that tissue dies, so do they. And yet this thing was alive even after Mr. Patterson had been dead for over twelve hours. It's the strangest thing I've ever encountered."

"Is it alive now?"

"No. It died shortly after I finished the autopsy. But I plan on performing a whole series of tests on it."

Murdock nodded. "Good. Let me know what you find."

194

CHAPTER THIRTY

Tim sat on the living room sofa and listened to the sounds of the old house settling around him. Every creaking joint, every knocking pipe, got his pulse pounding, and he wondered, when the time came, would he be able to distinguish those sounds from Trell's stealthy approach?

He'd managed to slip away from Trell at the compost dump, but could he really expect to get away with that twice? Sooner or later, it would come for him, and when it did, there was nothing he could do to stop it. That was the cold, hard truth. And since he was being honest, he might as well prepare himself for a slow and horrible death. Because that seemed to be the way Trell rolled.

For all he knew, Trell might already be inside the house. Or maybe it lurked in the backyard, watching him through the living room window. Studying him. Like an insect in a jar.

He glanced at the window, but all he could see was a reflection of himself slouched on the sofa like a scared little boy.

From somewhere behind him came a sudden *Click! Click! Click!*

He whirled around.

Nothing.

Probably just the radiator.

It did that sometimes when the heat kicked on. And it was a chilly night, so that made sense. Right?

His eyes shifted back to the window. He didn't like the idea that Trell might be lurking right outside, watching him. So he switched off the light and sat in the dark. But was that really such a good idea?

What monster didn't love sneaking into a house when it thought everyone was asleep?

Speaking of which, why had his parents gone to bed so early? And what was with them, anyway? Dragging him from place to place like an old suitcase. What good was it to ask his opinion if they never listened to his response? It was just a formality to them, just another box to check. Like forwarding the mail.

As the people of Glenwood vanished one by one, his parents just sat around waiting their turn because they'd made a decision and, by God, they were going to stick to it. Talk about being stubborn. And of all the places they could have gone, his Dad had to choose Glenwood.

There's nothing out there, Tim had said. *It'll be so boring.*

God, he'd give anything now for it to be boring.

A scream rang out from the street. Tim jumped off the couch and raced to the door, his heart thumping like ghetto bass. A little girl was running toward his house, her arms flailing, her nightgown flapping in the breeze.

"Sarah!" Tim cried, and rushed outside to meet her. He lifted her up, and she wrapped her arms around him and buried her face in his chest, hot tears streaming from her eyes.

"What is it? What happened?"

She could barely speak, but Tim deciphered the only three words that he needed to hear.

Monster ... Got Daddy ...

A glare of headlights washed over them. Tim shielded his eyes as a police cruiser turned the corner and pulled up beside them. The window rolled down and a cop with thinning gray hair leaned toward them. "She the girl I just heard screaming?"

Tim nodded. "She said someone hurt her father."

"Where?"

"On Pennybrook Road. Number ..."

196

"102," Sarah said.

The cop studied Tim for a long moment before shifting his gaze to Sarah. "You know this kid?"

"He's my friend," Sarah said.

The cop squinted at Tim. "What's your name?"

"Tim Hanson."

"You live in that house?"

Tim nodded.

"Okay, Tim. Take the girl into your house and lock the door. Don't open for anyone except the police. Got it?"

"Got it."

The cop flicked on his flashers and sped off down the street.

CHAPTER THIRTY-ONE

Jay surfed through the channels, clicking up and down and back again. Not a thing worth watching, which was just as well since he wasn't in the mood anyway. It was just something to keep his mind occupied, something to make him forget that he hadn't had a drink in over twenty-four hours, hadn't had a drink since he missed the call that could've saved Frank's life, the call that could've saved all their lives.

He licked his lips. God, he could use a beer right now. A nice, cold one to take the edge off.

Give it a rest, would you? Learn some self-control.

A few days ago that voice would have pissed him off. But not tonight. Tonight, he recognized it as the voice of his younger self— back in the days before the bottle became an addiction, back when his will was still his own.

He had liked himself then, respected himself. Too bad he could barely remember what that felt like.

Eight years of my life. Stolen because of my father. If he hadn't been such a drunk, hadn't passed a gene along to me ...

But no. He wouldn't pursue it. It was time to stop blaming others for his problems, time to own up, take responsibility for his own faults, his own actions. That was the only way to beat this thing, the only way to reclaim his life. If somehow he could do that, if somehow he could resist the temptation, keep himself sober, then maybe he could protect the kids. Maybe he could find a way to defeat Trell.

It would take a lot of smarts, a lot of guts—things he feared he didn't have anymore—but he had to try ... because he didn't want to end up like his father, didn't want to die a worthless drunk. This was his chance to make up for his mistakes, to right his wrongs. And if he had to die, then he would go out fighting and die sober.

Great pep talk. But how do you plan to kill Trell?

Fair question. Randy had shot it with a .357 Magnum. Maria had run it down with a car. But Trell had just shrugged it off and lumbered back into the woods.

Jay unfolded Frank's note and angled it into the lamplight. What was *Trell Arrow Wol* supposed to mean? And what about those runes and the obelisk with the key at its center? Was it the beginning of a sentence that explained how to kill Trell? Was it some kind of secret weapon or phrase that would send Trell back to where it came from if uttered three times?

The sudden stomp of footfalls on the porch startled the paper from his hand. He jumped to his feet and stared at the door just as someone began pounding on it

He snatched the gun from the coffee table and stalked to the door.

"Open up, Jay. It's Tim."

Jay reached for the doorknob ... and hesitated. What if it wasn't really Tim? What if Trell was controlling him?

He cocked the gun and cracked open the door.

Tim pushed his way inside, leading Sarah by the hand. "Trell seized control of her mom. Tried to kill her, but her dad got in the way."

"Oh my God. Is he okay?"

"Don't know. Cops are there right now."

Christ, Jay thought. *Thank God I passed on that drink.* "Sarah? Are you okay?"

She glanced up at him and burst into tears.

He wrapped his arms around her and hugged her tight. "It'll be all right. Everything will be okay." He bit his lip, feeling like he might start crying himself. How could anyone hurt such a sweet little kid? What kind of monster could do this to her?

But, of course, he knew the answer to that. They all did.

***

Tim studied Jay as he comforted Sarah. If he was drunk, it didn't show. Not in his voice or his movements. And there didn't seem to be any beer cans lying around, no bottles of liquor in sight.

Give him another hour. Then he'll be crawling around on all fours, singing sailor songs and hitting Sarah and me up for money.

He glanced out the window. Sirens warbled in the distance. "I don't think we can stay here much longer. Trell knows where we live."

"Where do you suggest we go?"

"Doesn't matter. Anywhere. At least until we figure this out."

Jay nodded. "You're probably right. We need to buy more time."

Sarah wiped her eyes. "What about Daddy?"

"We'll find out how he is," Jay said. "I promise."

She sniffled. "And Mommy?"

Jay crouched down beside her. "The only way we can help her is by killing Trell. And to do that we need to get out of here for awhile."

"Okay," Sarah said. "But I'm scared."

"So am I. We all are. But we won't let anything happen to you. I promise."

"Should we leave tonight?" Tim asked.

"The sooner the better," Jay said.

"All right. I'm just going to run to my house real quick and grab some things." He paused when he reached the door. "I'll call Maria too. Tell her we'll swing by her house."

"Okay," Jay said. "Hurry back. And be careful."

***

200

The phone rang a moment after Tim closed the door, making Jay and Sarah both jump. Jay grabbed it before it could ring again, and was surprised to hear Crystal's voice.

"I don't want to give you the wrong idea by calling, but you still have a lot of my stuff at your house."

"Uh-huh."

"I'm coming over tonight to get the rest of my things."

"Tonight?"

"Is that a problem?"

"It's ten o'clock."

"So? Am I interrupting your beauty sleep?"

"Tonight's not very good for me."

"Dare I ask why?"

"Cut it out, Crystal. Just come by in the morning."

"I won't have a chance in the morning. I'm coming over now."

"Crystal—"

But it was too late—she'd already hung up.

CHAPTER THIRTY-TWO

Murdock had just pulled away from the Glenwood Country Inn when the radio squawked on the dash. The dispatcher's voice cut through the static. "Potential homicide. 102 Pennybrook Road."

Christ! Here we go again.

He pinned the pedal to the floor, and the Impala's tires screeched against the pavement, belching smoke into the air. The car raced down the blackened stretch of road, the sound of the revving engine loud in his ears.

He snatched the CB from the dash and asked for the name of the officer calling in the report.

The dispatcher rustled through some paper. "Officer Andrews."

Murdock strangled the steering wheel. "Andrews is supposed to be covering nine South Maple. Tell him to get his ass back over there!"

The Impala careened around the corner and barreled into the straightaway. Murdock floored the accelerator and the car surged forward. "Come on, come on." He veered onto Elm Street and the car fishtailed across the double yellow line, coming within inches of slamming into an eighteen-wheeler.

He had to get to Gallagher's house, had to get there fast.

Maybe he didn't realize Andrews left. Maybe he's passed out drunk.

But all Murdock kept picturing was Gallagher fleeing the scene, his only suspect getting away.

"The hell he will." He flicked a switch and the sirens screamed to life. The car shot like a bullet down the street.

***

The thing that was not quite Lenny Archibald shambled in the moonlight. Its destination loomed in the distance, the windows of the house glowing with bright yellow light. It could smell the three inside and knew that they were to die—the Dark One had commanded it.

It stalked toward the house with Randy's gun cradled loosely in its hand. When it spotted a figure lurking near the walkway, it raised the gun and pulled the trigger.

CHAPTER THIRTY-THREE

The stomp of footsteps announced a visitor on the front porch, and before Jay could even peek through the blinds, a key slipped into the lock and the door swung open.

Crystal's eyes swept the room. "From the way you acted on the phone, I would have thought you changed the locks."

"Hello Crystal." He tried to sound annoyed, but didn't really succeed.

"Don't worry, I'll only be a few minutes. I just need the rest of my clothes."

"You shouldn't have come here, Crystal."

"What are you talking about?"

The flush of the toilet drew both of their glances.

Crystal arched an eyebrow. "And who might that be?"

Before he could answer, Sarah emerged from the bathroom, her eyes still red from all the crying.

"Sarah," he said, softly. "This is Crystal."

"Hi," Sarah said, and dropped her gaze to the floor. She was trying so hard to be tough. The poor kid had just watched her mom stab her dad and somehow she was holding it together.

Crystal grabbed Jay by the arm and pulled him out of earshot. "What's a little girl doing here all alone with you?"

He could see by the look in her eyes that she thought the worst. Christ, how could she? After all these years? "Come on. You know better than—"

A gunshot sliced through his words.

"Jay, what—"

The door flew open and Tim collapsed onto the floor, his eyes wide with shock.

Jay rushed over to him. "Tim! Are you okay? What happened?"

"Lock the door! Hurry!"

Jay scurried crab-like across the floor and slammed the door shut.

"Someone shot a cop," Tim said. "I think I was next."

Jay blinked at him. "You weren't hit?"

"No."

Crystal clutched Jay's arm. "What's happening?"

"We're getting out of here."

"What are you talking about?"

He thought about the LeBaron rusting in the driveway and wondered if it would start. "We'll need your car."

"My car? What do you mean? We can't go outside! Are you crazy?"

"Listen to me. We have to get out of here. If we don't, we're going to die."

"But the police will—"

"The police can't protect us from what's out there."

Crystal turned to Tim for confirmation, saw him nod, and didn't say another word.

"All right," Jay said. "Good. Did you park in the driveway?"

"Yes."

"Okay, let's go."

"Which way?" Tim asked.

"Through the cellar. It's got a door leading to the driveway."

"But what if whoever shot the cop is waiting outside?" Crystal asked.

"If it's still out there," Jay said, "it'll probably come through the front door or the back door."

Crystal raised an eyebrow. "Why do you keep saying 'it'?"

Jay ignored the question and stalked to the cellar door in a crouch. He held it open and waved them all forward. "We'll keep the lights off. I don't want it to know we're down there."

The old boards creaked beneath their feet as they descended into darkness. In a few moments, they stood on the concrete floor of his dungeon-like cellar. It smelled damp and musty, as if rainwater had leaked through the foundation.

"Stay close," Jay said. "And watch out for low pipes." He scanned the darkness for any sign of Trell. It could be anywhere down here. Lying in wait, its red eyes closed until the moment of attack.

He led them through what felt like an ancient crypt, navigating around a maze of boxes, tools, and lawn furniture. They arrived at the door an eternity later, and as Jay struggled with the reluctant slide bolt, the ceiling came alive with the sound of pounding footfalls.

Sarah let out a whimper.

"It's alright," Crystal said. "Just stay quiet."

Jay drew the gun from the waistband of his jeans and cracked open the door. A slant of light from a nearby street lamp filtered through the gap. He glanced back at the others and saw that Crystal held the car keys in her hand. "Ready?" he asked.

They all nodded.

"Okay," he said. "Let's go."

They hurried into the driveway, sand grating beneath their shoes. A strong wind gusted at their backs as the frenzied music of his neighbor's wind chime carried through the night.

A car screeched to a halt in the street.

Crystal unlocked the doors to her car.

The screen door flew open with a crash. A kid with spiky blond hair charged down the length of the porch, laughing and screaming in turn.

Jay raised the .45 and waved them forward. "Get in!"

"FBI! Hold it right there!"

Jay didn't even glance in the direction of the man in the street.

The kid leveled a gun at him, and Jay dove to the ground just as the kid fired. The bullet struck the pavement and sprayed jagged bits of concrete into the air.

The engine roared to life behind him. He tucked into a ball and rolled to the other side of the car. When he stood, he saw the kid standing at the edge of the porch, the muzzle of the gun pointed right at him.

He had time only to think, *That's Lenny Archibald from 2nd period Geometry.*

And then the gun went off with a thunderous roar. The bullet whined past his shoulder, so close he felt the breeze as it sliced through the air. Blue-gray smoke billowed from the muzzle of Lenny's gun, curling into the air in lazy tendrils. Through its hazy screen, he watched Lenny's eyes grow wide and his body jerk back as another shot rang out from the street. A circle of blood formed on Lenny's tee-shirt and spread in all directions like a blooming rose.

Jay yanked open the door and jumped into the passenger seat as Lenny doubled over the porch railing and fell face first into the driveway. Crystal shifted into reverse and stomped on the accelerator. The car screamed out of the driveway.

Murdock holstered his gun and climbed into a black Chevy.

"What's happening, Jay? Who was that?"

The car barreled down the narrow street at better than sixty miles per hour.

Blue flashers kicked on behind them. Murdock's car was a quarter of a mile back, but gaining fast.

Crystal applied the brakes.

"No!" Jay shouted. "Don't stop!"

"But it's a cop." She began edging over to the side of the road.

"Listen to me, Crystal. Do not stop this car."

"He's right," Tim said. "We need to keep moving."

"What's wrong with you guys? It's just a—"

Something huge darted from the shadows and rushed past the passenger window.

Sarah screamed.

"What was—"

It landed on the roof with a crash, its massive weight pulling the car to the right. The roof buckled inward, and the four of them ducked their heads and screamed as the car swerved across the road.

"Get it off! Get it off!"

Trell's claws pierced through the roof, and metal groaned as a strip of steel tore back like an old pop-top.

Jay kicked off a shoe and smacked it against Trell's claws.

"What are you doing?" Tim yelled. "It's not a bug!"

"You got any better ideas?"

"Yeah, shoot it!"

He'd completely forgotten about his dad's .45. But where was it? He glanced down and saw it slide under the seat—just out of reach—as Crystal swerved onto the shoulder.

"Do something!" Crystal shouted.

"Buckle your seatbelts!" Jay grabbed the wheel from Crystal and yanked it to the left. The car veered across the double yellow line and ran Murdock off the road just before striking a tree at twenty miles per hour.

The car hit the tree with a sickening crunch that sent them all rocking forward. The air bags deployed, then rapidly deflated. Steam rose from the Volvo's crumpled front end in billowing clouds.

Jay glanced at the roof and could see pinpricks of stars through the holes that Trell's claws had made. "I think it's gone," he said. "Everyone okay? Crystal, can you back up?"

But she didn't seem to hear him. She just stared forward, her eyes vacant.

"Crystal! Get us out of here!"

Something rustled in the woods nearby.

"Hurry," Sarah said, pressing her head against Tim's chest.

Crystal shook herself out of a daze and pressed down on the gas. The tires spun, but the car didn't move.

"I hate to point out the obvious," Tim said, "but it's coming ... and I'm guessing it's pissed."

Crystal mumbled something to herself, shifted into reverse, and stomped on the accelerator.

At first the car refused to move, refused to budge even an inch. But then the RPM gauge climbed higher, the tires dug in, and the front bumper slipped free of its embrace with the tree.

The car shot back with a sudden jolt, zoomed into the street, and almost veered off onto the other shoulder before Crystal jammed it into drive and peeled off down the road.

And as the car raced into the darkness of night, leaving Murdock's Chevy lying on its roof in a ditch, tires still spinning, Jay hoped that the agent's death would be quick.

CHAPTER THIRTY-FOUR

She ran.

Under a violet sky flecked with twinkling stars.

Fleeing the world. Fleeing herself.

But these horrors she couldn't escape.

A slant of moonlight shone through the canopy and fell upon her. Tears blurred her vision. Leaves crunched beneath her racing feet.

Maybe she could break free of its power, run far enough to sever the chains that bound her. But as she ran, she could hear its laugher, its awful voice calling to her through this blackest of nights.

Evil.

Inside her. All around her.

Evil.

Controlling her mind. Controlling her body. Leaving memories like fingerprints.

Do you feel it, Margaret? Can you see it?

She weaved through a maze of trees, tearing through a forest cloaked in shadows. A vision appeared in her mind, and she watched herself plunge a butcher knife into Nick's stomach. She could feel his blood—hot and slippery—flowing over the back of her hand.

A stitch burned in her side, and she drew her breath in shallow gasps. But she continued to run…because she didn't know what else to do. Didn't know where else to go.

And still the memories came. Parading before her eyes, one after the other. Haunting visions that should have driven her insane, but would not.

I won't let you go crazy, Margaret. I won't let you take the easy way out.

And then her mind brought her back to that dark place, the place where the horror began.

***

She could feel cold emanating from slick black walls, could hear water dripping in muted plops, could feel wetness seeping through her paper-thin cotton nightgown.

Where am I? How did I get here?

She drew a deep breath and collected herself, gaining her feet with the aid of a slime-coated boulder. Its touch sent a shiver through her body.

Water rippled behind her, and she whirled in the direction of the sound.

A creature rose from the depths of the pool, water beading off its massive head. Ribbons of moisture spouted from its flaring nostrils and sparkled in the phosphorescent light.

She screamed in terror, the sound echoing throughout the cavern.

The thing before her uttered a guttural laugh. Its eyes fixed upon her, forced her to walk forward. Commanding her to move against her will.

She suddenly remembered having seen the creature before, remembered it looming over her in the backyard, the lid to a trash can dangling loosely in her hand.

The black goo. Sinking into her eyes.

And then she lay down on the cold stone and spreads her legs apart.

The creature climbed out of the churning water. Are you ready for me, Margaret?

***

"Make it stop. Please, God."

But if God was listening, He didn't make His presence known. Her world was one of darkness now, and as she ran through the maze of towering trees, she feared she would never again see the light, never again be free.

I won't let it control me anymore. I won't let it make me do those horrible things.

But from somewhere inside her mind, the voice of the Dark One spoke to her.

Don't do it for me, Margaret. Do it ... for the baby.

And then something slipped inside of her. A thread of sanity snapped like piano wire. She grabbed a large branch from the ground, intending to murder the life within her. But an unseen force seized control of the branch, and instead of striking her in the womb, blow after blow smashed into her face until she saw the world through a bloody haze.

Her foot caught beneath a log and she fell headlong into the dirt. She scrambled back to her feet and ran. And as she ran, the voice inside her laughed.

And laughed.

And laughed.

CHAPTER THIRTY-FIVE

The world spun. Around and over and under. Metal crumpled and groaned. Glass shattered, rained down like glittering jewels.

How many times had the car flipped? Murdock wasn't sure he knew, wasn't even sure how it'd happened. His mind was cloudy. It was hard to think.

Dust hovered in the ruined interior. He hung suspended upside down, his head just inches from the roof. Both windshields had blown out on impact, the weight of the car collapsing the roof, blocking any chance of escape through the windows.

The driver's side door then.

He clicked on the dome light—surprised to find that it still worked—and scanned the door to see if it got smashed shut. But it looked okay. The only thing that seemed out of place was a strip of steel molding encased in vinyl, the tip of which had curled toward him. A droplet of blood glistened on the molding. He touched the steel tip and his fingers came away bloody.

He was injured, then. But how badly? He knew better than to think he was okay just because he couldn't feel anything. The combination of shock and adrenaline was more effective than morphine when it came to blocking out pain in the short-term. He had once watched a perp run three blocks after two .38 slugs had ripped through the man's thighs.

He glanced down at his left side and swore. A crimson blotch stained his shirt. A stab of pain shot through him when he drew a deep breath. Had he punctured a lung?

Christ.

He reached for the seatbelt, braced himself with one hand over his head, and triggered the release. The belt let go with a loud snap and he fell the remaining two inches to the roof. He absorbed half of the force with his hand and the other half with his head.

He rolled over and groaned. Safety glass grated on the roof where he lay. Beads of it clung to his cheek. His mind began to clear as the pain in his side intensified. He reached for the radio on the dash and called for help. Then he began the task of wriggling out the door.

It was a lot harder than he'd expected. The door would only open halfway, and his large frame filled nearly the entire gap. He tried to crawl out on his hands and knees, but the car—which was part way on the road and part way on a steep embankment—began to teeter. One wrong move and it might flip over on him.

A few minutes later he had done it. He lay spread eagle on the glass-littered embankment. His side throbbed with each ragged inhale and exhale. He stared up at the dark sky and wished he had never come to this god-forsaken town.

His leg hurt. The pain had surfaced as soon as he left the car. It was his knee. He must have smashed it against the steering column when the car flipped. It felt broken. Christ, maybe even shattered. How had he not felt it until now?

A distant streetlight flickered, revealing brief glimpses of the surrounding woods. He struggled to recall the moments before the accident. He'd been chasing Gallagher, fighting to catch their speeding car until the woman driving began to slow down. Then something had darted out of the shadows—something big like another car pulling out from the side of the road.

Except it hadn't been a car. It was ... a ... a ... He shook his head. Christ, what the hell was wrong with him? He couldn't have seen it. It wasn't possible. But it had looked so real. Like some abomination straight out of hell. It had attached itself to the Volvo's roof, leaping from the ground and sticking there like a fly. Then the car cut in front of him and he swerved into a ditch.

It didn't happen. It couldn't have.

But he drew his gun anyway, thankful that it hadn't slipped out of the shoulder holster when he wriggled out of the car.

Something moved in the woods. The crunch of leaves silenced the crickets.

Murdock sat up, ignoring the bright flash of pain in his knee. He caught a glimpse of movement, a dark shadow lurking among the trees. And then the streetlight winked out and everything went black.

He pictured Frank Patterson's mutilated body, blood pooled beneath his missing legs. Dr. Weisman's words whispered to him.

The puncture wounds suggest that the teeth of this particular animal were barbed.

Sweat seeped from his pores and beaded on his brow. It turned ice cold in the gusting wind. He glanced at his watch. His back up should be arriving in a few minutes. Five or six at the most. Why had he made his voice sound so calm when he radioed in?

A rustling emanated from the woods. He sat up, but could see nothing. And then on his left, he heard whistling. The wind carried the melody to his ears. He recognized the tune—an old song from the Blue Oyster Cult.

Murdock brought up the gun. "FBI. Don't move."

But the whistler kept coming, his face obscured by shadows.

"Stay where you are. One more step and I'll shoot!"

The whistler stopped in his tracks, and a moment later the streetlight winked on.

"Calhoun? Christ, you scared me half to death." Murdock lowered his gun. "How did you get here? I didn't even hear you pull up." He chuckled to himself. For a minute there, he'd really let his imagination run wild. "Hey, give me a hand, will you?"

Calhoun drew to a halt several feet away. He crouched down, resting his hands on his knees, and Murdock thought he saw a strange look in his partner's eyes, a look like ... well, like madness.

"I didn't come here to help," Calhoun said.

"What are you talking about?"

"I came here to watch."

"Watch what?"

"Your death, of course." And then he began to sing. *"The curtains flew and then He appeared ..."*

"What are you doing?"

"Said, *'Don't be afraid ...'*"

Something sprang from the shadows, something huge and black. Murdock raised his gun and squeezed off two shots before the beast pounced on him, its claws plunging into his flesh like daggers.

The flickering light illuminated its face, and as saliva dripped from its jaws in frothy lines and its rank breath plumed into his face, Murdock wished the street light would go off. Wished that the darkness would hide the horror of this thing.

But when it stepped onto his legs and began tearing strips of flesh from his chest, Murdock knew that his fate was to die slowly. He stared up at the cold, twinkling stars and heard Calhoun laughing and singing from somewhere far away.

"Come on, Murdock ... don't fear the Reaper."

CHAPTER THIRTY-SIX

"Excuse me?" Jay said. "Could you repeat that?" He adjusted the volume on his phone and stepped behind the gas pump as an eighteen-wheeler roared past, pulling a whirlwind of litter in its wake.

"Let me check the patient list. Hold on please."

"Thank you." Jay watched the truck hurtle down the blackened stretch of the Mass Pike, its taillights winking as it crested the hill and disappeared.

He noticed Sarah peering at him through the rear window, and he wished that Samuel hadn't dragged her into this. What could possibly be gained by involving her? He offered her a smile as he waited for the nurse to come back on the line, but he regretted the gesture immediately. What if she thought he was smiling because he'd gotten good news? What if she thought her father was okay and then he had to tell her that he wasn't?

"Come on," he muttered, leaning against the battered Volvo.

The nurse returned to the line, but unlike the last three hospitals, this one had a listing for Nicholas Connelly.

"They just wheeled him out of surgery."

"So he's okay?"

"I'm sorry, but I can't tell you any more than I already have. Would you like directions to the hospital or shall I have the doctor call you back?"

***

The motel occupied a run-down concrete block just off the highway in a depressed area of Worcester. A convenience store stood across from the motel parking lot, its barred windows reflecting the flashing red glare of a stoplight. An abandoned factory loomed atop a

217

hill nearby—its crumbling smokestack pointed like a leper's finger to the sky.

Jay let the curtain slip back over the window, blocking the view of both the city and the graveyard of flies trapped between the screen and the glass. When he turned around, he found Crystal staring at him. She looked shell-shocked.

"This is what you meant when you said it wasn't a 'who', but a 'what' that was responsible for the disappearances?"

Jay nodded.

"And the boy? He's real too?"

"Yes." Jay glanced through the door to the adjoining room where Tim and Maria sat on the bed, comforting Sarah. At Tim's insistence, they had picked up Maria on their way out of town. "You couldn't see him because your mind wasn't open to the possibility. But I think if I showed you the picture now, you would see."

"Then why was I able to see the creature that jumped onto the roof of the car?"

"Because it's not dead. It's here, in the flesh. Samuel's not a physical presence like Trell is."

"It has a name?"

"Sit down, Crystal. I didn't want to get you involved, but it's obviously too late now." He told her the whole story, leaving out nothing except for the reason he missed Frank's phone call on the night of his murder.

When he finished, Crystal stared at him with her mouth agape. "What are we going to do? Do you really think it won't stop until it's killed the whole town?"

"I don't think it'll stop at Glenwood. Three hundred years ago, it wiped out an entire settlement. If the Washakas hadn't stopped it, it would have moved onto the next settlement or the next tribe."

"Do you think it can stray far from its cave?"

"No, but I'm not sure it matters. We know that it's used people like Frank to bring victims to its lair, so it can do plenty of damage just by staying put."

"But how did this all start happening again?"

"Good question. I wish I had an answer. But I'll tell you something that bothers me. Frank said that Trell draws its strength from killing, but I think it's more than that. Killing amuses it. Trell's alone in our world, and we're its entertainment."

"That's a scary thought."

"I know," he said, draping an arm around her shoulder.

"I'm sorry I didn't believe you before."

"I wouldn't have believed me, either." Their eyes met, and he had the strongest urge to kiss her.

"Do you think she'll be okay?" Crystal motioned to Sarah, who was crying against Tim's shoulder.

Jay nodded. "She's a tough kid. I just hope her father pulls through."

After they had stopped for gas, Sarah asked if they could go back and look for her cat. When Jay told her that it was too dangerous, it somehow snapped her out of her shock and made everything real for her. She'd been crying ever since. Even from the other room, the sound was heart-wrenching.

He pulled Crystal into a hug and lost himself in the warmth of her skin, the scent of her hair. This time, he couldn't fight back the urge to kiss her.

She stiffened against his embrace and turned her head away. Not exactly the reaction he was looking for.

"I can't, Jay. I'm sorry." She got off the bed and folded her arms across her chest.

"But I'm not drinking anymore. I haven't had a single drop in two days. And I don't want to, either."

219

Okay, that was a bit of an exaggeration. He hadn't had a drink, but he *did* want one. Several times in the last two days, he'd pictured himself sitting on a barstool at Malley's, drowning his problems in a frosty mug of Sam. Fortunately, his desire to protect the kids had won out, but how much longer could he keep it up?

"I'm glad you're trying, Jay. I really am. But I came over tonight so I could finally put you out of my life. I know that sounds harsh, but it's the truth."

"Is that what you really want?"

"I think it's for the best."

"Okay. Fine," he said, and stormed out of the room.

Where had he gone wrong? On the drive to the motel, all he could think about was how the night's events would bring them closer, how fate had dealt him one last chance for a happy life.

So much for that theory.

He took a seat on the bed next to Sarah. "You doing okay?"

Sarah looked up, rubbed her eyes. "I want to see my Dad. And I'm scared for my Mom."

"I know, hon, but she'll be okay."

"Samuel said killing the monster is the only way to help her."

"Wait a minute—you talked to Samuel?"

Sarah nodded.

"When?"

"Earlier tonight. He woke me up and told me the monster wanted to make Mom hurt me."

"Did he say anything else?"

She furrowed her brow and thought hard, biting her lip. Finally, she looked up. "He said blood makes it stronger and a pool stains its life."

Jay thought about the dark waters that Frank had described, how Trell had risen up from the pool. "Stains?" he said. "Are you sure? Or was it 'sustains'?"

"Yeah, that was it—sustains."

Jay scratched his head. "So blood makes it stronger and the pool sustains its life."

"If that's true," Tim said, "why haven't any bodies been found? If it's like a vampire, wouldn't it leave behind bodies after it drank their blood?"

"Maybe it has to kill them in the pool," Jay said. "Maybe it's something about the water." He thought back to the story Frank had told him. "That has to be it. Frank told me Trell forced him to bring children to the cave. If it's to get stronger from their blood, then it has to be spilled in the pool."

"So how do we kill it?" Tim said. "Drain the pool?"

"Maybe. The other day Maria hit Trell with a car, right? And you said it was hurt?"

"Yeah, I saw it limping into the woods."

"But it wasn't limping tonight."

"Are you saying it uses the pool to heal itself?"

Jay nodded. "It makes sense, doesn't it? If we shoot Trell and then block it from going into the pool somehow, keep it from healing itself, then we might have a chance."

"But what if it's already so strong that bullets can't hurt it?"

Jay turned to Sarah. "Did Samuel say anything else?"

She thought for a moment. "He said he couldn't stay in our world much longer."

Jay frowned. There was still so much they didn't know, so much they needed Samuel to tell them. He stood up and peered out the window. Shadows draped the parking lot. Could Trell have followed them all this way? Could it have sent someone after them, an assassin?

He dismissed the thought. No one had followed. His eyes had been practically glued to the rearview mirror the whole ride up. He'd seen nothing suspicious, no cars that had stayed with them for any length of time. They had even backtracked on the Pike and headed

221

west for a few exits. That's where he'd filled the tank, called the hospital, and used an ATM. If the police accessed his phone or ATM records, they'd think he was headed west toward Albany instead of east toward Boston. Plus, before leaving the gas station they switched off cellular data so that no one could track their phones.

They would be safe here. For a few days, at least.

So why did he feel so edgy?

Because you want a drink. Am I right, boy? Why don't you slip out and pop into that discount liquor joint we passed on the way to this roach motel?

But he ignored the voice. He had to concentrate on their situation, keep his mind clear. But these thoughts kept circling his head, buzzing around like mosquitoes. Sometimes he felt like slapping himself in the face until the voices shut up, hitting himself like a raving lunatic. If that was what it took to end the war inside him, he would do it in a second. He just wished it were that simple.

"Arrow wol," Jay said, pacing in front of the window. "I wish I knew what that meant. Any ideas?"

No one said anything.

He sighed. "It's got to mean something. Why else would Frank write us a message in his own blood?"

***

Twenty-seven. No, twenty-eight.

That was the number of bed springs Jay could feel poking into his back. He turned onto his side and glanced at the door to where Crystal slept. Tim was fast asleep on the bed next to his. The sound of his deep, easy breathing drifted through the room.

How can he sleep? After all that's happened, after all we're up against, how can his body allow it?

But the answer was simple. Tim's body knew how to sleep on its own, not like Jay's, which depended on alcohol to put it to sleep.

The night before, he'd lain awake for hours listening to the sound of his wristwatch ticking on the nightstand.

You want some sleep? Then have a drink. Half a bottle of Jack and you'll be sleeping like a baby.

If this room came equipped with a minibar, he'd probably do as the voice advised. He wished he was stronger than that, wished he had the power to resist such temptation, but lying here in the dead of the night, he felt spineless and weak.

It didn't help that he was sleeping alone. If he could just curl up next to Crystal, feel the heat of her body against his, he was sure it would keep his demons at bay. Maybe even help him get some sleep.

A rough jangling of metal broke him out of his thoughts. He threw off the covers and rolled out of bed. It sounded like someone fumbling with a ring of keys. A moment later, he heard the exterior door to the girls' room open and then shut.

Jay snatched his gun off the nightstand and circled around Tim's bed to the door connecting their rooms. As he reached for the knob, he heard the click of the lock being engaged. He yanked the door, but it wouldn't budge.

Through the layer of steel came a throaty chuckle. "Too slow," a man's voice said.

Jay swore and dashed for the exterior door.

Hang on, Crystal. I'm coming.

He rushed out into the night, stepping barefoot onto a concrete walkway littered with cigarette butts. He blinked at the light cast by the sodium arc lamps and braced himself against a blustery wind.

The door to the girls' room was locked, but Jay could hear the man's voice through the paper thin walls, the sound rising and falling as he paced about the room. A tiny fraction of his body showed through a gap in the curtains.

How did it find us, how did it track us here?

223

COLONY OF THE LOST

Jay could hear Crystal trying to reason with the man. He could picture her sitting on the bed in her white tank top, her eyes reflecting a mix of fear and determination.

"Don't do this," she said.

"The Dark One commands your deaths."

That voice. It was so familiar. It sounded like—

"Listen to me," Crystal said. "I need you to fight it. You can stop this. Do you hear me?"

"The reign of the One and the Many is at hand."

"I know you don't want to hurt me, Steve. Now please ... put the gun down."

Jay could see Steve's silhouette through the gap in the blinds. He positioned the muzzle of his dad's .45 a fraction of an inch from the glass.

It's not Steve. Not anymore.

But that was only partly true. Steve was in there somewhere, banished to some subterranean level while Trell controlled his body like a mad puppeteer.

I don't have to kill him. If I can just get the right angle...

The gun boomed like a thunderclap as he squeezed the trigger. Shards of glass flew from the window and billowed out the curtain, giving him a better view into the room. Blood sprayed from Steve's shoulder, the force of the shot knocking him off balance, sending him stumbling into the wall.

Crystal sprang off the bed and charged into Steve.

"Sarah!" Jay yelled. "Open the door!"

Sarah scurried across the room, but Maria swept the girl into her arms and pulled her back onto the bed like a lioness taking down an antelope.

"It's me!" Jay shouted. "Open up!"

224

Jagged bits of glass clung to the window frame like rotted teeth. Jay knocked them loose one by one, smacking them with the butt of the gun.

Inside the motel room, Crystal and Steve grappled for the gun in a sinister ballet.

Tim appeared beside Jay a moment later, his hair sticking up in sleepy corkscrews. It would've been comical if not for the scene unfolding before them. "Maria!" Tim yelled. "Open the door!"

To Jay's surprise, she responded to Tim's voice and flung the door open.

Jay stepped inside and leveled the gun at his fiancée and his best friend and waited for a clear shot.

Tim rushed past Jay and dipped his shoulder for a tackle.

Steve swung Crystal around, and Tim plowed into her and sent them both crashing into the bedside table. They collapsed onto the floor in a tangle of limbs.

Steve stepped aside and grinned, his eyes gleaming red.

Jay sucked in his breath. They were dealing with Trell now. Not just one of its minions. "Drop the gun!" he yelled. "Now!"

Trell turned toward him, its lips curling into a grin. "You wouldn't shoot your best friend, would you Jay? Huh, old buddy?"

"You're not Steve. Not anymore."

"Steve is not dead. He simply obeys my commands. If you shoot this body, I will abandon it. And who do you think will feel the pain? Who do you think will feel the agony of another gunshot wound? So go ahead and shoot, Jay. It matters not to me."

"If I shoot, you lose your opportunity to kill us."

"Do I? You seem so sure of yourself. Don't you think I'll find you again? Weren't you wondering how I found you tonight?" It pointed to the TV. "I brought you a little present. Slightly used, but I don't think the motel clerk will be needing it now that I slit his throat."

Jay glanced at the TV. A bottle of Jack sat atop the console.

"Your favorite, isn't it? Old No. 7. What do you say we make a bargain? Their lives for that bottle. It's yours if you walk away from here. Whatever happens when you leave is of no consequence to you. What do you say? Thirsty?"

"I don't drink anymore." He tried hard to ignore the need raging inside him, the need that urged him to abandon his friends and take a sip.

If I have a swig of that, I probably will leave them, probably will let them die. That's how messed up I really am.

"Drop the gun, Trell."

"My, my, did someone grow a spine? It doesn't suit you. You're a lousy fighter. Always were. But you make an excellent drunk. Almost as good as your old man." It pointed the gun from Crystal to Tim and back again. "So who shall I kill first? The bitch who left you or the kid who thinks you're a worthless loser?"

"How about you kill yourself," Tim suggested. "See if maybe you can get it right this time." He rose to his feet. "What kind of monster are you, anyway? You couldn't even kill a nine-year-old girl in her sleep."

Trell pointed the gun at Tim. "Why don't I do us all a favor and shut that smart mouth of yours? What do you say, Tim? Are you ready to die? Or will you wet your pants again like that time in the library?"

Jay cocked his dad's .45. *God help me*, he thought, and pulled the trigger.

Steve's chest erupted in a geyser of blood. The force of the blast sent him stumbling against the wall. He fired a wayward shot into the ceiling before dropping the gun and collapsing to the floor, his back tracing a bloody smear down the wall.

Jay tossed the gun onto the dresser and sank to his knees beside Steve. The glimmer of red had vanished from his eyes. Jay pressed a hand over the wound and could feel hot blood soaking through his fingers.

"Hang on, Steve. We're gonna get you some help."

It seemed like an effort, but Steve lifted his eyes to meet Jay's gaze.

"I'm sorry," Jay said.

A ghost of a smile touched Steve's lips. "Not your...fault. Should've ... listened ..." And then Steve's head dropped to his chest and his eyes stared at nothing.

Jay lowered his head into his hands. What had he done?

"Jay look out!"

Crystal's warning caught him off guard. He didn't have time to react, didn't have time to think about what could be wrong. All he could do was throw his arms over his head and wait for the danger to pass.

He heard a creak of bedsprings, followed by a muted *whump*! as something heavy struck the carpet. He whirled around and saw Sarah sitting on the edge of the bed, her chest heaving, the bedside lamp gripped in her hands like a club.

Maria lay sprawled on the floor beneath her, a gun just beyond her reach. After a moment, she dragged herself into a sitting position, but Crystal jumped on top of her and pinned her to the ground.

"She tried to shoot you," Sarah said. "She had a gun hidden under her pillow."

Tim shook his head. "I don't understand it. When could Trell have gotten to her?"

Jay grabbed his gun and stood up. "I don't know," he said. "But we'd better get the hell out of here."

227

CHAPTER THIRTY-SEVEN

Sarah turned away from the glare of oncoming headlights and rested her head against the door. She wished she could fall asleep, get even just a few minutes of rest, but every time she closed her eyes she saw Daddy or that man Steve all covered in blood.

She'd probably have nightmares because of it. But it would be nothing compared to if Daddy died. Because who would help with her nightmares then? Who would sit by her bed and hold her hand until she drifted back to sleep?

Rain fell from the sky, and had been since they left the motel. Fat drops pelted the car, beating against the windshield like a drum. Sarah glanced out the window. There were no lights or buildings—just trees. Thousands of them crowded the road, whizzing by in a blur. She imagined them coming to life like the trees in the *Wizard of Oz*. Except instead of throwing apples, these trees would drag the car off the road and smash through the windows with their spindly branches. They'd reach inside to grab her and—

She turned away from the window and tried to clear her mind by picturing Jenny sitting beside her. But she couldn't recall Jenny's face in enough detail to really bring her to life. Her features were all blurry, like looking through Daddy's glasses.

She hated to admit it, but Jenny was gone. She wasn't real anymore. And probably never would be again.

I think I'm growing up. But not in a good way. Not in a way that Mommy would have wanted.

A tear slid down her cheek.

Please let Daddy be okay. Please don't let him die.

Crystal turned around in the front seat. "Are you okay, Sarah?"

228

She nodded, even though it was a lie.

Maria leaned forward, her hands cuffed behind her back. "Your Daddy's dead, Sarah. I bet his corpse is stinking up the hospital already."

Tim clamped a hand over Maria's mouth and held her against the seat. "She doesn't mean it, Sarah. Trell is controlling her."

Sarah stared down at her feet. "I know."

"Do we have anything to gag her with?" Jay asked.

"Like what?" Tim said.

Crystal pulled opened the glove compartment. "I've got some masking tape in here." She tossed it to Tim, who caught the roll on his finger.

Jay glanced into the backseat. "Don't listen to her, Sarah. Your father isn't dead. The nurse said he was heading into the recovery room."

Tim ripped off a few strips of tape and pressed them over Maria's lips. "She won't bother you again. I promise."

"Thanks," Sarah said.

No one spoke for a moment, and then Tim said, "I thought she'd snap out of it after awhile, you know...the way Frank did."

"A lot of time has passed since Trell took control of Frank," Crystal said. "You guys said yourselves it's gotten a lot stronger since. I guess that means its control over people is stronger too."

"But I still don't get it," Tim said. "If Trell was controlling her, why did she open the door for me?"

"I think Trell was afraid of blowing her cover," Jay said. "If we managed to get away from Steve, it didn't want us to get away from her too. It wanted to save her until the time was right. If Sarah hadn't hit her with that lamp, she probably would have killed us all."

Everyone fell quiet after awhile, and Sarah sank back into her thoughts. Mom was out there somewhere, doing all kinds of bad things for Trell.

Does she know what's going on? Does she see all the things it's making her do?

She hoped not. She hoped Mom was asleep while Trell moved her body around. She tried to remember what she and Mom had last talked about before Trell took over. But she couldn't do it. They hadn't spoken much these past few days. Ever since Mom began to feel sick, Sarah had tried not to get in her way.

If only Sarah had known then what was happening. Maybe she could have stopped it. Maybe she could have warned Daddy.

Then he wouldn't be hurt, wouldn't be in the hospital.

But that probably wasn't true. Even if she had warned him, Daddy wouldn't have listened. He didn't believe in anything like that—not ghosts, not monsters, not invisible friends, nothing. He would have told her it was all her imagination, just a nightmare that seemed real, but wasn't.

I wish I were home. I wish I could wake up and see that none of this really happened.

She kept picturing Mom wandering around in the woods, talking to herself like a crazy person, her nightgown stained with blood. She thought back to the night that Mom had come into the house all covered in mud, remembered the trail of footprints climbing the stairs. But most of all, she remembered the way Mom had looked at her when Sarah opened the bedroom door. Mom's face wasn't just angry—it was scary. But it was even more than that, more than she liked to admit.

Evil.

She didn't like thinking something like that about Mom, but it was true. Every time she thought about that night, she pictured Mom's eyes and how they had seemed to turn red as Sarah closed the door. She'd thought it was her imagination then, but now she knew better.

The car continued through the rain. Sarah could feel Maria watching her. She didn't dare turn around, didn't dare look Maria in the eye.

I want to go home, she thought again, and pictured her special place by the stream. She could almost feel the spongy moss beneath her fingers, could almost smell the scent of the woods. She imagined dipping her toes into the water while Mr. Whiskers chased a bug in the grass.

I hope he'll be okay by himself.

She felt the car begin to slow down, and when she looked up she saw that they had turned off the highway. A few minutes later, Jay pulled into the parking lot of a 7 Eleven. It looked like it was still open.

"Why are we stopping?" she asked.

"To get some food," Jay said. "Aren't you hungry?"

"A little bit."

"I'll wait with Maria," Jay said. "You and Tim can go inside with Crystal to pick something out."

Sarah nodded, anxious to get out of the car.

"I can stay with Maria," Tim said. "I don't mind."

"You sure?" Jay asked.

"Yeah. Don't worry. Go ahead."

"All right," Jay said. "Just be careful."

***

Tim cast a sidelong glance at Maria, who sat still as a statue beside him. Her eyes were open, but they seemed vacant, and he feared that Trell's withdrawal may have left behind nothing but an empty shell. Earlier, as they got ready to leave the motel, Maria had thrashed around the floor like an animal, and the evil he glimpsed in her eyes was so intense he could barely stand to look at her. It was such a stark contrast to the sweet, pretty girl who had kissed him on the lips outside of history class.

The attack at the compost dump had brought them closer, and being with her felt natural, without any of the awkwardness that usually came with a new relationship. She was interesting to talk to and actually appreciated his sense of humor. He was falling for her, and he had a feeling that she might be falling for him too. Unfortunately, in the last twelve hours, she had gone from making out with him to trying to murder him, which definitely introduced a level of complexity to the relationship.

At this point, he really wasn't sure what to say to her. He had zero experience when it came to dating girls possessed by demons, so he was at a loss for typical conversation starters. In the end, he settled for resting his hand on her thigh, which drew no reaction whatsoever.

He made an attempt at eye contact and saw that the tape he'd applied earlier had lost its stickiness. Half of it now dangled from her lips and fluttered as she exhaled. He was debating whether to press it back on when she suddenly turned toward him, her eyes blinking.

"Tim? What happened, where are we?"

Tim jerked back in surprise. He fingered the door handle, ready to make a quick escape should it become necessary. "We were attacked at the motel and had to leave. We're in the car now."

She struggled to raise her arms. "Why am I handcuffed?"

"You don't remember? Trell got a hold of you somehow. It must have happened after I left your house. Also, you tried to kill us."

"Oh my God, Tim. I didn't hurt anyone, did I?"

"No, but it was close."

"I'm sorry, Tim. I didn't know what I was doing. I swear."

"I know," he said. "It's not your fault."

Maria bit her lip and blinked, as if fighting back tears. She glanced down at the space between them. "Are you afraid of me?"

"No, it's just—"

"You are, aren't you?" She began to cry.

"I'm sorry. Don't cry. Please?" He slid his body next to hers and draped an arm around her shoulders. "It'll be all right. I promise."

She looked at him, her eyes brimming with tears. "I'm scared, Tim."

"So am I," he said, and kissed her forehead. She raised her lips to meet his. He pulled away the tape and kissed her long and hard.

She broke away for a moment, kissed his chin, and then slid down to his neck, her breath blowing hot against his throat. She kneeled on the seat and straddled him, arching her back so that her breasts pressed against his face.

"Let me out of these cuffs, Tim."

"Uh, I don't think that's a good idea."

"Please, Tim. We might never get another chance."

"I don't know ..."

"I need my hands, Tim. I want to make you feel so good."

She used her body to push him against the door. He pulled up his shirt and she trailed hot, wet kisses down to his naval. "The cuffs, Tim."

He reached into his pocket for the keys. "How about I move them to the front?" She nodded, and he re-cuffed her hands in the front. Then he slipped the keys back into his pocket.

Maria pulled down the neckline of her blouse and exposed her breasts. "Do you like what you see?"

"Yes," he gasped.

"I think you're going to like this even more." She unzipped his pants and wriggled them down to his knees, taking his boxers with them. "Close your eyes, Tim."

He felt her lips on his inner thigh, and his whole body shuddered.

"No peeking," she said. "Just lay back and ..."

Tim opened his eyes at the tinkling of metal and saw that Maria had escaped from the cuffs. Her right hand was drawn back over her shoulder, clutching the hilt of a hunting knife.

Tim swept out his arm as she brought the knife down, deflecting it so that the blade only grazed his shoulder. He shoved Maria onto the floor, threw open the door, and dove into the parking lot. He landed headfirst in a puddle and rolled onto his back as cold rain pelted his face. He tried to stand, but tripped over his pants and fell down again.

Maria jumped out of the car and pinned him to the ground, her right foot pressing down on his groin. "What do you think, Tim? Which head shall I cut off first?"

"Drop the knife!" Jay shouted.

Tim let out his breath in a gust of relief. *Thank God*, he thought, as Jay ran toward them with his gun drawn.

Maria lowered the knife and backed away.

"Get out of here," Jay yelled. "Go!"

Maria snarled at them before withdrawing into the street.

Tim hiked up his pants and climbed into the car.

"Nice job on watch," Jay said.

Crystal shook her head. "Looks like he fell for the oldest trick in the book."

"Why were his pants down?" Sarah asked.

Tim pressed a hand over his shoulder. "Can we change the subject, please?"

***

The first traces of dawn brightened the sky as Jay navigated Crystal's battered Volvo past the skyscrapers of downtown Boston and checked them into a motel near the airport. With two double beds and a sleep sofa, they were able to squeeze into a single room. And with the blackout curtains drawn tight, everyone was asleep within an hour of check in.

Everyone except for Jay.

His ears still rang from the exchange of gunfire earlier in the night, and even with his eyes closed and the pillow covering his head, the phantom echo of the night's fatal gunshot still haunted him.

I killed him, he thought. *I killed Steve.*

And in his mind's eye, he kept seeing Steve thrown back by the force of the bullet, his blood spattering the wall in a crimson arc. How could he break it to Gloria? How could he even begin to explain what'd happened?

He'd known Steve since before they could walk. Growing up, they practically lived at each other's houses. He still remembered that Wednesday night was meatloaf night at the Callahan residence. Who would have guessed that Steve's mom cooked all those extra meals for the boy who would one day kill her only son?

Steve was gone. Just like that. All it took was a tiny movement of Jay's index finger.

Christ, why did it have to be Steve?

Because Trell likes to play games, likes to watch you suffer.

He recalled the bottle of Jack that Trell had placed on the TV. He imagined the amber liquid sloshing around inside the glass, clambering up the sides, begging to be set free.

You wanted that drink, didn't you, boy? You wanted to grab hold of that bottle and never let go. Well, it ain't too late. Liquor stores'll be opening up in a couple hours. These guys will never know you were gone.

I don't want it.

The voice of his father laughed—a hard, raspy sound like the rustling of dead leaves. *Sure you do. You want it so bad you're drooling. You can't lie to your old man. You want it ... and you always will.*

I won't end up like you.

Only 'cause Trell's gonna kill you first.

235

He glanced over to where Crystal lay on the bed, one hand curled beneath her cheek, a serene expression on her face. "I love you," he whispered. "I know I screwed things up, but I love you. I always have." He closed his eyes and thought back to the moment they shared alone after check-in this morning. He'd gone into the bathroom to get Sarah a glass of water, and Crystal had followed him.

"Hey," she'd said. "Are you okay?"

He nodded without turning, not wanting her to see him cry.

"It wasn't your fault, Jay. You did what you had to do. No one blames you for that."

"I blame me." He wiped his eyes with the heel of his hand and caught a glimpse of himself in the mirror. He looked worn and haggard, his face covered with stubble. "I could have stopped this days ago. Frank called me right before he died to explain how to kill Trell. But I didn't answer the phone. You know why? Because I was drunk. Passed out on the couch, drinking myself into oblivion while people were dying." His chest hitched with sobs.

Crystal pulled the door shut. "Shh." She held his head against her chest. "It's all right. You made a mistake. But you're fixing it now. I know it's hard for you not to have a drink, probably harder than I could ever imagine. And I know I didn't say it before, but I'm proud of you for trying."

He forced a smile. "I love you."

"I know," she said, softly. "Maybe in time ..." She shook her head. "Let's not talk about this now. We should get some sleep." She kissed his cheek. "You need a shave. And a shower. Make you look a little less like a fugitive."

He drew back the shower curtain. "Plenty of room in there. We could help each other get those hard to reach places."

"Nice try." She picked up the glass that he'd filled for Sarah. "Don't drown in there."

"There's safety in numbers."

"Good night, Jay."

He smiled now at the memory, his eyes still focused on Crystal.

I better get some sleep.

But he wasn't having an easy go of it. And the way things looked now, there was a very real possibility that he might never sleep again.

CHAPTER THIRTY-EIGHT

In the blackened night of the new moon, the storm raged. It came in gusts and swells, the wind whooping and hollering like a warrior in the throes of battle. Thunder rumbled in the sky as a curtain of rain beat down upon the earth.

Chief Skatchawa sat in the quiet gloom of his study and sketched by the glow of a gooseneck lamp, a charcoal pencil clutched between his leathery fingers. It had been a long time since he created a new piece. His days of drifting across the land and moving from town to town on the money scraped together from the sale of his art were long behind him. These days he only sketched when his mind was troubled, only sketched on those nights when he was haunted by demons past or demons present.

He glanced down at the paper and watched his sketch begin to take shape. It was the way he always worked. He simply placed pencil against paper, and his hand would move of its own accord, as if guided by an unseen force, tracing out lines and curves until a recognizable picture emerged.

The pad on his lap displayed a portrait of an aging warrior scarred from battles past and wizened by the passing of the ages. He could only be seen from the shoulders up, his strong jaw and chiseled features centered on the page.

As the Chief listened to the wind-swept rain drum against the windows, a gradual uneasiness stole over him. Voices whispered in his mind, cries of men long dead, restless spirits that haunted his thoughts. He tried to drown it all in his sketching, tried to purge the demons through his art, but it wasn't working.

He saw the face of the teacher's friend, his eyes crazed and desperate as he spoke of death and destruction ... and of a creature called Trell.

The legend doesn't refer to a name.

The lie echoed in his ears.

How many people dead? How many—

A crash emanated from outside. The Chief jerked upright in his chair. The pencil dropped from his fingers and rolled onto the hardwood floor.

His eyes shifted to the window and strained to see through glass painted black by night. But he could make out nothing. Even the stand of birch at the outer fringe of forest was invisible to him, a distance of twenty paces veiled in darkness.

Probably just the barrels toppled by the wind.

But his pulse quickened nevertheless. He glanced at the pencil coming to a rest between his feet. He dared not pick it up, dared not move for fear of masking a sound of danger. He sat still and listened to the sounds of the night, the voice of the storm.

How can he know? How is it possible?

The legend was not well known, not even among the members of the dwindling tribe. Only a handful of elders knew the story, and even fewer knew of its name.

How then?

Because it's true. It's back. Somehow... it lives.

No. It was impossible. He scanned the room, his eyes sweeping the shadows. The urge to rush out of his chair, draw the blinds, and switch on all the lights was maddening. But he fought to keep the temptation at bay. He would not lose himself to irrational fear, would not succumb to demons of his own making.

The back door rattled in its frame, a persistent banging inconsistent with the rhythm of the wind. The Chief stared through the shadowy hallway, his eyes narrowed to slits. The hairs at the nape of

239

his neck prickled in response to what stood behind the flimsy shield of aging pine. He drew a deep breath. Sweat pooled beneath his arms. His heart pounded faster than it had in years, beating in his chest like a war drum.

The demon. Returned from the spirit world.

The Chief slipped out of the chair and crept across the room. A dagger hung on the wall, mounted between an oil painting of the Berkshires at dusk and a sketch of an eagle in flight. He drew the knife from the worn leather sheath, the buffalo bone hilt smooth and reassuring in his hand. The blade gleamed in the light, and he thought suddenly of the days of his youth when he had hiked through the forest with this very knife, searching for adventure and dreaming of the battles his grandfather's blade had witnessed.

And then the door crashed open, the wood splintering into a throng of jagged projectiles. Rain swirled in through the gap. The wind swept it into the walls, shrieking and moaning like a thing alive. Lightning flashed in the sky, lashing out like a serpent's tongue. The momentary brilliance revealed a form hulking in the doorway, a dark silhouette of a creature crouched on all fours.

Chief Skatchawa trembled at the sight of it, but somehow held his ground.

The demon growled, a heavy clicking that emanated from the back of its throat. It approached slowly, and when it lifted its head from the shadows its red eyes burned like fire. Water dripped from its body, its black scales reflecting the light of the gooseneck lamp. Spiked plates lined the arch of its back, a low ridge that bristled when it moved.

When it stepped fully into the light, Chief Skatchawa felt his bowels loosen. He stood paralyzed, his jaw hanging open. It was a creature unlike any he had ever imagined, a ghastly fusion of claws, scales, and teeth—a creature built solely for death.

It halted five paces away from him, its lips parting to reveal row upon row of jagged yellow fangs. A squealing sound escaped its chest, and before the Chief could react, a jet of liquid shot from its throat and struck him in the eyes.

Chief Skatchawa stumbled into the kitchen table, but managed to catch himself before falling ... avoiding what would've been a very costly mistake. He cleared his eyes of the burning goo and stared directly at the beast through a murky haze. "How did you find me?"

The creature's voice boomed within his mind, vibrating his skull from the inside out. "I am the Hunter and the Hunted, and all things in between. But you should know that, shouldn't you, Skatchawa?" It stepped toward him. "Your people were so proud, so certain they could destroy me. But where are they now? Who amongst you remains?"

"There are some," the Chief said. "There are those who still remember ... those like me who know the name *Trell*."

"Impressive, Skatchawa. I was sure you would have forgotten. So much of your way of life perished in the war with the white man. They destroyed your land. They did everything your people feared and worse. They killed more of you than even I. But all that is in the past. My strength has grown considerably since then. Your spirits and potions cannot stop me now." Its jaws twisted into a grin. "But you don't remember the magic of your ancestors, do you Skatchawa? You are as helpless against me as that drunkard, Gallagher."

"What do you want?"

"Are you really so ignorant? For over three centuries, I lived a waking death, struggling against the poison your ancestors unleashed upon me, struggling to build up strength enough to rise from the waters once more, to break free of the spirits that chained me." Its eyes narrowed to slits. "Revenge is what I seek. Revenge for my torment, my pain."

The Chief drew a deep breath and thought about Gallagher. *I should have believed you. I should have told you what I know.* He bit his lip. *May the spirits guide you. It is too late now for me.*

And then Chief Skatchawa raised the blade of his grandfather. Uttering the war cry he'd learned as a youth, he charged the demon and lunged for the glistening scales between its eyes. But its scales were like armor. The knife barely left a scratch before Trell's jaws clamped around his arm and crushed his bones into splinters.

But the Chief would not scream, would not give the beast what it so desired.

It roared and flipped him into the air, hurling him to the floor like a rag doll. It slashed his face with the swipe of a paw and stomped on his chest until his body snapped and crunched and spewed blood.

But still he would not cry out, would not beg for mercy. And as his body was kicked for the last time, he caught a final glimpse of the sketch that he would never finish.

My greatest work, he thought, and closed his eyes. And in the ensuing darkness, he could still see it—a sketch of an aging warrior, his wizened face proud and defiant until the very end.

COLONY OF THE LOST

CHAPTER THIRTY-NINE

Sarah crept along a wooded path, picking her way through a dense gathering of trees. A canopy of intertwining branches blocked out the sky, making it impossible to tell whether it was day or night. She saw no signs of life in this place. No birds or squirrels. No bugs of any kind.

And she heard nothing—not chirping, not scurrying, not buzzing. It was quiet. Dead quiet.

But even so, she sensed that she was not alone.

Sarah ...

A voice drifted to her from somewhere far away, and she followed the sound of it, letting it guide her through the tangle of underbrush. Time passed, but she couldn't tell how much. She traveled miles, yet never grew tired.

Am I dreaming?

Before she could answer her own question, she spotted the owner of the voice near a giant oak.

Samuel.

That same blue light shone around him, fading in and out like the rhythm of a beating heart. A man stood beside him, and as she drew closer she saw that it was Jay.

Are we sharing the same dream?

"The pool," Samuel said to him. "It is a place of great power, the source from which the beast derives its strength—this creature born of the Land of Demons. It must be destroyed."

"But how? We don't even know where it is or what Frank's message means."

"You must destroy the gateway. You must cut off the source of its power."

"I don't understand. Please—I need you to explain."

Samuel gestured to the woods around them. "This world ... it is but one of many. And yet there is a single point where all such worlds meet."

"Are you saying that Trell's pool lies at the nexus of these worlds?"

"Yes."

"But the runes, the obelisk ... Arrow wol—what do they mean?"

Samuel's lips pressed into a tight purple line. "All that I know, I have told you. There are secrets that the beast guards dearly, secrets that are yet to be revealed. But there is a price. There is always a price." He glanced into the forest. A ground fog had crept in and swirled about their feet. "Take heed, for there are forces drawing me from the world of the living, forces I cannot resist much longer. I must go now."

"Wait! You haven't told me anything. Tell me how to kill it!"

"You must find a way. If your people are to survive, you must find a way."

Jay's body began to lose its definition—first blurring, then becoming transparent, until finally he vanished into the mist.

Samuel glanced at Sarah. "Come. Our time grows short."

"Where are we going?"

"There are things I must show you, things you must remember at all costs. You must open a space in your mind. Are you ready?"

She nodded.

"Follow me. We must walk the path of the wolf."

Mist rose from the ground and formed into a thick gray wall that blocked the way forward. Samuel drifted toward it, his aura coloring it blue. For a moment, Sarah just stood there watching. Then she drew a deep breath and hurried after him.

The mist wrapped around her like a cool, wet blanket, so dense she could barely see. She soon lost sight of Samuel and wandered ahead blindly, a claustrophobic panic stealing over her.

What if she never found her way out?

But then the mist vanished as quickly as it came and she found herself standing waist-deep in a thicket of thorny vines. She spotted Samuel moving ahead of her, his body passing through the brambles as easily as if he were made of the mist.

She followed him, hurrying now, not wanting to lose sight of him again. Thorns bit into her ankles and snared her feet, sinking into her flesh like teeth, but the pain seemed somewhere far away. When at last she caught up to Samuel, he stood before a large boulder. Vines covered the jagged rock in twisted ropes of green.

"Here," Samuel said, sweeping aside the vines.

Sarah craned her neck and saw that it was actually two boulders leaning against each other. *A cave,* she thought, and followed Samuel through the dark opening.

The glow from his body lit up a small section of the narrow passageway, and Sarah could see their shadows creeping along the walls and floor—large and misshapen like the monster that lived here. She could hear the slow drip of water from somewhere up ahead and felt a cold wind blowing into her face. Her heart thumped in her chest. She wanted to turn back, but knew that she couldn't. Mom was depending on her … and so were the others.

The floor of the passageway sloped downward, and as she followed Samuel further into the cave, the light from the entrance disappeared behind them, leaving only the strange pulsing of Samuel's aura. Up ahead, dark patches lined the walls on either side, and as they drew closer she realized they were tunnels. She counted five on the left before Samuel steered her into the third one.

Darkness pressed in all around them, and even the light cast by Samuel's aura wasn't enough to chase it away. They continued through a maze of twisting black corridors and intersecting tunnels until they came to a huge cavern lit by a glow similar to Samuel's.

"Here," Samuel whispered. "The lair of the beast. My prison for centuries. Remember the way, Sarah. Remember it well."

***

Jay awoke slowly, fighting his way back to consciousness, fearing that he might never wake from this dream. Bright sunshine lanced in through a gap in the curtains. He shielded his eyes and glanced around the room. Tim, Crystal, and Sarah sat on the sofa bed, their eyes glued to the TV.

"Turn it up," Tim said.

Crystal adjusted the volume and glanced at Jay. "It's about you."

Jay scurried to the foot of the bed. The TV showed an attractive newswoman standing on the tangle of Jay's front lawn. She motioned to his house with a sweep of her hand. "Police announced early this morning that they are looking for this man."

A picture of Jay appeared in the upper right hand corner of the screen, a picture taken last year for the faculty section of the yearbook. In it, he had the beginnings of a five o'clock shadow and dark circles beneath his eyes.

"While police would not comment as to whether Jay Gallagher is a suspect in the recent disappearances that have stunned this historically quiet town, one source confirmed that he *is* wanted for questioning. When police arrived at the scene last night to question Gallagher, they were shocked to discover that a crime was already in progress.

"Moments before their arrival, an armed youth shot and killed Glenwood police officer, Douglas Sandler, who was conducting a routine patrol of the neighborhood. The youth then broke into

Gallagher's residence and fired several shots from a handgun, and although details are still sketchy, preliminary reports indicate that the gunman was a former student of Gallagher's.

"Police opened fire on the gunman, killing him instantly, and during the chaos, Gallagher fled the scene in a black Volvo."

The camera zoomed in on his front porch for a close up of the bullet hole and the dark swatch of blood smeared against the shingles.

"Police believe that Gallagher is traveling with a former girlfriend and two others, but would not comment as to whether they are considered hostages."

The reporter motioned to the street, and the camera followed her gesture. "As you can see here in front of me, the streets of Glenwood are deserted. One can only speculate as to whether people have packed up and left in the wake of this ongoing tragedy or whether they are at home, locked behind closed doors.

"It's been three weeks since the first disappearance, and since then nearly fifty people have gone missing, although police suspect the actual number may be higher. To date, police have uncovered the mutilated bodies of four victims, but no trace has been found of the others.

"The FBI has recently joined the investigation, and yesterday the Governor called in the National Guard to patrol the streets."

The camera switched to a middle-aged man in the newsroom. He sat behind a desk as people bustled about in the background. He adjusted his glasses and gazed into the camera with an expression of deep concern. "Nancy, how have officials responded to rumors that the deaths and disappearances might be linked to cult activity?"

"Well, Peter, police have not ruled it out, but as I said, this is a very strange and complicated case. There are all sorts of rumors flying around. Earlier, I spoke with one man who swore that the town had been overtaken by aliens. Again, some very bizarre circumstances in this case, but Channel 6 will continue to sift through the information and bring you up to date coverage. Reporting live from Glenwood, I'm Nancy Wellington."

Crystal shut off the TV and tossed the remote onto the bed. "Every cop in the state must be looking for us by now."

Jay chewed his lip. "We need to ditch your car. Or at least switch out the plates."

"We have to go back to Glenwood," Sarah said. "We have to find the cave."

Jay and Sarah exchanged glances. "The dream," he said. "Is that what Samuel showed you? The cave?"

Sarah nodded.

"Did he show you where it is?"

"Only part of the way. But he showed me where it lives on the inside."

Tim furrowed his brow. "What are you guys talking about?"

Jay explained what he'd learned from Samuel in his dream. When he finished, Sarah recounted what Samuel had shown her in the cave.

"So you think we should head back to Glenwood?" Crystal asked.

"Not yet," Jay said. "We still need to figure out where the cave is and what Frank's message means. And we're going to need supplies. This isn't going to be easy."

CHAPTER FORTY

Margaret Connelly ran through a forest cloaked in night's shadows, racing along a path lined with crooked trees. They appeared ghastly in the failing light, gray trunks twisted and gnarled, knotted bark scrunched into rough-looking faces. They glared at her in the dismal gloom, branches flexing and clenching, rattling like bones.

Behind her, the Dark One followed.

A dream, she thought. *Just a dream.*

And she knew that she was both right and wrong.

The trees loomed over her, reaching for her with spindly fingers, groping for a hold of her clothes, a hold of her hair. Branches smacked against her face. Roots snaked around her feet.

Behind her, the Dark One laughed—a deep growling like the grinding of rocks.

Margaret screamed, but knew there was no one to hear, no one to help.

The Dark One emerged from the shadows, its red eyes gleaming.

Almost time, it whispered. *Almost time.*

***

Margaret came awake with a start. She rolled onto her back and stared at the morning sky through a screen of trees. Birds flitted about the budding branches, oblivious to the evil that lurked beneath them, indifferent to the death that stalked so many. Watching them, it was hard to believe that anything could be wrong in the world.

I wish I were like them. I wish I didn't know what was happening.

She knew she shouldn't be thinking such things, knew that it would do more harm than good, but she couldn't help it. Her world had been torn apart. Nick lay in the ICU, stabbed by her own hand, and Sarah was on the run, confused and afraid, certain to be an orphan.

Why did this have to happen? What did she do to deserve this?

If only she hadn't taken out the trash that night. If only she'd let it slide until the following week. There was plenty of room in the other barrels—it could have waited.

Don't do this to yourself. For whatever reason, Trell chose you. What's done is done.

She glanced at the swell of her belly peeking through a rip in her bloodied nightgown and wrinkled her forehead in disgust. It had grown rapidly in the last few days, tripling in size almost overnight. She guessed she had gained nearly thirty pounds and hoped to God it was near full term. Any bigger and it would never come out ... at least not in any way that she could survive.

I'm going to kill you. I'll find a way. I swear to God I will.

She glanced down at her hands and wasn't at all surprised to find crimson stains on her palms. How many had she killed last night? How many had she brought to the pool so that their blood would drip into the water and fuel Trell's strength?

She closed her eyes and opened her mind, and the memories returned to her in a flood of images, a grisly kaleidoscope of death. If she wanted to discover how to kill the demon, she had to endure the pain of these memories, had to sift through them in search of clues.

She saw herself breaking into a house in the dead of night, creeping into the children's bedrooms while they slept. She pressed strips of duct tape over their mouths and zip-tied their wrists, all before they had a chance to come fully awake. Then she carried them outside, roped them together, and dragged them into the woods, their eyes bulging as their muffled screams went unheard.

Enough!

She closed her eyes and hugged her knees as hot tears rolled down her cheeks. She wondered if she'd be better off being ignorant like the others. They numbered in the hundreds now—soldiers of Trell, ordinary people turned into slaves. Leading loved ones to their deaths.

But none were quite like she, none had moments of clarity, moments when they were truly themselves again. It was because Trell had come to her in the beginning, back before it had gained enough strength to survive on its own. It had chosen a select few to bring victims to the pool so that their blood could counter the effects of the poison and fuel its strength. What had become of the others, she didn't know. Most likely, it had killed them. They would have posed a danger to it, knowing what they did about its origin, its purpose. So far, it had spared her...but only because she carried its child. Once it was born, it would kill her too.

Maybe it could hear her thoughts, or maybe it was just coincidence, but a sharp pain flared in her uterus, so intense she fell back against the ground and screamed. After it passed, she sat up slowly, fearing that the slightest motion might set it off again. She closed her eyes and drew a cautious breath. She'd experienced these pains on and off for days now, pains she had at first thought—*prayed*—were the onset of a miscarriage. When she first felt them, she began to push, trying with all her might to expel the creature from her body, picturing a mini Trell writhing in the dirt, kicking and mewling. But it didn't happen. After a minute or so the pain subsided. Since then, it had returned every four hours. Just like clockwork.

A frightening thought began to take shape in her mind, a thought she'd tried for days to suppress. But now she couldn't hide it from herself any longer. The cramps were too regular to be punishment from Trell, too scheduled to be retaliation for something she did or thought. And there was one more thing—the pains felt like needles clamping down on her flesh, gnashing and tearing before moving on to another location.

It's feeding. Not on the nourishment my body provides, but on me. Biting my flesh, drinking my blood.

She shook her head and closed her eyes.

It hurts more each time ... and it just keeps getting hungrier.

CHAPTER FORTY-ONE

Tim lay sprawled on the sofa and stared up at the ceiling with his hands laced behind his head. He was alone in the room, all by himself for the first time in what seemed like years. The quiet sounded strange, almost too peaceful.

Like the calm before the storm, he thought, and pictured a dark mass of thunderheads gathering in the sky.

He was grateful for the occasional sound that filtered in from the street outside—the honking of horns, the screeching of tires. Listening to the city traffic, it was hard to believe that just a couple hours away, a creature from another world lurked in the woods, killing anyone who crossed its path.

It was crazy. But somehow true.

He glanced at the wound on his shoulder and thought about Maria. He imagined her walking along the Mass Pike, hitchhiking back to Glenwood.

Let me out of these cuffs, Tim. I want to make you feel so good.

He thought back to the first time he'd ever seen her. She was sitting on the bleachers in gym class, wearing spandex shorts and a pink tank top. She glanced over at him, smiled, and asked if he was new there.

No one else at school had given him the time of day. Most of the kids ignored him completely, either too cool or too shy to bother being friendly.

He hoped she was okay, hoped she was too far from Glenwood to do any killing for Trell. He had to get her back, but there was only one way to do that.

Kill it.

But how? It was too strong now. Bullets probably wouldn't even hurt it. And even if they did, how could they prevent it from going into the pool to heal itself?

Destroy the gateway. Cut off the source of its power.

Samuel's words. But what did they mean? Where was the gateway? And how could they destroy it?

He wished he could've been in the dream with Jay. He would have forced Samuel to give them at least one useful piece of information.

And speaking of useless information, how did Frank's message fit into all of this?

Maybe it doesn't mean anything. Maybe Trell wrote the message to throw us off track, keep us running around in circles until it murders the rest of the town.

He glanced at the clock. Why weren't the others back with lunch yet?

Maybe I should just go. Leave while I have the chance.

The thought came out of nowhere, but he quickly dismissed it. He couldn't let them face Trell on their own, couldn't just walk away with Maria in her condition. Like it or not, he was part of this thing. And, yes, he was afraid ... but so was Trell. Why else would it single them out? Why else would it demand to know what Samuel had told them?

Even Jay seemed committed to seeing this thing through. Tim couldn't stand him when they first met, had written him off as a worthless drunk. The guy had no real reason to fight Trell, nothing he stood to lose should he give in—no family, no job, no girlfriend. But somehow he found the strength to sober up and defend the town that had alienated him.

He never thought he'd say it, but the guy was actually a good role model. Unfortunately, his lunch-getting skills were terrible. Seriously, how long did it take to find a McDonald's?

What if the cops recognized Crystal's car and pulled them over? Or what if Trell's assassins found them?

He pictured Sarah, Jay, and Crystal slumped forward in the car, the side windows spattered with their blood, the doors riddled with bullet holes.

He shook the image from his mind and grabbed his backpack off the floor. Tucked into the front pocket was the trail map he'd copied at the library. He pulled it out and unfolded it carefully, smoothing out the creases on his legs. The map showed the region of Washaka Woods from Elm Street Park to the foot of the Berkshires. A network of trails snaked between a cluster of ponds, and color-coded symbols differentiated the walking trails from the biking trails.

He studied the map closely, his eyes poring over every square inch. Just as he was about to fold it up and put it away, something caught his eye.

He shook his head. "I don't believe it. There it is."

***

By the time the others returned with three bags of McDonald's, Tim was ready to pass out from hunger. "What took you guys so long?"

"Sorry," Crystal said. "We had to get Sarah something to wear besides a nightgown. Also," she said, pointing at Jay, "Magellan over here got us lost."

"I didn't get lost. We just got turned around because of all the one way streets."

"Well," Tim said, "while you guys were out joyriding, I figured out part of Frank's message."

Jay unwrapped a cheeseburger. "Seriously?"

"When am I not serious?"

Sarah surprised him by smiling. "You said before you had fourteen toes."

"What did you find out?" Jay asked.

Tim spread the map over the bed, and they all crowded around for a closer look. He traced a finger along one of the trails and tapped the spot where it was labeled. "Check out the name."

"Arrow," Crystal said.

"Now look at this one," Tim said. "See the trail that intersects it up here?"

Sarah glanced up at him. "Wolf. That's what Samuel said in the dream—follow the path of the wolf!"

"That's got to be it," Jay said. "Arrow Wolf. Frank was trying to tell us where it lives."

Tim nodded. "The cave must be right here. Just off the path where they intersect."

"But what about the runes?" Jay asked. "And the obelisk? Anything like them on the map? In the legend, maybe?"

Tim shook his head.

"I have an idea about the runes," Crystal said. "While Jay was driving around in circles, I thought back to a paper I did in college on the origin of language. I did most of the research at the Boston Public Library, and I remember coming across books on the language of ancient civilizations. Things like hieroglyphics and Druid runes."

"I doubt we'll find a match in any book," Jay said. "According to Samuel, Trell comes from another world, and the pool lies at the nexus of who knows how many worlds. The runes could be symbols from any one of them." He shook his head. "That sounds so crazy, doesn't it?"

"All of this is crazy," Crystal said.

Tim shrugged. "It may be crazy, but if we don't do something soon more people will die. And that includes us—we know too many of its secrets. Besides, I've heard people say that Egyptian hieroglyphics may have originated with aliens. I know it's a long shot, but I think we should at least check out the library."

"I agree," Crystal said.

"So do I," Sarah said.

Tim nodded. "So first the library, then the cave."

"Look," Jay said. "You guys need to understand that whoever goes into the cave will probably never come out again. If anyone's going inside, it should be me. Tomorrow, we'll drive back to Glenwood together. Anyone who chooses not to go into the woods can go home or go back to the city where it's safe. I want you to think about that very carefully ... because it might be the last decision any of you ever makes."

CHAPTER FORTY-TWO

The cabin lights flickered as the train plunged into the tunnel, the walls shuddering as the engine shifted gears. Jay stared out the window and watched graffiti zip past in a swirl of color. As the station fell away in the distance, the darkness of the tunnel transformed the window into a mirror. In it, Jay could see Tim, Crystal, and Sarah sitting in the seats behind him. They were all thinking about the cave—he could read it on their faces. But there was no reason they all had to go. If his Dad's .45 wasn't enough to kill Trell, then whoever went with him would die.

He glanced up at an advertisement posted above the window—a public service message for Hepatitis B. The photo depicted three teens with haunting yellow eyes. The image reminded him of the people in Glenwood who were under Trell's control, and he pictured Steve grinning in the motel room, a gun pointed at Crystal. He willed the memory away, but not before hearing the phantom echo of the gunshot and seeing Steve's blood splatter against the wall.

He drew a deep breath and bit his lip against the threat of tears. An ad for Dewar's scotch whiskey hung on the wall beside Crystal. He stared at it for a moment before a swell of anticipation bloomed in his stomach, and he had to glance away.

The craving was still there. Diminished, yes, but still there. He wondered if it would ever vanish completely.

I don't want to relapse, I don't ever want to be that person again. But what if I can't help it?

The T driver announced the stop with what sounded like a mouthful of marbles. Tim stood up and translated. "New England Medical Center. This is us."

When the doors opened, they followed Tim into the station. Sarah wrinkled her nose as they climbed the stairs to the street. "I smell pee."

Jay chuckled to himself. "I'm glad to see the Orange Line hasn't changed a bit since college." He glanced at Crystal. "Remember the night I took you to see *Cats*?"

She smiled. "You thought you were going to hate it until you saw how tight the girls' costumes were."

That was a good night. After the play, they dined at a rooftop restaurant and gazed down at the city, sneaking kisses and pointing out all places they'd been together. It seemed like such a long time ago.

"So where is this place?" Crystal asked.

"Between Chinatown and the Theater District," Tim said. "I'm not sure of the street, but I'll know it when I see it."

They were searching for a store owned by his friend Bill Dexler's father. "He's a little crazy," Tim said as they walked past a fenced-in parking lot. "Bill lived with his mom, but he'd visit his dad twice a month on Sundays. Every once in awhile, I'd go with him. He fought in the Gulf and sometimes thinks he's still there. And for some reason, he always calls me Dave."

Crystal rolled her eyes. "Sounds like a great guy."

They found the place ten minutes later on the ground floor of a run-down apartment building. A tattered green awning hung over the door, and steel security shutters were raised three quarters of the way above a plate glass window. Graffiti covered the visible portion of the shutters, and a rust-flecked sign dangled from chains near the door, its left side pocked with bullet holes that may or may not have been intentional. The sign read: *Dexler Gun and Survival Specialty Store.*

"Nothing special about this place," Jay muttered, looking through the window at a mannequin sporting combat fatigues and a gas mask.

A bell chimed as Tim held open the door for the others. Inside, metal racks sprang up from the carpet like toadstools, overflowing with second hand army uniforms, camouflage, and survival gear.

A smell reminiscent of moldy sweat socks permeated the air, and as Jay gazed at a rack of tattered old jackets he imagined bums wandering in off the streets to sell their clothes for a buck or two.

Except for a hunched old man lingering over a display case filled with World War II memorabilia, they had the place to themselves. Behind the counter, past an old keypunch cash register, an impressive array of weapons hung from the wall—bows, swords, daggers, axes … even a savage-looking mace.

As Jay studied these, a wiry man with gaunt features emerged from an interior office with a cigarette pinched between his lips. He drew a deep drag and blew smoke from the corner of his mouth. When he saw Tim, he leaned against the counter and smiled.

"That you, Dave?"

"More or less," Tim said, his cheeks flushing.

"How the hell are you, boy?" He clapped a hand on Tim's shoulder. "Been awhile since you was here last. Billy said you moved out of town."

"Yeah, we moved to Glenwood a few weeks ago. It's near the—"

"Glenwood? Ain't that the town with all them people missing?"

"That's kind of why we're here."

Dexler raised an eyebrow and motioned toward the others. "They from Glenwood too?"

Tim nodded and made a quick round of introductions. "There's some pretty crazy stuff going on there. It's not safe, especially not for us."

"So you want to protect yourselves, am I right? Want to buy a gun or two without waiting around for no permit to be approved?"

Jay felt the corners of his mouth curl into a grin. Finally, something looked like it might go their way. "We don't want to cause you any trouble. But if you could help us out, that would be great."

"No trouble at all, so long as you understand you were never in here, never met me."

"It won't be a problem," Jay said.

"Then that'll work out just fine," Dexler said. "Because you never seen me, and I certainly never seen your picture on the news." He winked at Jay. "Now that we got that settled, you can follow me to the merchandise."

Dexler led them into an adjacent room where the walls were lined with guns stored in locked cases. He brought them from case to case and spoke of caliber, recoil, and sights with a gleam in his eye.

"Now, this," Dexler said, "this here is an assault rifle with a removable laser sight."

"What about ammo?" Tim asked.

"What about it?"

"We need something that will really penetrate, you know, like armor-piercing bullets."

Dexler brayed laughter. "Armor-piercing bullets? Just what the hell've you got yourself into, boy?" He mussed up Tim's hair, then held up a hand. "No, no, don't tell me. I'd rather not know."

"All right," Tim said. "So I guess that means you don't have any."

"Here? Hell no. I keep all the illegal shit in the safe out back."

***

The Boston Public Library was a mammoth stone building that lay in the shadow of the Hancock Tower, just a short walk from the upscale stores of Newbury Street. It always reminded Jay of a fortress with its thick slabs of concrete, its giant oval doors, and its wrought iron sconces perched above the entryway.

Inside, at the research terminal, Crystal jotted down the location codes of some books she'd found. Then she led them down a series of corridors before emerging into a courtyard bursting with the vibrant colors of tulips and daffodils in full bloom.

Sarah stopped a moment to sniff the flowers, crouching down at the edge of a cobblestone walkway.

"It's beautiful," Crystal said, gazing at the fountain in the center of the courtyard. "You'd never even know you were in the city unless you looked up at the Prudential Tower."

Jay nodded, but said nothing. They would be heading back to Glenwood just before dawn tomorrow and the odds were whoever entered the cave would never see daylight again. He wondered if Tim and Sarah really understood that. At their age, he had believed himself to be invincible, always climbing to the tops of trees and scaling cliffs in the deep woods, never once doubting that he'd make it home before dark without a scratch. During the long summer days before high school, he and Steve used to pedal their bikes along deserted country roads and race each other through towns twenty miles from home, cutting across railroad tracks at full speed, daring the oncoming trains.

He gazed at Tim, who had hoisted Sarah onto his shoulders so she could reach for a butterfly. *I can't let them go into the cave. I can't take their childhood away from them.* But even as the thought entered his mind, he feared it was too late. With all that had happened, all the violence they had experienced so far, it was a wonder they could even find it in themselves to smile.

Crystal touched his shoulder and, for the time being, all his dark thoughts drained away. He squeezed her hand and smiled. The words "I love you" formed on his lips, but he choked them back, fearing they would only be wasted.

"Come on," he said, and started toward the door at the opposite end of the courtyard. "Let's see if we can find anything helpful in those books."

***

A series of arched windows lined the wall of a cavernous reading room. Their table sat in a row of what seemed like hundreds occupying a room almost as long as a football field. Several stacks of books teetered on the table before them, books with titles like *Symbols of the Ancient World, The Book of Runes,* and *Ciphers of the Occult.*

Tim leafed through the appendix of a book entitled *The Language of Ancient Civilizations.* He tossed it onto the table and folded his arms. "Who are we kidding? We're not going to find anything in these books." He motioned to the tattered slip of notebook paper upon which Frank had scrawled his final words. It gave him the creeps just looking at it. He couldn't help but picture Frank dipping a shaky finger into the ruined mess of his legs before tracing his message in bloody finger paint. "Those runes are probably older than any of the civilizations in this book, maybe even older than this world."

Jay marked his page with an index card and set down the book he'd been reading. "It says here that the ancient Egyptians decorated their obelisks with hieroglyphics that depicted the pharaohs giving offerings to the gods. It says that was the whole purpose—to raise the pharaohs to the heavens and show them mingling with the gods. I can't find any hieroglyphics that resemble a key, though."

"I didn't have much luck either," Crystal said. "I looked through a book on Druid runes and another one on Scandinavian runes, but nothing matches the symbols on that paper."

Jay frowned. "What if we can't kill Trell without knowing what this message means?"

"I don't know," Tim said, "but I don't think we're going to find anything in here. And the longer we wait, the stronger Trell gets."

Crystal nodded. "I think Tim's right. We have to save Maria and Sarah's mother before it's too late."

At the mention of her mom, Sarah's lip began to tremble. Crystal draped an arm around her shoulder and hugged her tight.

Tim glanced up at the towering rows of stacks and imagined what it would be like to be trapped in here alone. In his mind's eye, he saw the lights click off and the room go dark. He imagined Trell's claws clicking against the tiles as it stalked him through the maze of stacks.

The hunt is finished, Tim. But the killing ... the killing is just begun.

He shook the image from his mind and pushed his chair back. "I'm ready to get out of here," he said. "Who's with me?"

COLONY OF THE LOST

CHAPTER FORTY-THREE

They moved like phantoms in the dark of night, slipping through the deserted street, faces obscured in a veil of shifting moon shadow. Stars twinkled in a velvet sky, and the bright arc of a crescent moon peered through the drifting cloud cover.

A breeze blew from the east, ruffling Jay's hair as he slid the last box into the trunk of the car Dexler had loaned them. The late model Dodge made Jay's LeBaron look like a luxury sedan by comparison. According to their deal, if Jay failed to return for Crystal's Volvo in a week, Dexler would own it.

Jay closed the trunk and rubbed his hands briskly against the cold. A muted click carried through the silence—the back door of Dexler's Gun and Survival Specialty Store closing behind its owner and leaving the four of them alone.

They stood in a rough circle around the rear of the car, each glancing at the other, no one saying a word. Their breath plumed out before them in rolling waves of white vapor. Jay glanced at Tim and Sarah and saw them as he had first met them, the astonished look on their faces as they ran into each other in the midnight woods, drawn together by the ghost of a child dead to this world for centuries.

Why us, Samuel? Why in God's name did you choose us?

But the boy's words drifted back to him, faint and distant, like the whisper of an autumn breeze. *It is not I who sought you, but you who sought me. You have the vision. You see what others cannot.*

That was the grim reality of it. Each had seen Samuel for his own reasons, each had been drawn into this nightmare that wouldn't end.

Oh, it'll end soon, boy. But I think you know that already.

265

Jay ignored his dad's voice and wondered how he'd come to be haunted by these ghosts. He stroked the trunk of Dexler's car with his index finger, cutting a slick track through the coating of dew. The sun would rise in a couple hours and spread like fire across the horizon. And here he was, standing in the dark with his ex-fiancée and a couple of neighborhood kids, leaning over a car loaded with a cache of weapons.

He shook his head and grinned into the dark. How many charges would he be brought up on if the police happened by? How many felonies had he committed so far?

After the others piled into the car, Jay lingered a moment longer. He opened the trunk and rechecked their supplies. He'd arranged them neatly on the gray carpet, wedging towels between the boxes to prevent them from bouncing around. He took a mental inventory of what they would carry into the cave: four heavy-duty lantern style flashlights, a Glock nine millimeter with laser sight, pepper spray, a stun gun, a high powered assault rifle loaded with armor-piercing bullets—cop-killers, Dexler had called them—and, of course, his Dad's .45.

This last weapon he'd tucked into the waistband of his jeans. He could feel the cold steel of its muzzle pressed against his flesh. The safety was on, but it was loaded, ready at a moment's notice should Trell send another of its assassins after them.

And then there was his insurance policy, his plan B, tucked under the false bottom with the spare tire, wrapped carefully in the towels he'd swiped from the motel. Two hand grenades.

Live ones, Dexler had cautioned. *You know you only got three seconds before the sons-of-bitches explode?*

Jay nodded. He knew all right. But there was no other alternative. If Trell's scales truly protected it like armor, then it was their only option—an option that would likely kill them, but an option, nonetheless. He let out his breath in a shaky sigh and closed the trunk with trembling hands. The sky was lightening in the east, the stars already fading from view.

Soon now. One way or another, it will end soon.

He bit a fingernail and spit into the dark.

You're wasting your time, boy. Give up this hero business and buy yourself a drink. Make your dear old dad proud.

A hand settled on his shoulder, and he nearly screamed. He groped for the butt of his gun and whirled around.

Crystal's eyes dropped to his hand. "What exactly are you reaching for?" she asked, but her voice quavered so much neither one of them cracked a smile. "Are you okay?" she asked, finally.

"I'm fine. It's them I'm worried about," he said, gesturing to the car. "And you. I can't let you guys go with me. It's too dangerous." He glanced down at his feet. "The truth is, if I hadn't been drunk when Frank called, we'd know how to kill Trell. So this is my mistake, my responsibility."

"We're all involved now, Jay. And if the kids go, I go."

"You can stop them. I'll pull over at a gas station, leave the three of you stranded."

But Crystal shook her head. "It's not my decision. Tim's old enough to know what he's doing. And in a weird way, I think Sarah is too. I want to stop her. I want to stop them both, believe me. But they each have someone they're trying to save. I don't think I can deny them the right to try."

"But they're just kids! Talk them out of it—they'll listen to you."

"Damn it, Jay. Don't you think I've tried? You think I want this to happen?" A tear rolled down her cheek.

"Hey." He slipped an arm around her waist. "I'm sorry you got caught up in this. But please think about what I said. The kids may hate you for the rest of their lives, but at least they'd be *alive* to hate you. Someday they'd thank you. Someday they'd thank us both." He kissed her on the forehead, then gazed into her eyes. "I love you, Crystal."

He placed a finger over her lips before she could respond. "Take the kids. Save yourselves. In a couple years, you'll find someone who loves you the way I never could. You'll settle down ... forget all about me."

She wiped her eyes with the heel of her hand and sniffled. It was moment before she spoke. "You're not scared?"

"Not as much as I thought I'd be. It's funny, before Trell came along, I was dead. If I didn't drink myself to death within six months, I would have found some other way to finish the job. But now ... now I feel alive again. It took all this to wake me up—knowing that I was the only one who could protect Tim and Sarah, knowing that I was all they had. It saved me, Crystal. Death doesn't seem so bad now because it's on my terms. Does that make any sense? After all these years, I finally have a choice. I finally have control over my life. And this is what I choose. This is my destiny."

He grinned, and it felt awful and wonderful at the same time.

CHAPTER FORTY-FOUR

Her stomach quivered as the thing inside of her fed. The outline of its body bulged against her flesh, providing a momentary glimpse of the horror within. Pain shot through her womb and radiated to every extremity, but she separated herself from it and thought of a place far away, a place where the demon couldn't hear her thoughts. It was her sanctuary, a desperate handhold on the last thread of sanity ... a thread that had worn precariously thin.

Ghostly slivers of moonlight filtered through breaks in the budding canopy, combining with the wind to create a host of shadows skittering across the forest floor.

Come, Margaret. The time draws near.

The Dark One commanded her to move through the underbrush. Thorns pierced her legs, and Margaret could feel rivulets of blood trickling down her calves.

It's forcing me to the cave. Maybe for the last time.

She ordered her legs to stop, and for a moment they obeyed. But the victory was short-lived, and just as she had learned before, no act of defiance ever went unpunished.

Her knees buckled and she dropped to the ground, her face striking the damp earth. Invisible hands tightened around her neck and choked her until her lungs burned for want of air. Bright bursts of purple light exploded before her eyes, and she could feel herself slipping away.

Go ahead and kill me! I dare you!

The Dark One squeezed tighter, so tight she thought her windpipe might break. But then it relinquished its grip and left her gasping and wheezing, her head swimming in a fog of pain. She rolled onto her side and struggled to her knees.

Not finished, Margaret.

Her hand closed around a jagged rock, its underside coated with a scrim of mud. She raised the rock above her head and laid her other hand on top of a boulder.

No, please!

The Dark One laughed. *Smash, smash, Margaret.*

Her arm dropped like a hammer and the rock smashed into the back of her hand, breaking at least two metacarpals. She clutched her ruined hand to her breast and screamed.

Come, Margaret.

She got up. Not because she wanted to. Not because the pain was too much to bear sitting still. She got up because it forced her to. That was a half hour ago. Now, as she staggered through the woods, her mind in that dark, secret place, cut off from Trell's probing touch, she could feel her hand throbbing.

A crippling pain stabbed her belly, and she had to steady herself against the trunk of a pine. After a few minutes, the pain subsided and she felt a strange sinking sensation inside her.

Contractions. I'm having contractions.

Tears welled up in her eyes, but she refused to let them flow. Trell pulled her away from the tree and forced her into a march. She thought of her family and how much she wanted to see them again. She imagined Nick lying in a hospital bed, leads taped to his chest, monitors recording his vital signs. She wanted to sit beside him, kiss his forehead, hold his hand.

And she thought of Sarah, her sweet little girl. Somehow they'd grown apart over the past couple years, and she wished more than anything that she could go back and make it all better. She'd spend more time with her, hug her more often, play dress up, be a little less strict.

I love you, baby. Please stay safe ... wherever you are.

The entrance to the cave loomed ahead through a cluster of birch. If Trell got its way, she would die in there ... alone, and in the dark. Yet she marched toward Trell's lair on traitor legs, tears rolling down her cheeks.

Darkness smothered her as she squeezed through the opening, and she knew she had to stay strong. She drew a deep breath and retreated into that secret place in her mind. She told herself that she could do this, that she could put an end to this nightmare.

I know about the amulet, Trell—its origin, its power, the Life Force. I know all of your secrets. And I'm going to kill you. I swear to God, I will.

CHAPTER FORTY-FIVE

No one said much during the drive back to Glenwood. Jay played the radio awhile, tuned to a classic rock station, but Crystal turned it off when the Rolling Stones came on, singing *Sympathy for the Devil*. "Too close for comfort," she'd said, and that had been that.

The eastern sky brightened slowly, and as dawn approached, the car cruised along the Mass Pike at just a hair above the legal limit, the miles melting quickly away. At one point, a state police cruiser fell in behind them, blue lights flashing, sirens wailing.

Jay switched on his blinker and began pulling over, but the cop blew past them, apparently en route to some other emergency. Jay exhaled sharply and loosened his grip on the steering wheel. In the back seat, Tim shook his head. "I don't know if we just got real lucky... or real *un*lucky."

Jay's vote was for the former. If they got arrested, nothing would stand in Trell's way, and Glenwood would become every bit as desolate as the lost settlement of Freetown. If that cop had pulled them over, Jay could imagine himself drawing the .45 from the waistband of his jeans and leveling it at the cop's chest.

I can't let you take us in. You have no idea what's at stake here.

And if the cop didn't stand down? Could he bring himself to shoot? Could he take one life to save thousands?

"We're running low on gas," Crystal said.

Jay glanced at the gas gauge and nodded. He turned off at the next exit and steered the car into a Shell station. He cut the engine and waved a ten-dollar bill at Crystal. "Mind putting this on pump three?" No sense filling the tank beyond what they needed to get to Glenwood.

272

She unbuckled her seatbelt and reached for the bill. "You guys want to come with me? Pick out something for breakfast?"

"Why?" Tim asked. "So Jay can take off without us?"

Crystal did her best to appear confused. "What are you talking about?"

"I heard you guys earlier. You're terrible whisperers, by the way." He folded his arms. "I'm going to Glenwood."

"No, you're not," Jay said. "Get out of the car. All of you."

"I'm not leaving," Tim said. "Trell turned Maria into one of its assassins. And, by now, it's probably gotten to my parents too. I can't give up when there might be a chance to save them. Besides, what makes you think we'll be any safer staying behind? It tracked us here from Glenwood. How do you know it won't kill us after you drive off?"

"It found us through Maria," Jay said.

"You don't think it has some of its assassins driving around looking for us?"

Jay scratched his head. The kid had a point. "What about you, Sarah? Don't you want to stay with Crystal? She can protect you while Tim and I go into the cave."

"I'm coming too." There wasn't a hint of doubt in her voice.

"You realize this isn't a game? We're going into the cave and we might never make it out again."

"I know," she said. "But I think our best chance is to stick together."

Jay shrugged. "All right then. I hope you know what you're getting yourselves into ... because I sure as hell don't."

***

A security checkpoint blocked the road as they crossed the town line into Glenwood. Two National Guard Humvees were parked side by side in opposite directions. For a moment, Jay considered shifting the car into reverse and trying another way into town, but then he noticed that the trucks were empty, the door to the nearest one glistening with blood.

Jay exchanged a glance with Crystal before steering the car onto the shoulder and rolling past the Humvees. They cruised slowly through neighborhoods shrouded in shadows, passing homes that were eerily silent in the predawn gloom. The streets were empty—not a car on the road, not a single pedestrian in sight.

People should be getting ready for work now.

But he didn't see any lights burning. Not a single one. It seemed as if the entire population of Glenwood had vanished, and he imagined this same location centuries before when the French fur trappers found the settlement of Freetown deserted, all traces of life frozen in time—doors open, wood half cut, place settings laid out for dinners that would never be served.

"Place is like a ghost town," Tim said.

Jay nodded. Whoever hadn't fled town was either dead or under Trell's control. He braked suddenly, swerving to avoid a kid's bike lying in the middle of the road. Twenty yards farther ahead, a doll lay on its back, its glass eyes staring up at the sky.

"Do you think we're too late?" Tim asked.

Jay glanced at him in the rearview mirror. "I don't know."

They passed through the center of town, through the ghost-like silence, and turned onto the road leading into Elm Street Park. Jay pulled over next to an overgrown field. "Last chance to change your minds."

"I'm going," Tim said.

Sarah nodded. "So am I."

"All right," Jay said. "But I don't know who's crazier—you guys for wanting to go, or me for letting you."

They climbed out of the car and stretched their legs, the scent of pine wafting out of the forest. It always seemed stronger to Jay after spending time in the city, and he found it oddly comforting, even now.

He closed his eyes and turned his face into the breeze. God, it felt good to be alive, good to be aware of the world around him.

Do you really want to do this? Do you really want to die?

But he ignored the voice and focused his attention on the woods before him, on the vast expanse of forest that had stood for centuries, a silent witness to the slaughter of so many. The mountains loomed beyond the trees, basking in the blood-red glimmer of the rising sun. A host of rose-colored clouds scudded across the sky, and Jay thought of a saying he'd first heard years ago: *Red sky at night, sailor's delight. Red sky at dawn, sailor be warned.*

There's a storm coming all right. I just hope we're ready for it.

Sarah's voice broke him out of his thoughts. "This is where we met," she said. "Where we first learned each other's names."

Jay nodded. He remembered that night well. They had emerged from the woods right over there, just past the white gazebo and the cluster of crooked birch. He'd been so relieved to see the yellowish glow of streetlights, so happy to be away from the smothering darkness of the crowding pines.

"All right," Jay said. "Let's get this over with." He popped the trunk and doled out the weapons, handing the rifle to Tim, the Glock to Crystal, and the stun gun to Sarah. Then he strapped on a holster and slid his dad's .45 into it. He showed the grenades to Tim. "Let's put these in your backpack for safekeeping."

Tim turned around, and Jay zipped the grenades into the front pocket, tucking them behind the bag of bagels they'd bought at the gas station minimart.

"I'll try not to fall on them."

"Probably a good idea," Jay said, ruffling Tim's hair. He kneeled down beside Sarah and helped her strap the stun gun into a holster. "You remember how the man showed you to use that?"

She looked at him with her big brown eyes and nodded. "I remember."

275

"Good." He kissed her on the forehead and stood up.

Crystal squeezed his hand. "Let's get moving."

Jay nodded. He admired her courage. He admired all of their courage.

***

The forest swallowed them, its dense tangle of trees closing around them like the jaws of some ancient beast. They walked along a narrow dirt path in columns of two—Jay and Tim in the lead, Crystal and Sarah trailing a step or two behind. Dust spiraled up from their heels and drifted through the air like smoke.

Tim walked with the trail map open in front of him, the rifle slung over his right shoulder. "We stay on this path for a mile," he said. "Then we turn left onto Arrow."

The morning grew hot as the sun climbed into the sky. Slants of light pierced the canopy and dappled the forest floor in a patchwork of gold. Crickets chirped in the grass—seemingly all around them—and birds flitted from branch to branch, the woods echoing their song.

Just another day to them, Jay thought, wiping sweat from his brow. He scanned the forest, studying the shadows in the deep woods, looking for any sign of trouble. *I should've come here alone.*

Something rifled through the underbrush and streaked into the path ahead of them.

Tim dropped the map and stumbled backward, nearly tripping over Sarah.

Jay drew his gun and leveled it at what turned out to be a squirrel. It twitched its tail at them before darting back into the brush.

Crystal placed a hand over her heart and drew a deep breath, the hollow of her neck glistening with sweat.

Jay bit his lip. A squirrel? How could they expect to stand against Trell if they nearly died from fright when a squirrel crossed their path?

You picked the wrong guy, Samuel. I'm not the hero type.

That's right, boy. But you're the drinking type. Just like your old man.

Tim picked up the map and shook it free of dust. "You should have shot it," he said. "Blown the furry little rat to kingdom come."

Jay holstered his weapon and wiped sweat from his eyes. God, this weather was crazy—cold one day, hot the next. Typical New England Spring.

They started out again, following the path as it sloped down a hill and curved around a bend. Soon they arrived at a crossroads marked by a weathered wooden sign. Jay could just barely make out the words—black letters painted on white—Arrow Lane.

They drew to a halt and exchanged glances.

"Keep your weapons ready," Jay whispered.

They crept along more carefully now, sticking close to the tree line, watching and listening for the slightest movement, the slightest sound. No one said a word ... not even Tim. The woods were thicker here, the trees crowded together. Underbrush grew in a wild tangle and, in some places, spilled over onto the path. The canopy was denser too, the branches of pine, spruce, and oak joining together to form a screen that shut out the light.

Silence crept in like a fog. Jay couldn't hear a single cricket, a single bird. It was as if every living creature had fled ... or had been killed. Shadows lurked everywhere, dark things brought to life by the wind through the trees. Jay suddenly felt as if they weren't alone. Sarah must have felt it too because she drew closer to him and pressed her body against his side. He stroked her head with his free hand, his dad's .45 clutched in the other.

Give me the strength to protect them. Please, God ... if you're listening.

He tried to shake the feeling that they were being watched, that they were being hunted, and although he was scanning the area for danger, he didn't see the thing behind the tree until it was too late.

It pounced on him with such speed that all he saw was a blur of black before hitting the ground. The jolt of the landing knocked the gun from his hand and made his teeth clack together.

Something rock-solid drove into his stomach, and his breath escaped his lungs in a choking whoosh. The thing climbed on top of him, pinning him to the ground, and all Jay saw was a tangled mane of hair as it clawed at his neck and strangled him. He thrashed his body, trying to throw the thing off him, but it was just too strong.

I'm going to die, he thought. *Right here on the ground while everyone watches.*

But then he heard a searing crackle, caught a whiff of ozone, and the thing tumbled off him. He scrambled to his feet and retrieved his gun from the ground. Then he stepped back and took his first good look at his attacker. "It's human?"

"I don't know if I'd call it that anymore," Tim said, motioning to the crumpled form with Sarah's stun gun.

Crystal wiped blood from Jay's cheek. "Are you all right?"

"Yeah," he said. "Just a little freaked out."

Somewhere through the trees ahead, a twig snapped.

"Quick!" Jay said, "Hide!"

They dropped to the ground and scrambled into the underbrush as a dozen or more of Trell's assassins loped around the bend—some on all fours, others hunched like mountain gorillas. Their clothes hung in tatters, revealing bodies coated with dirt.

Crystal gasped. "It's turning them into animals."

But Jay knew better. It was Trell's way of humiliating them, Trell's way of asserting its dominance over the human race.

In the ferns beside him, Jay's attacker began to stir. But Tim was on it in an instant, zapping it in the neck with the stun gun.

Trell's assassins shambled down the path, their eyes darting left and right, nostrils flaring. The pack hissed and snorted and drew to a halt just ten yards from their hiding place. The leader paused to sniff the air.

Jay held his breath and lay as still as possible, his belly pressed against the ground. Sweat seeped through his pores and trickled down his ribcage, creating a maddening itch.

Come on, keep going, keep moving.

But the things on the path weren't ready to leave just yet. They split up and waded into the waist-high underbrush. Jay watched them through a screen of fern. There was no way he and the others could take them all on. He might be able to fire a shot and scatter them, but what if Trell ordered them not to flee? What if it commanded them to fight to the death?

One of the things headed right for them, wearing nothing but a pair of soiled underwear. Jay drew his gun from the holster and had a vision of Steve spinning into the wall, his blood splashing the air.

The thing took another step, and Jay got a better view of its face. His jaw dropped open.

Oh my God ... that's Ron!

The principal of Glenwood High paused, one foot poised above the ground. It tilted its head to the side. Listening. And then all at once, as if orchestrated by some unseen conductor, Trell's assassins gave voice to a chorus of grunting. The sound rose like a wave into the forest, startling more than a few birds from their perches.

The Ron-thing echoed the grunting before lumbering back to the path, snarling and clenching its fists.

"It's him," Sarah whispered. "It's Samuel."

Jay spread apart a veil of fern and saw Samuel moving through the pines, that strange blue glow pulsing around him.

"I see him," Crystal said. "Jay, I can see him!"

"He's leading them away," Jay said.

279

They watched Trell's assassins retreat into the trees and disappear. After a few minutes, Jay stood up and looked around. They were alone. "Come on. Let's get out of here."

They stayed close to one another as they crept along Arrow Lane, their eyes sweeping from left to right, searching for whatever horrors might be lurking among the shadows. But they saw nothing.

The trail narrowed as it wound through a dense tangle of brambles and cut through the heart of an old-growth forest. The smell here was earthy, almost mineral-like. Moss grew thick on the sides of rocks and trees, and plump white mushrooms sprang up from dark soil.

An intersection loomed ahead. A sign for Wolf trail hung on a tree at eye level. The faded black lettering reflected a narrow swatch of sunlight that had found its way through a gap in the canopy.

Sarah drew to a halt as they rounded the bend. She pointed to a spot in the woods. "There it is."

"The cave?" Jay asked.

She nodded. "It was in the dream. Samuel showed me."

Jay had pictured something bigger, something more ominous—like a yawning black maw carved into a mountain of stone. But this didn't even look like a cave. It was just two boulders covered in tangled ropes of ivy.

Tim scratched his head. "Looks like a giant Chia Pet."

Jay detected a blur of motion from the corner of his eye. "Did you guys just see that?" Before anyone could respond, he caught a glimpse of a man slipping behind the boulders. He motioned for the others to get down. "Hand me the stun gun."

Tim passed it over.

"Be careful," Sarah said.

"Do you think it saw us?" Crystal whispered.

"I don't know," Jay said. "Maybe."

Tim stood up. "I'm coming with you."

Jay shook his head. "I need you to stay here and be ready with the rifle."

"All right," Tim said, gripping the gun in both hands and taking up position behind a tree.

"Just don't shoot unless it gets past me."

"Got it."

Jay gave him a nod and squeezed Crystal's hand. "I'll be back."

Will you, boy? Will you really?

He stepped into the thicket separating the path from the cave and moved against the wind, using it to conceal the sound of his approach. With the stun gun gripped in his right hand and his Dad's .45 holstered at his hip, he stole from tree to tree in a low crouch, wincing at every twig that snapped beneath his feet.

Not exactly an Injun, are you boy?

When he reached the tree closest to the cave, he paused to wipe his sweaty palms on his jeans. Then he peered around the trunk and saw what appeared to be the caveman version of his favorite bartender.

Bill Malley stood beside the cave, wielding a machete and grinning like a lunatic. He wore tattered jeans and no shirt, his barrel of a chest streaked with dirt. Dried clumps of mud dangled from the curls of his chest hair.

Jay froze, and for a moment, he and Malley locked gazes. Then Malley made a throat-slitting gesture with the machete, and charged.

Jay stumbled backward into the brambles, gritting his teeth as the thorns ripped into his calves. Malley closed the gap quickly, the machete slicing through the air in a blur of blue steel.

From somewhere behind him, Crystal cried out in warning.

Jay fell against a tree and ducked as the machete sliced into the trunk above his head, sending chips of bark raining into the air. He lost his balance and fell into the dirt, the stun gun tumbling from his hand.

Malley yanked the blade free and stepped over him. Jay shifted his weight and rolled to the left as the machete clanged against a rock and produced a shower of sparks. He snatched the stun gun from the dirt just as Malley hoisted the blade over his head.

Jay thrust his arm upward and planted the stun gun against Malley's groin. A blue spark jumped between the leads with an electric crackle, and Malley collapsed in a heap.

Jay staggered to his feet and was joined by the others a few moments later.

"Does anyone else smell burnt wiener?" Tim asked, letting out a nervous laugh.

Jay glanced into the woods beyond the path. He thought he could hear the distant sound of grunting. "Come on," he said. "We don't have much time."

CHAPTER FORTY-SIX

Margaret lay on the cold, hard stone and breathed in shallow and rhythmic gasps. Crippling jabs of pain ripped through her womb, and she focused her attention on the stalactites suspended above her. Water rippled in the pool beside her, and the pale blue phosphorescence that radiated from its edges cast a host of shadows crawling over the cavern walls.

It's soaking in the pool. Feeding off the power, channeling the strength into its body.

It was the magic of this place that made it possible, the convergence of worlds, the overlapping of gateways. The pool had kept Trell alive throughout the centuries. Nurturing it, healing it … somehow transforming the blood of the dying into a form of energy that it could absorb through its skin.

The rippling water built into a churning roil as the Dark One emerged from the pool. An ice-cold spray of water splashed onto Margaret's face, sending a chill through her body. She turned her head away and allowed herself to descend into that secret place where the beast couldn't hear her thoughts.

Greed.

It would be Trell's downfall. Maybe not today, maybe not for a thousand years, but one day it would exact its price. She was certain of it, for she knew of the dual nature of the pool, of the magic that the Dark One had added to it.

Does it know I've picked its brain? Does it know about the secrets I've stolen?

Pain flared in her uterus, a simultaneous stabbing and sinking that wrenched her out of her secret place. Her eyes fluttered open, and

283

her surroundings drew slowly into focus. Trell loomed over her, its eyes gleaming in the shadows. Its rank breath plumed into her face as its lips spread apart in a maddening grin, revealing row upon row of jagged fangs.

Its voice boomed in her mind, so loud that it rattled her teeth.

Soon you shall bear witness to the ancient ritual ... life from death and death from life.

The amulet dangled from Trell's neck, so dark and shiny it was camouflaged against the surrounding scales. It swung before her eyes, the polished obelisk reflecting the phosphorescent glow of the pool. She tried reaching for it, but she couldn't seem to lift her arms.

Beautiful, isn't it? Trell said. *A souvenir of the old world, the spoil of my greatest battle. I would tell you the story one day, but I believe you already know it, don't you?* Its lips twisted into a freakish grin. *But no matter. It will all be over soon. So lie back, Margaret, and relax. This child will be born whether you want it or not.*

CHAPTER FORTY-SEVEN

They stood waist-deep in the tangle of underbrush, huddled shoulder to shoulder before the cave. They could hear Trell's assassins grunting in the distance, becoming more agitated by the second. Tim cast a nervous glance into the woods. His eyes swept across the trees as he unzipped his backpack and passed out the flashlights.

Jay noticed a tremor in the boy's hands, but said nothing. Instead, he shifted his gaze to the faces of those in this unlikely group, the charges of a boy dead to this world for three centuries, a boy murdered by the very beast they had come here to slay. "All right," he said. "Last chance."

"You've already heard my answer," Tim said. He clicked on the flashlight and ducked inside the cave.

Sarah peered up at Jay. "Will you hold my hand?"

"Of course," he said, taking her hand. "Well?" he asked, glancing at Crystal. "What about you?"

She held his gaze for a moment. "I'm gonna stand by my man," she said, and surprised him with a kiss before slipping into the cave.

For a fleeting moment, Jay forgot all about Trell, all about the danger they were about to face. But then he glanced at the dark gash between the boulders and wondered how many people Trell had dragged through that opening over the centuries, how many children had it slaughtered within those walls?

Anger welled up inside him, for the time being drowning out the fear. He kissed Sarah on the forehead. "Come on," he whispered.

Darkness smothered them as they entered the cave, the change so sudden that Jay felt as if someone had thrown a hood over his head. Even with the flashlights, it still took a minute before his eyes adjusted

285

to the darkness and he could finally discern the faces of Tim, Crystal, and Sarah standing before him.

It was cool in here, almost cold. A breeze gusted from some subterranean level, the damp air wafting the earthy scent of minerals. Jay shone the flashlight overhead, illuminating the craggy black rock of the ceiling. The passageway appeared to be no more than eight feet high by ten feet wide. He wondered if it narrowed at any point, forcing them to crawl. He saw by the look on Crystal's face that she was thinking the same thing—she was claustrophobic. He reached for her hand. "It'll get wider," he said, although he didn't have the slightest idea if that was true.

Tim ran his hand over the wall and studied the damp residue on his palm before wiping it on his shirt. "Destroy the gateway," he whispered. "Maybe it has something to do with the runes."

But Jay only shrugged. He didn't have a clue what it meant.

They crept along the passageway, Jay and Tim in front, Crystal and Sarah trailing a step behind. They walked for a long time, the floor of the cave sloping ever downward, descending deeper into the heart of the earth. Jay trained his flashlight on the blackness ahead, the beam lancing through the dark like a laser. The others had their lights switched to the lantern setting, which threw off a warm glow in a ten foot radius.

Sarah nudged Jay and whispered, "What if there are more of ... of them in here?"

Jay bit his lip. What could he say? That they were like sitting ducks with the lights on? That Trell's assassins would see them a mile away?

We should have asked Dexler for night vision goggles. How did we not think of that?

"I think Samuel led them all away," Tim said. "But if not, we'll get them before they get us."

286

"Right," Jay said. He hoped the lie made Sarah feel better, because it only made him feel worse. He drew a deep breath and tried to steady his nerves. Somewhere in this darkness, somewhere deep in this labyrinth of stone, was Trell.

Christ, Jay thought. *Are we playing right into its hands? Is this what Trell wanted all along?*

In the back of his mind, the voice of his dad cackled.

What would it take to defeat Trell? Was Tim right? Would bullets be useless? And even if they somehow managed to wound it, wouldn't it just heal itself in the pool?

There were too many questions and not enough answers. How could he have been so stupid? Here they were, wandering through the depths of some nameless cave—a recovering alcoholic, two kids, and a woman all of one hundred and fifteen pounds—carrying guns and grenades on their way to battle a creature from another world, a creature that shouldn't even exist, but somehow did. Their plan was to march right up to this creature, this beast with no known weaknesses, confront it on its own turf ... and they no longer had the element of surprise.

You really screwed yourself this time, boy. I told you not to come down here, told you not to get involved. But you didn't listen to your dear old dad, did you?

Jay ignored the voice and instead listened to the sounds that permeated the inky darkness—the muted plop of slow dripping water, the hollow grinding of pebbles beneath their feet. He drew a shaky breath and focused on banishing the fear from his mind, on willing his legs to move forward, conscious of the fact that he was the leader of this group, the commander of this unlikely bunch, knowing that if he faltered, if he showed any sign of fear or weakness, they wouldn't stand a chance against Trell.

Sarah tugged at his shirtsleeve. "This way."

Jay nodded, knowing that she was reliving the dream that Samuel had given her, knowing that their fate might well depend on what this little girl remembered. And so he led them through a passageway on the left, its ceiling lined with stalactites. He clenched his jaw as they crept through the tunnel and tried to shake the feeling that they were walking right into a trap.

But it was too late to turn back now, too late to even consider it.

He tightened his grip on his dad's .45 and swallowed, trying to force some moisture back into his throat. He was beginning to sense a presence in this place, beginning to feel the evil that dwelled here. It prickled the hairs at the nape of his neck and made his heart thump hard in his chest.

"We're getting close," Sarah said.

Jay nodded. He had guessed as much by the smell. He had noticed it only moments before—a damp, musty odor mingled with something rotten. Like a dirty cage at the zoo.

They continued along the passageway. A series of tunnels appeared on their left, yawning like hungry, black mouths. Something caught Jay's eye in one of the tunnels, and he drew to a halt.

"What is it?" Tim asked.

"I thought I saw a gleam of red ... almost like eyes watching in the dark."

"I don't see anything," Crystal whispered. "But let's keep moving just in case."

What if it follows us? Jay thought. *What if it blocks our only way out?*

Before he could finish the thought, a woman's scream rang out from somewhere ahead of them, echoing throughout the passageway. Even in the dim glow of the flashlights, Jay saw a spark of recognition flash across Sarah's face.

"Mom!" she cried.

And before Jay could do anything to stop her, she dashed ahead into the darkness. "Sarah, stop!"

But she didn't listen, and a few moments later they heard the crack of plastic, the tinkling of glass ... and then Sarah was gone, vanished into the darkness as her flashlight winked out.

"Sarah!" Jay yelled.

But the girl didn't answer—she only screamed.

Jay charged through the tunnel, running too fast to react to anything that the flashlight might reveal in his path. Soon, the tunnel began to brighten—not from the light of day, but from a pale blue phosphorescence that emanated from somewhere up ahead.

He stumbled into an enormous cavern and almost tripped over Sarah's broken flashlight. Tim and Crystal appeared beside him a moment later, but he barely noticed their presence as he glanced up at a vaulted ceiling lined with dripping stalactites.

The cavern stretched back at least a hundred feet to the far wall where a still, black pool shimmered like onyx, its edges radiating a bright band of phosphorescence.

A woman lay beside the pool, sprawled on the floor with her legs spread apart. She wore a tattered white nightgown, stained with what could either be dirt or blood. Sarah kneeled beside her, her profile half-obscured by the swell of the woman's stomach.

Jay set the flashlight down and held his dad's .45 in both hands, his eyes never leaving Sarah's mother. She was a servant of Trell now. She was its eyes and its ears, its teeth and its claws. And even in her current condition, she would be dangerous.

Tim exhaled sharply. "Sarah never said anything about her mom being pregnant."

Jay raised the gun and stared down the sight. "I have a feeling this is something recent. Something very recent."

CHAPTER FORTY-EIGHT

Mom!

The word drifted through the swirl of fog that clouded her brain, the sound so weak and distant she thought for sure she had imagined it. But when the cry repeated itself a moment later, she knew it had to be real. Someone had entered the cave, someone Trell hadn't invited.

Sarah?

Margaret struggled into a sitting position and propped herself up on elbows trembling with fatigue. She glanced about the cavern and saw that it was empty. Trell was nowhere in sight. But she knew it wouldn't have strayed too far—not with the birth of its child so imminent.

Somehow Sarah had found her, she and the others that Trell hunted. Somehow they had made it to this awful place. But they couldn't possibly know what they were up against, couldn't possibly know how to kill it. She'd have to find a way to tell them, find a way to bypass Trell's control of her. But how was she going to do that? How could she possibly break free of it ... even for an instant?

A contraction wracked her body, and she clenched her fists in agony. This intensity of this labor was unlike anything she'd ever experienced. Birthing Sarah felt like menstrual cramps in comparison.

That's because it's tearing me up inside. Feeding on my flesh.

From the corner of her eye, she saw Sarah step into the cavern, the eerie blue light falling upon her. She tried calling out to Sarah, but a stabbing pain ripped through her womb, and she bit her tongue and pounded her fist into the ground.

Sarah dropped the flashlight and screamed.

When the contraction passed, Margaret sat up and held out her hand.

Sarah took a tentative step forward. "Mom? Is that you?"

"Yes, honey, it's me. For now. You understand how it makes me do things I don't want?"

"It made you hurt Daddy."

"Yes," Margaret said, and felt sickened by the memory.

Sarah's eyes swept the cavern. "Where is it?"

"I don't know. The pool, I think. The others are with you?"

Sarah nodded and drew closer. She seemed to consider if this was wise, but sat down beside her anyway. She glanced at her mom's nightgown. "What's wrong with your stomach?"

Margaret bit her lip to keep it from trembling. "It put a baby inside me." She lowered her eyes, not wanting to see Sarah's reaction. Sarah knew where babies came from—they'd had the talk just last month.

"I'm sorry," Sarah said.

It was such a grown up thing to say, such a brave thing, it nearly broke her heart. She took Sarah's hand. "You have to be strong now. You have to—"

"Sarah?" a man's voice called. "Come over here."

They turned toward the passageway where a man stood framed in lantern light, his gun aimed at Margaret.

"She's dangerous, Sarah. Remember who controls her. Remember—"

The words died on his lips as the surface of the pool came alive with a churning roil.

Margaret grabbed Sarah by the shoulders and locked eyes with her. "You've got to go to them, Sarah. And whatever happens, remember that I love you. Remember that I would never hurt you and that—" she whispered, pointing to her neck, "Get Trell's amulet, free the Life Force—"

291

A scream erupted from inside the pool. Water shot into the air like a geyser and rained down in a torrent. Sarah sprang to her feet and scrambled away, racing into the man's arms. He folded her into an embrace and then stepped protectively in front of her.

Margaret drew a deep breath and thanked God for this man. She didn't know who he was or how he came to know Sarah, but it gave her hope to know that there was still some goodness left in the world.

Trell would punish her now, but she didn't care. She had tricked it, had beaten it at its own game. Dizziness washed over her, and she felt suddenly disconnected from her body as Trell seized control. It commanded her to lie down and spread her arms out in the form of a cross. She wanted to tell the others what needed to be done, but she couldn't move, couldn't speak. It was up to Sarah now.

It lifted her head into the air and smashed her face against the stone, breaking her nose with a sickening crunch. And as blood trickled into her mouth and drained into her throat, she could hear it cursing her in the Ancient tongue.

But in her mind, she screamed in triumph.

How do you like that, Trell? You should've seized control when Sarah walked into the cavern. But you wanted me to suffer, didn't you? Wanted to hear me explain how you raped me. But you lost, Trell. You underestimated me ... and now your secret is out.

***

An icy rivulet of water trickled down Jay's cheek as Trell rose from the depths of the pool. Until now, Jay had only caught shadowy glimpses of the beast on the side of the road, and the sheer size of it shocked him.

It stood nearly six feet tall, its massive head crammed full of jagged fangs skewed at oblique angles. It crouched on all fours beside the pool, its forepaws twice as long as the rear so that it was standing

292

semi-erect. Grayish green scales covered its body, and the arch of its back bristled with spikes.

My God, Jay thought. *It's a killing machine.*

Trell lowered its head and gazed at them, its eyes glowing like the embers of a freshly-stoked fire. A gravelly sound emanated from its throat—something midway between a laugh and a growl.

Crystal reached for Jay's hand and squeezed it, and Sarah pressed her face against his stomach. He could feel her hot tears soaking through his shirt. She was trying to tell him something, but he couldn't quite make out the words.

Deeper into the cavern, Sarah's mom moaned. She sat up suddenly, as if yanked by invisible wires. Then her jaw dropped open and her mouth began to form speech in the clumsy way of a ventriloquist's dummy.

"You have arrived just in time to witness Margaret birth a most extraordinary child. How convenient that you will be present for its first feeding. As you'll soon discover, the child will emerge quite ravenous. So please, step inside, and partake in the ancient ritual of death begetting life."

Trell bounded over to Margaret in two quick leaps, moving with a fluid grace that belied the creature's size.

It's fast, Jay thought, and felt a sinking in his stomach. *Too fast.*

He raised his dad's .45 and aimed for the scaly ridge between its eyes.

All right, you son of a bitch. Let's see if you're faster than a speeding bullet.

The gun exploded with sound as he squeezed the trigger. The force of the shot snapped Trell's head back a fraction of an inch. A split second later, something whizzed past Jay's ear, and he realized with dawning horror that the bullet had ricocheted off its face.

Trell's lips twisted into a freakish grin. "Did you really think you could just walk in here and dispense of me with those pitiful weapons? It appears that you came all this way ... just to die."

Jay lowered the gun. Blue smoke curled up from the muzzle and swirled into the air.

Tim swung the rifle off his shoulder. "Where's Maria?"

"I'm afraid your precious Maria met a most unfortunate demise. But perhaps you can take solace from knowing that you're close to her final resting place, for her blood swims in these very waters, her bones rot in their dark depths. I can still hear her screams echoing off these walls. Such a beautiful voice. Such powerful lungs."

Trell inched closer, its eyes gleaming. "I forced her here under my power, but relinquished control as she entered the cavern. She tried to fight me, Tim, tried to flee. But she died. In the end, they all do— even you. And in your deaths, I will grow stronger. I have lived in this cave a thousand years. I will live here a thousand more. Nothing can stop me. Not you, not your guns, not Samuel."

"Is that so?" Tim asked. "You ever hear of armor-piercing bullets? Think you can guess what that means?" He squeezed off two shots in rapid succession, twin reports pealing like thunder.

Trell rocked back on its hindquarters, its blood spraying the air. A scream rose from its throat as it leaped off the ground and jumped high into the vaulted ceiling.

Tim followed the arc of its flight, planting one foot forward, anchoring the butt of the rifle against his shoulder. He fired again. Missed. The bullet hit rock and ricocheted back, whining through the air.

Trell crashed into the water with a gigantic splash that left Jay and the others dripping wet. Then it sank beneath the surface and disappeared, leaving only the rippling water in its wake.

The four of them glanced at one another. "You hurt it," Crystal said. "I saw it bleed."

"Yeah, but now it's healing itself," Jay said, his eyes fixed upon the pool.

Tim crept forward, aiming the rifle into the water.

"Don't get too close," Crystal said.

Sarah tugged at Jay's arm, her eyes brimming with tears.

"What is it?" Jay asked. "Are you okay?"

She tried to speak, but her chest kept hitching with sobs. "Mom said ... to ..."

"Take a deep breath," he said. "Try to relax." He shifted his gaze back to the cavern, his eyes moving from floor to ceiling.

Destroy the gateway.

What gateway, Samuel? I don't see any gateway.

He turned toward the pool and studied the aura of blue that glowed around its edges. *Could that be it?* Jay wondered. *Could the pool be the—*

Somebody screamed.

Jay whirled around and saw Crystal restraining Sarah. "What is it?" he asked.

Crystal motioned to Margaret with a nod of her head. "Baby's coming."

Tim raised the rifle. "I've got a bad feeling about this."

"So do I," Jay said.

Margaret pulled up her nightgown and exposed the bloated mound of her belly. Something wriggled just beneath the surface of her skin—an alien form swimming in and out of focus.

"My God," Jay muttered.

A claw pierced her abdomen from the inside out, sending a droplet of blood running down her side. Margaret screamed as the claw sliced down the length of her stomach, cutting through layers of fat and muscle with a wet, ripping sound.

Sarah screamed and tried to rush forward, but Crystal held her back.

COLONY OF THE LOST

A creature emerged through the bloody slit, wriggling and writhing until it dropped onto the floor. It resembled a miniature Trell, its reptilian body coated in a glistening slime of blood and afterbirth. It tilted its head in Jay's direction before propping its forelegs on Margaret's belly and tearing a sliver of flesh from her womb.

Sarah's mother—still screaming—batted the creature with her fists, but it only buried its head deeper into her womb like a lioness devouring its prey.

Tim scrambled toward the edge of the pool. "I can't get a clear shot!"

"Please!" Sarah yelled. "It's killing her!"

Jay lunged forward and kicked the creature in the face. It latched onto his foot and clung to his sneaker like an alien barnacle. He kicked his foot back and forth, trying to shake the beast loose, but it held fast, squealing and hissing.

Water crashed behind him as Trell erupted out of the pool.

Christ, is it healed already?

Jay stumbled toward a cluster of stalagmites and kicked his foot against it, smashing the creature's head into the daggers of limestone. The creature lost its grip and fell to the ground, and Jay stepped back and unloaded his weapon into it. Black blood sprayed into the air and ran down Jay's face in hot rivulets.

The creature rolled onto its back, gave a spastic kick, and then lay still.

Jay backed away from the carnage, wiping its blood off his face.

"Look out!" Crystal yelled.

He glanced up and saw Trell galloping toward him. A deep growl emanated from its throat. He ejected the spent clip and slapped in another, squeezing off a shot that ripped into its jaws.

Trell reared back, writhing its head to and fro. Then it shrugged its massive shoulders and glanced down at the child lying near it.

Jay retreated further into the cavern and took up position behind a cluster of stalagmites.

Go on, he thought. *Try to save it.*

Trell snarled at him, then snatched the child in its jaws and bounded back toward the pool. After it vanished beneath the surface, Crystal rushed to the water's edge and filled her hands with water.

"What are you doing?" Jay snapped. "Are you crazy?"

"It's for Sarah's mom."

Before Jay could argue, Crystal tiptoed away from the pool and poured water over Margaret's ruined abdomen. Sarah and Tim quickly followed suit. Margaret was alive but unconscious, and the water seemed to stop the bleeding.

Sarah kneeled down beside her mom and kissed her on the cheek. "Please don't die," she whispered.

Jay reached for Sarah's hand. "I'm sorry," he said, "but we've done all we can for now, and we can't forget that Trell still controls her."

Sarah allowed Jay to pull her up without another word, and the four of them hurried back to the mouth of the cavern. Jay nodded to Tim. "Be ready with the—" His gaze dropped to Tim's arms. "Where's the rifle?"

Tim stared down at his feet. "Trell jumped out of the pool and I just … I dropped it. I was trying to get a better angle to shoot that thing, and I got too close to the water. I'm sorry."

"The gun fell in the pool?"

Tim nodded.

Christ, Jay thought. The rifle was the only weapon that seemed to have any effect.

"Will those bullets work in either of our guns?" Crystal asked.

Jay shook his head. "I don't think so."

A shuffle of footsteps emanated from the tunnel behind them, the sound mingled with a distant chorus of grunting.

Jay sucked in his breath. Trell's assassins would be here any minute. He had to do something. They were running out of time, running out of options.

Across the room, Margaret stirred. "The amulet, Sarah. Tell them …" Her words trailed off into a wheezy gasp.

Sarah glanced at Jay and made a grabbing gesture at her throat. "She said to pull off its—"

Trell rose out of the pool, ribbons of water spouting from its nostrils. It stepped toward them, its eyes burning with rage. "The child," it hissed, speaking through Margaret. "You murdered the child. And for that you shall pay."

Tim shook his head. "Just listening to you is torture enough. You wanna know something? You're nothing but a bully. And that was the ugliest baby I've ever seen. Looked like something a dragon threw up."

Jay nudged him in the ribs. "Careful," he said through clenched teeth.

"My, Tim, aren't you just full of bravado? But I'm afraid you can't fool me. Beneath all that tough talk is the same scared, little boy who wet his pants in the library. So tell me … how would you like to die? Shall I gut you like an animal, spill your steaming entrails onto the ground? Or perhaps I should rip out that wagging tongue of yours and strangle you with it. Seems rather fitting, don't you think? Or maybe I'll just kill you after I rape Sarah. What do you think? Would you like to see that, Tim? Perhaps she'll even enjoy it, perhaps she'll even scream my name in the throes of ecstasy, shout for me to push deeper as did that whore, Maria."

Tim yelled something unintelligible and lunged forward, but Crystal yanked him back just as Trell's forepaw raked the air, missing his head by inches.

Jay fired off three shots from his dad's .45, sending a hail of bullets into the demon's face. He reached into Tim's backpack and pulled out a grenade. "Hey Trell! Want to watch me destroy the gateway?"

He charged toward the pool and could hear Trell's claws clicking against the stony floor as it bounded after him. He needed to find the source of the blue light and destroy it, and if he had to sacrifice his own life in the process, then so be it.

He dove into the water and plunged into its icy depths, the shock of cold turning his body instantly numb. For a moment, it paralyzed him, but he fought through it and propelled himself deeper.

Somewhere near the surface, Trell crashed into the water after him.

Seconds crawled by. His chest began to tighten. He glanced behind him, searching for Trell, but he could see little in the murky depths. A minute passed. He could feel heat building in his lungs, could feel his throat constricting as his body begged for air. But he kept swimming.

Voices whispered in his mind, thousands of them jumbled together, voices of men, women, and children long dead, pleading with him in a half dozen different languages, begging to be set free.

Trell's victims. Trapped forever in this pool. People from different times, different worlds, here together, sharing the same fate.

The water brightened as he dove deeper. The shades of gray grew progressively lighter, transforming into the same pale blue luminescence of the pool's outer glow. The water was denser here, thicker somehow. He could discern objects drifting across his field of vision, clusters of gray that neither sank nor rose. The pressure in his ears grew painful. He pinched his nose, blew, and swallowed...and his ears equalized with a hissing pop.

He glanced behind him and saw the dark silhouette of Trell hovering in the water above. One of the gray things bumped against his shoulder. He pushed it away and realized after a moment that it was a femur. When the silt cleared and his vision came into focus, he saw

299

that there were thousands of bones suspended before his eyes, stuck like flies in honey, rotting slowly away in this watery grave. And then the phosphorescence brightened, sharpening until it formed a ring of pulsing blue.

He drove himself toward the light with a final kick ...

... And then he was falling.

His shoulder slammed into something solid, and he rolled onto his side and gasped at newly found air. The grenade rolled out of his hand and spun in a slow circle near his head. The pool was suspended above him, angled perpendicular to the ground like a ship's portal. Through the ring of pulsing blue, he could see the murky water, could see Trell's massive shape approaching the edge.

He dragged himself off the ground and staggered to his feet. He reached for the grenade and glanced quickly around. What he saw left him breathless.

Stars glittered in the sky above, billions of them scattered like jewels across a violet canopy, alien constellations lined up in dizzying complexity. A comet burned across the heavens, streaking through the sky as simultaneous explosions of color and light burst around it, giving birth to new stars, new galaxies.

Somehow in passing through the gateway, he had crossed into another star system. He was light years from home, so far from Earth it was beyond comprehension.

He glanced at his feet and saw that he stood on a platform of dark stone so smooth and polished it reflected the light of the stars above. On the opposite end of the platform rose twin pillars etched in intricate detail, covered in archaic designs that spiraled up to the base of an elaborate archway.

The platform seemed to hang suspended in space, surrounded on all sides by a kaleidoscope of stars. There were other platforms near his, dozens of them, all connected by a narrow catwalk, all with stone arches and gateways that pulsed a phosphorescent blue.

A sloshing noise drew his attention back to the gateway, and he turned in time to see Trell squeezing itself through the opening. It landed heavily on the platform, clots of liquid splatting down next to it like mucus.

Jay shoved the grenade into his back pocket and reached for his dad's .45. But the gun was gone, the holster empty ... lost somewhere in the pool.

The waters must have provided some kind of psychic connection, because Jay could suddenly hear Trell's voice booming in his mind.

"You cannot destroy the gateway. This is a place of power, a place of magic. And you are but a mortal."

"Then why did you follow me?"

"Look around you. You've got nowhere to run. No options remaining ... save for death."

Jay inched backward and glanced over the edge of the catwalk. The whole universe unfolded beneath him, an endless void flecked with the pinpricks of glimmering stars. The view gave him vertigo, and for a moment he thought he might tumble over the edge.

"Go ahead, Jay. Step off. See what happens. This place ... it is not space as you know it. It is a place of Limbo, a great void between worlds created eons ago by the Ancients. The concept of weightlessness does not exist here. If you step over the edge, you will fall. But there will be no bottom to hit, nothing solid to crush your bones against. You will fall forever, for all of eternity. Even after you have died of thirst, of starvation, your body will hurtle through the stars, disintegrating bit by bit."

Trell inched forward and grinned. "I've seen it happen."

Jay retreated another step and felt his back brush up against one of the pillars. He stole a glance at it, at the designs spiraling up to the arch above.

Not designs—runes!

Trell crouched on its hindquarters and prepared to pounce.

"Hey, Dragon Breath! You forget about me?"

Jay turned toward the gateway where Tim stood with a gun drawn, mucus oozing down his body. He held Crystal's Glock—the nine millimeter with the laser scope. The red dot glowed on Trell's forehead.

Jay was about to yell for him to turn back, that the gun might not even work after getting wet, but then he saw the bag of bagels ripped open at his feet.

Smart kid.

And then Tim fired. The bullet struck Trell between the eyes, sending it staggering back a step.

Jay dodged behind the pillars. He scanned the columns, searching for a match to the runes Frank had scrawled in his own blood. Each rune was set in a perfectly carved square. He found the first match halfway up the back of the nearest column. He touched the center with a trembling hand. It gave beneath his touch and sank partway into the pillar, a blue light tracing the rune's outline.

A second shot rang out behind him, followed by an ear-splitting shriek of pain.

"You'd better hope they make dentures in your size!"

Jay searched the column from left to right, his eyes poring over every inch. He found the second rune and pressed it. Blue light pulsed in the outline, crackling like electricity.

He crouched down, scanned the base of the column. Nothing. He moved to the next pillar, began searching at the middle, and then worked his way up.

Come on, come on.

He heard another shot, followed by another scream from Trell. But this time it seemed more angry than hurt. He spotted the final rune near the top of the pillar, one square below the base of the arch and at least two feet above his outstretched hand. He glanced back at Trell,

302

saw that it was halfway between him and Tim. It seemed to be deciding whom to go after.

Jay leaped into the air and wrapped his arms around the pillar. A few seconds later, he had shimmied his way up to where he needed to be.

"Jay, look out!"

Trell galloped toward him, saliva flying from its jaws in a frothy line.

Jay waited until it was directly beneath him before pressing the final rune.

Trell shrieked and launched itself into the air. Its claws raked his shirt and cut into his stomach like razors.

Tim fired off a round of shots, emptying the gun into the base of Trell's neck. Each shot stunned it for a moment or two.

Jay used the time to plant his feet on the pillar and propel himself over Trell. He landed a few yards in front of it, sprang to his feet, and raced for the gateway with everything he had.

He made it little more than halfway before the gateway flared a brilliant blue, the flash so bright it momentarily blinded him. When his vision returned, he saw that a ring of stone had appeared on the inner edge of the gateway. It was moving toward the center like the shutter of a camera, a waning circle that grew smaller by the second.

He could hear Trell behind him, growling as it shook off the latest round of gunfire.

Tim ejected the spent clip and slapped in another. "Duck!"

Jay dropped his head and continued running. Tim squeezed off one shot after another, the reports muted by the vastness of this place. In a moment, he was by Tim's side, and the gateway was more than halfway shut.

The gunshots slowed Trell. The bullets ripped into its jaws and shattered teeth. Tim had found the weakness in its armor, and the laser sight ensured that each shot hit home.

Jay grabbed the plastic bag and saw the other grenade sitting atop the bagels. *Breakfast of champions*, he thought, and dropped his own grenade inside the bag. Then he elbowed Tim in the ribs and pointed to the gateway. "Go!"

Once Tim was through the opening, Jay reached into the bag and pulled out the pins. Then he twisted the bag shut and threw it into the air. It soared over Trell and landed at the base of the pillars. The flat weight of the bagels kept the whole package from rolling over the side of the catwalk.

Jay dove through the gateway and kicked furiously through the water. A second or two later, the gateway slammed shut behind him with a reverberating bang. An explosion rocked the pool, and Jay and Tim spun through the water, carried by the shock wave that ripped through the underwater lair.

Jay glanced over his shoulder and saw that no light shone behind them, no ring of phosphorescent blue.

We did it! We destroyed the gateway!

He and Tim swam side by side through the pitch-dark waters. The pain in his stomach began to fade, and he could actually feel the wound closing.

But how? Hadn't they destroyed the gateway and cut off the source of the pool's healing power? Was this just a lingering effect?

His eyes detected a distant blur of light up ahead. They swam toward it, kicking hard, and then he and Tim broke through the surface, gasping for breath.

Crystal and Sarah staggered back from the pool. A wave of disbelief seemed to wash over them. "You're alive!" Crystal cried. "But you were gone so long."

Tim hoisted himself out of the water and rolled onto his back. "We did it," he said. "We destroyed the gateway."

Jay swam toward the edge of the pool.

"I think something's wrong," Crystal said.

"What do you mean?" Jay asked.

"Don't you hear it?"

Jay cocked his head to one side and could hear the grunting of Trell's assassins, their feet shuffling as they lumbered through a nearby passageway. He gave one last kick and reached for the edge of the pool.

How can they still be under its control?

A vice of teeth clamped down around his leg and ripped into his flesh like daggers. Crystal reached for him, but he was dragged away from the edge, thrashing and flailing, trying to keep his head above water. Then he felt himself rising into the air as Trell emerged from the pool, his leg buried to the knee in its jaws.

His mind could barely accept what was happening.

Looks like you're a goner, his dad's voice said with a chuckle. *And I thought I died badly!*

He glanced toward the passageway and saw Samuel enter the cavern, followed by a hundred or more of Trell's assassins.

"The amulet!" Sarah yelled. "Get the amulet!" She was jumping up and down and pointing to her neck.

Jay hung upside down from Trell's jaws. His leg had gone numb, and he felt that he might lose consciousness at any moment. Sarah's words had trouble penetrating the fog that swirled through his mind. An amulet? What amulet?

But then he saw it—a gleaming black obelisk dangling from Trell's neck. It reflected the light of Crystal's lantern and was obscured by the shadows of its head, partially covered by the folds of its skin.

An image of Frank's bloody sketch flashed through his mind—a picture of an obelisk with a key at its center. But what did it mean, and what was it a key to?

An explosion of gunfire startled him out of his thoughts. He grabbed the amulet and yanked the chain off Trell's neck.

A second gunshot shattered one of Trell's fangs. The beast reared backward and roared.

Jay's leg slipped free as it opened its jaws. He fell onto solid ground and rolled onto his side. The amulet tumbled from his hand.

Trell turned toward it, but Jay snatched it up before the beast could reach it.

"The Life Force, Jay! Set it free!"

And in that moment he knew exactly what Sarah meant. He held up the amulet and focused all of his energy on the polished black obelisk. Then he stared into its mirrored depths.

Set them free!

The amulet flared a brilliant blue. A shock of energy flung Jay backward and sent him sprawling.

Trell roared.

The water churned.

Blue light pulsed in the center of the pool and swirled into a spiral. Waves of water crested and broke, the blue light whirling into a frenzy. Then the light separated from the water and hovered above it.

The voices of the dead whispered praises of salvation, but then their tone changed and the light transformed into a glowing ball of rage, a mass of pure energy that bristled with power.

Jay was so focused on the light that he didn't see Trell until it was too late. The creature launched itself into the air, the muscles of its forepaws rippling. Jay tried to roll away, but he had nowhere to go. All he could do was cross his arms over his face as the creature's shadow fell upon him.

The Life Force came between them at the last moment, making a sound like the wind screaming through a canyon. It intercepted Trell and hurled the demon into the wall with enough force to bring down a stalactite. The pillar of stone crashed to the floor just a few feet from where Margaret lay in a semiconscious daze.

The Life Force coursed into Trell and ravaged the ancient creature. The mass of crackling light ripped through its body and tore through its eyes, nose, and mouth. Trell jerked and jittered as if electrocuted, its flesh searing beneath the writhing light. Its wailing screams echoed throughout the cavern.

And then the light spread out and broke apart. A swirling web of blue touched down on Margaret, entering her womb and coursing through her body. Another cluster zipped through the air and entered the wounds of Jay's leg, filling the bloody punctures with pools of phosphorescent blue.

A moment later, the light converged into a bright blue nexus and rose into the air above their heads. It emitted a dry crackle and split apart into thousands of bright spheres, which spread themselves throughout the cavern. For a moment, they hovered there, pulsing a brilliant blue, and then they shot up toward the ceiling and disappeared through the rock.

***

A hushed silence fell over them after the Life Force faded from view and the cavern dissolved into shadows. Jay knelt on the floor, still holding the amulet. It dangled from the chain and oscillated back and forth, reflecting the dim light of the lanterns. Somewhere behind them, water dripped from stalactites in a steady rhythm of muted plops.

Jay stared at the smoldering carcass of the creature that had once lived among these walls, the creature come from the Land of Demons. It lay still now, tendrils of smoke rising up from it in rippling waves. The afterglow of the Life Force was burned into his eyes, stamped across his field of vision like a photo negative.

Sarah was the first to break the silence. "Mommy?" She slipped out of Crystal's embrace. "Mom?" She ran to where her mother lay sprawled on the floor and dropped into a crouch beside her.

Margaret rubbed her forehead and glanced about the cavern. "Is it dead?" When Sarah nodded, Margaret flung her arms around Sarah and hugged her tight. "You did it, sweetie. You told them!"

Jay stood slowly, shifting his weight from his good leg to his bad. It felt a little stiff, but otherwise okay.

Crystal reached for Jay's hand and laced her fingers through his. "How did she know? How—"

Margaret spoke up. "It was the amulet that imprisoned the souls in the pool, the amulet that chained the Life Force to the water."

Samuel moved between them, his eyes dark and solemn. The aura of blue that had once pulsed so brightly around him was now barely visible.

"You didn't tell us about the amulet," Crystal said. "Why?"

Jay gazed at Samuel. "You didn't know, did you? It was one of Trell's secrets, one you said was yet to be revealed."

Samuel nodded.

"Then how did you escape?" Tim asked. "How did you break free if the others couldn't?"

But Samuel only shrugged.

Margaret struggled to her feet. "He escaped because the amulet fell off. The chain that had secured it was old, weakened over the years by the water." She shuffled toward them, her face bruised and swollen, blood caked between her teeth. "It was the Brakowski boy. He's the one who set Samuel free."

"But how?"

"He kicked off the amulet, broke the chain with his foot while Frank held him over the pool. But before it hit the water, before it sank, it touched Ryan ... and for an instant the two were joined. But that's all it took. Ryan's thoughts of freedom opened the gate for the split second there was contact, time enough for Samuel to escape into the world of the living."

She shook her head. "It was part of Trell's best kept secret—the dual nature of the pool. The overlap of worlds gave these waters a healing power. But the amulet added to that power. It trapped the Life Force of Trell's victims in the pool and allowed Trell to channel the strength into its body."

Jay turned around and saw that the former slaves of Trell had gathered around to listen. They looked shell-shocked, soiled, and withered. Like the survivors of a Nazi death camp.

A murmur went through the crowd. It began in the back and worked its way forward. The bodies parted one by one, stepping aside to open up a path.

Agent Calhoun staggered through the tunnel. His once slicked-back hair now hung in his eyes. He was limping a little, favoring his left leg. His eyes locked on Jay. "Gallagher! What the hell is going on here?"

Jay folded his arms and returned the agent's gaze. "You thought I was hiding something before. You thought there was something I wasn't telling you. Well," he said, and stepped aside, "there it is."

EPILOGUE

Sunlight filtered through the whitewashed slats of the gazebo, dappling the floor in a checkerboard of gold. From his vantage point, Jay could see a swatch of blue sky through the slats, as well as thin wisps of clouds drifting over Washaka Woods.

A warm breeze blew out of the east and ruffled his hair. In the crowd behind him, he could hear the murmur of guests, the giggling of children. Most of the town had turned out for the affair, the survivors of what the papers had called the most devastating encounter of man versus beast since the dinosaur age.

The FBI had covered up what they could—that Trell was a demon from another world, that it possessed the power to control people like puppets. As far as everyone knew, Glenwood had fallen victim to a previously unknown species of creature, a man-eating monster that scientists speculated was a fluke holdover from the Jurassic period. Even the former slaves of Trell didn't know the whole truth. Most of them remembered nothing of what occurred while under Trell's power, and that was probably for the best.

Tim had said just a few days ago that if the world wanted to know the real story, they'd have to read the tabloids. It was just a joke—and what did Tim ever say that wasn't—but it was true. One of the headlines had read: *Aliens turned my son into a killer zombie.* It turned out to be the most accurate account of what'd really happened.

In the aftermath of the tragedy, the media swarmed into Glenwood in a ratings frenzy and interviewed anyone even remotely connected to the story. Teary-eyed accounts were broadcasted all over the world. Exclusive footage was shown of men in orange hazmat suits hauling Trell's body out of the cave. They loaded it into the back of a military truck and drove away in an armed caravan.

Soon after the story broke, the charges against Jay were dropped. An FBI spokesman announced at a national press conference that Jay was involved in no wrongdoing and had, in fact, assisted in killing the beast. But even with the investigation now officially closed, questions still lingered about the man who had attacked Tim at the library and Jay at his house. The FBI took the position that these incidents were unrelated to what the papers referred to as the Berkshire Beast, although there were already a number of conspiracy theories circulating.

Calhoun told Jay later that the autopsy results confirmed that Trell's DNA was utterly alien, a fact that would never be released to the public. In the end, close to four thousand people died. Twenty five percent of the town's population—wiped out in a span of three weeks. A year had passed, and the town was just beginning to heal.

Crystal squeezed his hand and smiled, bringing his thoughts back to the present. She looked every bit as beautiful as he imagined she would.

"You sure you want to do this?" he asked. "I may not be as much fun now that I'm sober." He glanced over his shoulder and winked at Tim.

Tim gave him a thumbs-up sign and slipped his arm around Maria's waist.

Jay smiled as he recalled their reunion outside of the cave. Tim had spotted her wandering in a daze among the former slaves of Trell. He had stopped short at the sight of her. None of them had even considered that Trell had lied about her death to make Tim angry, to goad him into making a fatal mistake.

The minister glanced at Jay and Crystal. "The ring, please."

Sarah stepped away from the crowd upon hearing her cue. She waved to her mom and dad and mounted the stairs to the gazebo.

Jay smiled at Margaret. Her bruises had long since healed, her face radiant as she stood arm in arm with her husband, just a few yards away from Tim's parents.

He wished Steve could be here, Steve and Gloria both. But they were gone now, as was Crystal's sister. He closed his eyes and pictured the place of Limbo, the stone pillars rising from the catwalk, silhouetted against a violet sky flecked with twinkling stars. They were through one of those gateways now, somewhere behind a pulsing ring of phosphorescent blue.

He opened his eyes, returned once again to the world of the living, to a life blessed by a new beginning. Sarah stood between them, dressed in a flowered gown, her hair tied back with a white bow. He marveled again at how much she had grown in a year, both physically and emotionally. She seemed more confident now, more outgoing.

"Congratulations," she said, lifting the ring to the minister.

Jay smiled at her. So what if it wasn't traditional?

He glanced into Washaka Woods and thought about Samuel, the little boy who had first brought them to this place.

You opened my eyes, Samuel. You set me free, made me alive again.

He stared through the trees where the lair of Trell was no more, a fortress of rock reduced to rubble by dynamite.

Rest easy now, Samuel. You've earned it.

The minister closed the Bible and adjusted his glasses. "You may now kiss the bride."

Jay lifted Crystal's veil.

And I've earned this, he thought.

And then they kissed.

Made in the USA
Lexington, KY
20 June 2017